THE N

by Ben Osborne

CHAPTER 1

ELY PARK RACECOURSE.
Danny Rawlings wasn't to know someone was about to die.
Nothing indicated trouble was brewing. The capacity crowd was rightly humming with anticipation, the flag man in his white lab coat was ducking under the rails near the first hurdle, the starter in tweeds was counting down the seconds to post time at the foot of his rostrum and the seven runners were quietly circling.

Even the weather had behaved, just the odd puff of white dotting the brilliant blue sky. It felt more like Madrid in July, not Cardiff in late September.

Clearly the sun had brought the punters out, Danny reckoned, glancing over at the swirling mass of humanity in the grandstand quivering in the heat haze some three furlongs away.

He imagined similar scenes on the last incarnation of Ely Racetrack back in racing's heyday at this site over a century ago. It was a perfect setting for a day at the races. Even the ground was officially 'Good'.

Yet a part of Danny wanted this to end in hospital.

His hand felt a strip of flesh at the small of his back between the body protector and the waistband of his white breeches where he'd wedged a mobile phone. Weighing little more than that king-sized chocolate bar he'd foregone, it wouldn't show up at the weighing room scales.

Danny knew he'd be heavily punished if discovered with a phone out there on the racetrack, but he reckoned it was worth breaking the rules for this.

He then pictured wife Meg Rawlings lying supine in the maternity ward of Cardiff General. He'd reluctantly left her going into labour with her first child, Danny's second. He'd insisted the midwife call only if there was good news of a safe delivery with

3

both mother and baby doing well. He'd set the phone to vibrate. He longed to feel that buzz.

He'd begged Meg to book a spare rider so he could be at her side for the birth but she made a face that suggested she'd be better off without any more of his fuss-arsing. He could deal with the stresses of sport far better than the stresses of real life.

He ran a hand over the shiny black neck of exciting prospect Powder Keg and then down the white blaze on her face. After arriving to post early, he'd dismounted to take some weight off her small, narrow back. He'd gifted the filly to Meg, who was at the time her stable-lass and his girlfriend. Since then, the filly had become far more than a birthday present. What started out as her project soon turned into her passion and, much like Meg herself, the filly was now part of the family. Over the summer, the four-year-old had grown up mentally and physically. It was up to Danny, who was back in the saddle, not to undo all that good.

He knew Powder Keg had the form in the book to win this and last time he'd looked at the big screen, her odds of eleven-to-eight suggested she was widely expected to win. Oddly, knowing this added both confidence and pressure. It was his race to mess up. He also knew there were no certainties in racing. Standing in his way were eight hurdles of slanted timber panels framed by orange poles and an unbeaten filly named Maids A Milking – the seven-to-four second favourite ridden by rising star Micky Galbraith.

After Powder Keg had seen enough of the practice hurdle, Danny turned her to face the chief rival in the betting market. Both jockeys briefly held their mounts as still as living statues, like a showdown in some old Western.

Micky was better known as Concorde in the changing rooms. The green youngster lapped it up. He still reckoned it was for his 'smooth, slick style making the horses go supersonic'. It had gone too long unsaid for Danny to have the heart to reveal it was due to his beak-like nose.

Ignorance is bliss, he guessed, not wanting to hurt any feelings.

4

Danny adjusted his goggles for comfort and swallowed back the nerves.

When he felt a tickle run down his back, he tensed up. Soon as he discovered it was a bead of sweat and not the phone, he breathed out. He couldn't take any more false alarms.

He made one last turn and then they were called to walk in. The starter's hand came down and the tape went up.

The speakers bellowed, 'And they're off for the inaugural running of the fifty-thousand pounds added *Bet With RBOnline for the Best Value Welsh Champion Hurdle Trial* on this glorious day at Ely Park and it's warm favourite Powder Keg who has stolen something of a march on the rest. She's taken a three-length lead in this two-mile feature, but Micky Galbraith is quick to react and tucks Maids A Milking in her slipstream.'

Thereafter, Danny merely heard white noise. His focus was on getting his charge to the first hurdle on a perfect stride.

She was all about speed and Danny wanted to make the most of her quality by dictating affairs out in front.

He gathered the reins up neatly and flicked over the first flight of timber like he was on Big Buck's. He knew the collapsible three-foot of timber took less effort to clear, but in many ways that made it potentially more dangerous. The racehorses didn't always respect hurdles as much as the taller, more intimidating birch fences and were prone to fearlessly attack them at a greater speed. While they were designed to flatten if struck by the horses shin or hooves, he knew travelling at galloping speed a seemingly harmless contact could still propel the horse forward into a slip and slide, unseating the jockey. Only yesterday, he'd done something similar entering the weighing room, a harmless clip of a boot on the step quickly snowballed into a clown fall. 'Can't even weigh in without falling,' was all he'd heard from the lads that afternoon.

Powder Keg's quick, flicking action covered the sound surface like a hovercraft.

Back in March, similar trailblazing tactics had seen Meg fill a remarkable fourth in the hotly contested Triumph Hurdle –

the championship event for juvenile hurdlers – at the Cheltenham Festival.

Having already netted bumpers at Market Rasen and then Huntingdon before recently making a successful switch to hurdling in a Leicester maiden, he knew Maids A Milking was race-fit and a born winner. But the second favourite lacked the proven class of Powder Keg and he sought to exploit this by taking no prisoners out in front.

The final hurdle in the home-straight was the last to negotiate next time round. Powder Keg landed running.

Danny knew there was a long run to the next flight. He afforded a cheeky glance over at the sea of faces, many hidden behind cameras and phones. Even the glass balcony of the VIP box high up in the stands was rammed full.

Danny wondered if clerk of the course Keith Gosworth had finally calmed down. Apparently, bigwigs at the British Horseracing Authority, the BHA, had rolled into town and were somewhere on track. Something told Danny they weren't here on a jolly at this financially struggling track.

At least sunshine made everything look and feel better, Danny hoped.

Suddenly Micky came up broadside on his right to block the view.

'Daddy won't be pleased,' Danny said and smiled, 'your one needs holding up out the back. You *both* knew that.'

Out there in the field of battle anything goes, including sledging. Danny knew this the hard way. It was survival of the strongest in body and mind. This was no place for sporting gestures or goodwill.

Show me a good loser and I'll show you a loser, his dad used to say.

Without asking for any more, Danny soon found himself in the outright lead again. Micky had eased off. It seemed Danny had got inside the youngster's head.

Powder Keg was again allowed to coast along without the sideshow of another rival to distract and disrupt the rhythm of her jumping and stride.

He safely popped over the third flight. The cheering crowd told Danny there were no incidents in behind.

Powder Keg appeared to be enjoying this. It was no surprise as this place had become her second home. In lieu of helping to design the layout of both the hurdles and steeplechase tracks, Danny was allowed to work his horses there once a week and awarded the keys to the racecourse as a 'Racing Consultant'.

In the designs, Danny was adamant there'd be nothing to jump turning the side of the track. It was tricky enough trying to clear a hurdle at pace when the horse was balanced.

Seeing the paddock exit on the bend stretching away from the stands, Danny gripped the reins tighter.

Arriving at Silver Belle Stables, Powder Keg was a flighty, boisterous little madam, or as Meg put it, 'a right monkey.'

He couldn't do a thing with the filly and offloaded her to Meg, who gave the loving care and attention needed, including daily gallops and regular grooming, even when his wife was ill or feeling a bit low.

Kegsy's tantrums, particularly the kicking out and whinnying, were a memory now, as were the times she'd plant herself on the spot at the foot of the gallops.

She now knew her job and was rewarded with good food, attention and a radio tuned to BBC Radio Two in her box.

Over the summer, Powder Keg's regard for Danny also appeared to improve. He reckoned it was all the times the filly had seen the newlyweds show affection to each other around the yard. While in Kegsy's eyes, Meg would always be the outright leader of her herd, Danny had become the deputy.

Perhaps he should let Meg take over the licence but he then foresaw all the changing and feeding of the newborn. Suddenly looking after horses didn't seem such hard work.

He still sat quietly, tensed thighs ready to counter any jink right at the stable exit bend. The filly banked left, tracking the rail with no guidance from the saddle.

Swinging in to face two hurdles in the back stretch, Danny felt a presence on his right flank. He went a fraction wide, hoping to force any challenger even wider.

All's fair in love and racing, Danny reckoned. He was there to win for Meg, son Jack and the new baby on its way.

Any ground forfeited by taking a wider angle was offset by the momentum saved, as Powder Keg didn't have to change her lead leg to keep balanced. Her small, athletic conformation helped her easily make the transition from bend to straight and he'd successfully fended off any pretenders for the lead.

Down this far side of the track, there was no big screen to call upon. Neither could he feed off the crowd to forewarn of any move from behind.

He heard snorts of air and the thunder of hooves grow larger. When they'd safely negotiated the fourth hurdle, Danny looked back to see a flash of black and orange as the nearest pursuer pulled out more than a horse's width from the inside rail. It was Micky riding in the colours of his mother Maria, though there was no nepotism involved as, unlike Danny who took up racing to escape a life of drugs and crime, Micky was born and bred to ride. He was the son of ex-Flat jockey and current BHA chief Campbell Galbraith, who had clearly passed on his sense of balance, timing and touch in the saddle.

As Danny feared, Micky wouldn't surrender easily. He kept pressing for the lead but once alongside would then refuse to go by. Danny could see Powder Keg being lit up by these tactics. Micky had clearly been taught well as a race tactician.

Danny couldn't control the actions of others but wished he'd declared a pair of blinkers now.

Despite the gamesmanship, Danny found it hard to dislike Micky, who was his friend Stony's godson.

Campbell and Stony were locking horns on the racetrack back when Danny was skipping double maths for the motocross

8

park. Campbell had always been the better rider but it didn't stop the pair striking up an unlikely, albeit brief, friendship the season after Micky was born.

Micky had inherited some of that drive to succeed. Danny knew he was in for a fight.

He hoped all the exercise he'd put in up the valley slopes would pay off, not just for the horse's sake.

As if Powder Keg could sense a danger on her right, she effortlessly lengthened her stride.

With one last push and a feral growl from the saddle, the ground fell away. Danny heard a brush of timber and then a clatter as Powder Keg's drum and feet scraped over the other side. He'd forgotten he was no longer on the retired chaser Salamanca, but a hurdler not much bigger than a pony, at fifteen hands.

Danny felt a sinking feeling. Powder Keg's landing gear came out and the strong tendons in her front legs absorbed the jolting impact. He was shunted forward up the filly's narrow neck and tasted a mouthful of mane.

Fearing she'd crumple, he sat back to widen their centre of gravity. No way was he going to unseat. He couldn't bear to imagine Powder Keg bolting loose down this remotest part of the track to impale herself on the fence or collide with one of the tree trunks hiding the new housing estate built as part of the deal struck by the council to resurrect what was once Wales' number one racetrack.

Five gone, three to go, Danny told himself, just keep it together and we've got this.

Powder Keg's high head carriage meant Danny rode short with the reins. He crouched lower, peering between her pricked ears, almost acting like the sights of a gun. She got in tight at the final flight of the back straight, allowing Micky to move up sweetly on the outside.

Danny sat back and righted the ship.

On this section of the track he'd intentionally designed a gentle entry easing into the long turn for home in the hope runners attacked the bend and therefore began properly racing further out from the finish, avoiding any cat and mouse games. He asked Powder Keg to stretch her legs and the pair went on again into the bend. This was Micky's first sighting of this hurdles track and his inexperience was showing. He lacked Danny's track-craft.

They squared up for the final assault.

Winging the third and second last flights of timber, Danny was convinced he'd settled it, so he nearly did a double-take when he saw Micky alongside smiling back.

Danny didn't have the wind in his lungs to sledge the passer-by this time. He sank lower and began to row like Sir Steve Redgrave in one last bid to rescue the prize.

But he could see they were behind by a head, a neck.

Just a few strides before they had to leave the ground a final time, he felt a buzz against the small of his back. It was the message he longed for. In a stride, all the exhaustion had seeped away as his strong limbs found the boost needed. It was like he'd downed a vat of energy drink.

The renewed vigour appeared to transmit down the reins as Powder Keg found a second wind from somewhere, despite blowing as hard as him.

Meg's final words to him were, 'Don't go too hard on her, it's only a trial.'

The blowout would bring her on a treat for her next outing, he reconciled, as he continued to push the brave filly on. But he couldn't give up now they'd got this close.

He felt like he was on a daughter of the late Silver Belle.

Now the two leaders' heads were bobbing in tandem, Kegsy had made up the deficit.

'More!' Danny cried. 'More!'

Despite the temptation, he didn't call upon the whip as he knew she was already leaving everything she had out on the track.

Several strides from the red lollypop stick and the lighter line of cut grass marking the finish, Danny heard a loud pop. He feared something had snapped. He hoped it was the tack and not her cannon bone. But the sound had seemed to bounce off the overhang of the stands.

10

It was then he realised the cries from the crowd were now fuelled by terror, not excitement.

As he afforded the briefest glance across to his right, he saw Micky a neck down. Beyond, he saw the crowds were no longer looking back. They were running. They appeared to be scattering, fleeing. It made no sense. He wanted to stare at the scene harder to be sure it was really happening.

Two strides on, Danny looked up at the glass of the VIP box. There appeared to be a racegoer hanging by the legs from the balcony railing. He was being held there suspended by someone in the box. It appeared his jacket tail had fallen down over his head, revealing the back of a white shirt and the salmon pink lining of the suit. Could he really be that drunk?

From behind the suit jacket, there came a thin line of broken red down to the betting ring below.

Danny began to think exhaustion was playing tricks with his mind. No sooner had he lost focus, he'd lost the lead.

Seeing the finish line upon them, Danny pushed Powder Keg's neck. He wanted her small head down on the line.

Flashing past the post, instinct told him they'd rallied to get back up.

Above the cries from the dispersing crowd, he swore he heard a loud and lifeless thud, as if a sack of flour had been dropped from a great height. Then came the louder screams.

He'd leant forward and hugged Powder Keg, who'd slowed to a walk just yards after the line.

Again Danny looked up. There was no sign of the hanging grey suit from the balcony. His focus on the stands was then distracted by Micky offering a congratulatory hand, as if he knew the result too. He had clearly been brought up to be a sportsman in every sense.

'You'll go far kid,' Danny managed as their gloved fingertips touched.

When the Tannoy chimed, Danny leant back in the saddle, expected the announcement of a photo.

'This is a security announcement, would all racegoers please evacuate the racecourse as quickly and as calmly as possible and wait in the public car park until further instruction. This is a security—'

Danny had tuned out again. Powder Keg felt a bit wobbly, so he jumped off and began to lead her over.

The atmosphere there had changed from a party to a wake in seconds. Ely Park was certainly going to leave a big impression on the visiting BHA party. He looked up again at the VIP box.

Danny held back at first, waiting for the last of the tailed-off stragglers to complete. He glanced down the track. Even the ground-staff had refused to come out with pitchforks to tread in the scuffed turf.

His gloved fists still gripped the reins as tightly as when they'd cleared the final flight. Everything told him to get back on Powder Keg and gallop in the opposite direction to the unseen threat.

But the crowd had thinned enough to see the green of the picnic area, and he hoped the danger had too. He needed to respond to his phone someplace less public.

As he led Powder Keg onto the asphalt offshoot joining the racetrack and the parade ring at the back of the stands, he snapped away his tinted goggles, soiled by blades of grass and spots of earth. It was like leading a horse through the Somme battlefields. Men and woman were carrying children, racecourse security in orange hi-vis jackets were wheeling disabled racegoers from the ramped viewing gallery. They appeared to be fleeing for their lives.

He turned back to see Micky similarly transfixed. He'd also jumped off his horse.

A morbid curiosity made Danny glance over at the space between the bottom step of the tiered viewing gallery in the stand and the most sought-after bookies' pitches in the front row of the betting ring. There, he saw a green scrum of paramedics. Directly above, the VIP balcony was now empty. They'd clearly backed away from seeing the mess below. Danny felt the same way. A memory like that would take a second but last a lifetime.

Danny looked ahead to see clerk Gosworth charging down the path towards them. He was shouting something into the radio pinned to his green Ely Park fleece collar. His face was nearly as white as that thick cloud of hair on his head. Something told Danny the weighing in of the jockeys and the hosing down of the horses would have to wait.

From behind, Danny heard the creak of plastic. He looked back to see Micky had cleared the railing and was barging a way past the last of the racegoers. Had he seen the gunman?

'No, Micky!' Gosworth cried.

'Is the faller okay?' Danny asked Gosworth. He couldn't believe he was referring to a human and not a horse.

'He's dead.'

Danny glanced up to the VIP suite. 'Who was it?'

'Campbell Galbraith.'

CHAPTER 2

'Daddy!'

Danny felt small arms lock tightly round his left leg and anchor him there. He looked down at son Jack and then over at Meg, who was propped up by pillows on the only bed in this private room, small and dimly lit. She was cradling a tiny parcel of white.

He whispered, 'Did I miss anything?'

She smiled past tired eyes, face glowing radiantly. She mouthed the words, 'a girl'.

Danny ruffled Jack's blond hair and said, 'Looks like you've got a little sister, Jack.'

He felt as hot and nervous as he did just before the race. Hospitals always did this. As a jockey it wasn't the best phobia to have but for once this was the good kind of nerves. He quietly went to her side and hooked a finger over the blanket to see a tiny face, all pink and wrinkly, looking back up. He glanced adoringly between the flushed faces of mother and child.

He wiped a tear forming in both eyes and then let out a snotty laugh. Meg looked up and mirrored his smile. 'What are you thinking?'

'I'm thinking how good it is to be alive.'

She grinned even more. 'You won't be when you've got to send out both lots at first light.'

'Let's not talk shop now.'

'I'm just thinking of their future,' she said. 'We've got to make the yard work now more than ever.'

'She's got your looks.'

'Wish I was somewhere nearer her weight,' she said, voice small. 'Six pounds three ounces. Think my ankles weigh more.' She looked up at his studious face. 'Stop assessing whether she'll make into a future jockey.'

'Who said I was thinking—'

14

'I know you. Years of seeing what goes into running a yard, she'll probably end up running for the Black Mountains.'

'Anyway, Jack's the jockey, aren't you boy.'

Jack's head bobbed as he rocked in the plastic chair by the bed, arms and legs imitating his dad on the track, 'Giddy-up! Giddy-up!'

Danny smiled. 'Did it go well, love?'

'Not as well as Powder Keg,' she said. 'Let's just say, you weren't the only one in stirrups.'

Danny frowned. He suddenly felt a little light-headed and saw floating red dots. He slumped back in the other foam chair. Suddenly a flashback of Campbell leaking blood as he hung there filled his mind's eye. He'd never felt as flat straight after winning a big race.

He wondered what kind of a world he was welcoming a new life into.

'Is that all you could manage?' she frowned.

Danny swallowed. He thought he was going to be sick. 'It's just been a hell of a day.' He could almost hear the subsequent silence. 'But it's all good now. I'm thrilled, really I am.'

'Well, could you share it with your face?'

When Meg had moved in, Jack was at least old enough to reason with. Blissfully for her, she didn't know all the hard work that came before. That would soon change.

Danny bunched up the stems of the crappy garage flowers he'd bought in the rush there and lowered them into a jug on the bedside table. 'It's all I could get, sorry.' He was so low on energy he was tempted to finish the half-eaten cucumber sandwiches on a plate there. 'At least we can say goodbye to the food cravings.'

'That's my sister,' Jack screamed.

Danny swung him up to sit at the foot of the bed. 'I know Jack. And she's perfect, just like you. But remember what we said, whisper or she'll get upset.'

They all silently stared at the new addition to the Rawlings clan. For a precious moment, it wiped the memory of the race's aftermath. He guessed this is what they meant by the circle of life.

'God, I was bored waiting for it to happen, I swear that wall clock was stuck,' Meg said. 'And you know I get the fidgets when I'm not checking in on the horses. Please say little Tufty is still sound for her Worcester debut next week.'

'As a pound. Jordi sent her out for a spin this morning. She seems very well within herself, almost managed to keep up with the more experienced jumper Head Hunter,' Danny said. 'Don't worry so much, you'll make yourself ill. Believe me, in the first few months, we'll be the ones needing to be sound as a pound. She'll be squealing louder than the juvenile hurdlers.'

'Did you get the reading stuff?'

'Sorry love, my mind was on other things, I've got a racing paper in the car but it got a bit grubby and wrinkly from shower steam, been lying about in the weighing room, I'll check the hospital shop for a *Horse and Hound*.'

'Doesn't matter,' she said.

'Read this,' Danny said, and handed her a sample of the thousand business cards he'd ordered at the printers. 'What do you think?' he asked as she studied it, worryingly without response. 'Is it too obvious with the picture of silver bells either side of the name?'

'If we were wedding planners, yes,' she said, 'but we race horses, so no, it's not obvious … at all.'

'I had a choice of a galloping horse symbol too.'

'It doesn't matter, Danny,' she said, but barely seemed to have the energy to roll her eyes.

'With another mouth to feed, I have to do something.' Danny said. 'Several boxes are empty, and even a third of the owners we've got are behind on their bills.' His face fell.

'We've talked about this,' she sighed.

'You reminded me just then about making the yard work, I've got to chase payments, we don't want to be known as a soft touch, an easy ride, or there'll be a lot more than one in three,' Danny replied. 'It's the worst part of the job, I'd rather muck out.'

'That's the same with most yards, I saw a report on it in the racing press, we're not alone,' she reasoned.

'I'm not playing the victim.'

'I know Danny, it'll pick up,' she said. 'With Powder Keg among the ranks we'll be sorted. She'll keep the wolf from the door.'

'Mammy Meg?!' Jack cried.

Danny said, 'No Jack, there aren't any wolves, not in the valleys.'

'Hang on, aren't you the one supposed to be lifting my spirits,' she said and then failed to fight off a jaw-snapping yawn. 'Let's not talk shop, you said.'

'Have you thought again about a name?' Danny asked.

'Jill! Jill!' Jack screamed. 'Jack and Jill went up the hill.'

'We've been through this Jack, you know what happens to them,' Danny said. 'Jack fell down and brown his crown and Jill came tumbling after. We don't want to tempt fate.'

'You're getting suspicious in your old age,' she said.

'Guess so,' Danny said. 'Eh! What you mean old?'

He leant over and kissed her waxy forehead. 'Shall we go with our top girl name?'

She nodded. 'I'd like that.'

'She looks like a Cerys.'

'She does.'

'When can we leave this place?'

'They want to keep me in overnight,' she said, blinking her tired eyes. 'You best get home, we'll be fine here. You look like I feel.'

'Micky made me work for it.'

'Did you get chance to see him after?'

'I'd got the message from the nurse between the final two hurdles, so I came straight here. It's probably a good thing – what do you say to the poor lad. Especially as I'd just won the race and become a father,' Danny said. 'That's good news for me, irrelevant news for him. I might pop down there first thing tomorrow, before coming here.'

'Do you think that's wise?'

'I'm racing consultant there, I want the place to live. We've branded it a family friendly track. I dread to think how attendances will shrink after something like this.'

He gently picked up the small white parcel being offered up to him and needed no encouragement to cradle her in the warm light of the wall lamp.

'Hello you, little cutey Cerys, this is your daddy,' he said softly. He nearly couldn't get the words out, bursting with that much pride.

'You're my daddy,' Jack screamed, legs swinging from the chair.

'I'm both your daddies,' he said. He suddenly felt his legs start to tremble as he was blinded by another flashback from the bloody scenes of the track. He'd waited months for this precious moment but it was being tainted by the afternoon events.

Meg yawned and her eyelids finally began to lose the fight. Danny took the hint.

'Go now,' she managed. Danny sensed it was more an order than a suggestion this time. He laid baby Cerys in the cot bedside and trod lightly from there with Jack in tow. He was never one to refuse an invitation to leave a hospital, though with a heavy heart this time.

* * *

That evening, he slowly turned a tumbler of whisky under the desk lamp, splashing a golden lightshow across his white keyboard. The litre bottle of single malt was a birthday gift from Meg's father. Danny was left to ponder what sort of impression he'd made on her parents. His stomach wouldn't shut up. There wasn't much in the fridge. The supermarkets refused to deliver this far out in the sticks and he was simply too tired to go for a big shop that evening. In any case, he didn't know for sure when Meg

18

would be allowed home. At least it'll help keep the fat off, he thought. With so many lowly rated handicappers in the yard, he didn't want to take any rides with a risk of carrying overweight.

Danny knocked back a generous measure, but he was really knocking back the loneliness.

Since Meg and her mountain of dance dresses moved in, she'd breathed new life into him and the stables. It's like someone had plugged the yard into the mains.

Despite all the knockbacks and failures that a life in racing brings, her energy and positivity remained undimmed and just made him want to be a better trainer and more importantly, a better person.

In recent days he'd missed her infectious giggle bouncing off the walls and her sweet smell and the warmth of her body at night. With her not there, the yard seemed to have a colder, darker, just-got-back-from-holiday feel.

He'd put up with anything to be with her: those annoying stretching exercises in the way of the TV before dance classes or competitions, even her clumsiness. He'd lost count of the plates she'd smashed by accident. He said she'd missed her vocation in the Greek restaurant in town. She'd got her revenge by serving his dinner on Jack's plastic plate and beaker.

Despite hating hospitals, he couldn't wait to return there with an empty bag to take her and baby Cerys home.

Jack had made her a 'welcome home' card but was now in bed. He was that excited, Danny had to retell him the tale of a knight slaying a Welsh dragon in the valleys, while secretly trying to lose himself in that story too. Flicking the light off as he left Jack's room, he noticed his hand was shaking. He was still in shock from the Ely Park murder.

Countless times he'd fantasised about this day. Perhaps he'd built it up too much in his mind. But then, he could never seem to enjoy these life-changing events enough. He wished he could somehow pause or Sky+ them before the hard work really begun.

Moments before he'd heard of his dad's sudden death in a car crash, he was having a laugh with the lads at jockey school in Lambourn. Since then, he seemed wary of enjoying anything too much as he knew it probably wouldn't last.

He hoped Micky would cope better. He could see parallels between both their paternal relationships. Micky had also appeared to see his father as a friend, a confidante, an agent and a sports psychologist all wrapped up in one. He wondered whether the lad would still have the same love for racing now, or whether it had died with his father.

For Danny, the moments after the Welsh Champion Hurdle trial race were far from clear in his mind. That's perhaps why he kept replaying them over and over until his head hurt. It's as if his brain was trying to piece together the fragments of foggy memory to make some sense of it all. Perhaps seeing the chaotic and fatal moments from a different perspective might help make it go away.

His eyes were too tired to read the newspaper he'd picked up from the hospital shop. With the internet, print news had suddenly felt like yesterday's news. The paper would only have a preview of the Welsh Champion Hurdle trial not a review.

On the front cover of a red top on the desk, he noticed a photo of the Prime Minister Hugo Forster sinking a pint of lager on his way to see a gig, the next big thing Kiss The Trouble were playing. The headline was in a speech bubble: 'Lock up the lager louts!'

Danny presumed it was an ironic reference to a quote made by the PM about the youth drinking too much that caused outrage on social media earlier that year.

Typical politician, Danny thought; do as I say not as I do.

Finally the PC was ready. Danny reckoned he could boot up quicker in the weighing room.

Danny logged into a video-sharing site.

Along with his own website and joining various social media, he had put several sunny clips of the yard, hoping to attract reliable owners to fill the empty boxes in the new stabling block built on the proceeds of Salamanca, who was now happily enjoying his retirement in the lower field once graced by a previous stable star Silver Belle.

Now logged in, Danny saw the username SBStables appear at the top of the screen next to the search box, in which he typed: welsh champion hurdle trial. He filtered the search to videos uploaded in the last twenty-four hours to eliminate any preview clips for the race uploaded by form students or tipsters.

Just one relevant result came back. The rest were for Champion Hurdle Trials from other tracks and years.

Danny took another sip of whisky.

'Medicinal,' he muttered to himself. Perhaps he could drink himself to sleep on an empty stomach. He didn't much feel like returning to the kitchen. In his mind he had retired for the night and the creak of the staircase might wake Jack.

He clicked on the page of the relevant clip. Beneath the black inset screen was a timer that read: 0:00/0:27, a list of several usernames to have already viewed the clip and a zero alongside a tick symbol. Clearly none of those users had enjoyed the clip. Danny nearly didn't bother to click play. It was probably shakily shot by some drunk racegoer with a crap phone.

Danny waited for the clip to buffer. Forget superfast broadband, they felt lucky just to have broadband up here in the remote parts of the valleys.

The clip began to play, opening with a cacophony of cheers and yells as he made out his colours beside Micky clearing the final flight in unison. The tiny PC speakers crackled. Danny lowered the volume, mindful of Jack.

Jerkily, the camera tracked the protracted duel to the finish line, suggesting the director of these images had money riding on the result. Danny could see his green and brown silks regain the lead when a loud snap, like a firecracker, shot from the speakers. It made Danny sit up and wake up. This wasn't simply static or interference on the clip's sound. He had heard that same gunshot echo out from the stands in those dying strides of the race.

A stride on, the footage juddered violently as if there'd been an earthquake. Another stride and the viewpoint had begun to pan back over the white plastic railing, across to the picnic green, over to the asphalt offshoot, the disabled viewing platform and then spun right round to the betting ring before rising up above The Whistler bar on the first floor and the restaurant on the second to the long glass balcony of the VIP suite high up in the gods.

It seemed the director wasn't seeking out the gunman but the victim. There, Danny saw the VIP guest hanging like a piece of meat.

Danny felt uncomfortable watching these ghoulish last moments of a life and lunged forward to freeze the clip but the inset screen had already turned black. His username SBStables was added to the list below the clip.

He pictured all the cameras and phones he'd seen filming the finish. He wondered what it would take for some to stop filming and run for safety, clearly more than the sound of gunfire in the case of this person.

Frustrated, he quickly pressed replay, this time with the cursor over the pause button.

The twenty-seven seconds began to roll. Once again the footage turned from the horses to the drama unfolding the other side of the railing. Danny froze the film.

The speed of the moving camera made the single frame blurry but from this distance Danny could clearly make out the green of the picnic area. He could see families had already got to their feet and were fleeing the scene for their lives. Danny moved it on a few seconds. Toddlers could be seen hoisted under parents arms, flasks, champagne flutes and hampers were being knocked over, and plates of party food were upended. Punters were even clambering over the scattered benches to get one step ahead of the crowd in their desperate escape. He guessed panic in the immediate aftermath had sent many into fight or flight.

Danny pressed play again and soon paused. The clock now read 0:11/0:27.

By now, the more agile punters could clearly be seen clambering over the railings on to the asphalt path normally reserved for the returning horses. These were clearly regulars, knowing the path offered a fast-track escape route clear of the panicked thousands to the comparative safety and cover of the parade ring and exits round the back of the stands.

Whether out of shock or confusion a few just stood there transfixed in front of the betting ring, staring high up at the balconies. Off to the right, disabled race-fans were being wheeled down from the raised viewing platform by officials. From there Danny could see the fear in their faces, having to rely on the help of others to escape the melee.

What a mess, Danny thought, shaking his head. He knew the cash-strapped track was close to going under. He also knew another bad news story would finish it.

0:17/0:27. Pause. Although more distant and partly obscured by the blurred shapes of those rushing by in the foreground, Danny could see some punters standing in or near the betting ring had ducked and sought some cover behind the grid of electronic bookie boards topped by colourful signage and parasols, in front of their laptops hidden under small awning to record bets taken and to lay them off on the exchanges.

Danny unfroze the clip again.

In the gaps between the rows of bookies, he saw colours darting left as men in t-shirts and shorts and women in summer dresses made for the exit gates early.

0:25/0:27. Pause. By now the view was of the VIP suite balcony. He'd stopped the footage just frames before the tragic ending. Danny saw the grey suit hanging there. On the balcony, there appeared to be a woman. She had her sleeveless arms in a lock, like a bear hug, around both trouser legs. He could make out her slim figure hugged by a black dress and red hair, but the image was as blurry as his memories and her pale face was no more than a smudge, like an impressionist's brushstroke. The woman appeared to be the only barrier to Campbell falling to the concrete of the betting ring far below. He could see from an increasingly stooped posture she was always going to lose out to gravity.

He recalled the balcony had been full as they'd streamed past the grandstand on the first lap. He bet the deserters thought their lives were too good to cut short.

The woman had been left alone to save Campbell. She deserved a medal for bravery. According to Stony, the BHA chief had piled on the pounds since his last ride. There'd be no hope of her supporting that weight let alone reeling him in. He let the footage run out.

In the final second, Danny saw her grip loosen and for a few frames the body began to fall. Her hands went to cover her face, as if wanting the horror to go away.

Danny's imagination picked up not long after where the clip ended, with the green huddle of paramedics.

Poor Campbell, Danny thought. He recalled looking back on the asphalt path. *Poor Micky.*

For once he was glad the whisky was making him more tired than drunk. It would help him sleep tonight if nothing else. He needed to be bright eyed and in better spirits to welcome Meg and Cerys home tomorrow morning.

He closed the browser and sat back, heart thumping. He deleted his temporary internet files, as if attempting to cleanse himself of the horrible event.

There was a faint knock on his office door. Danny sat bolt upright. He looked around for something sharp. He downed the whisky and then held the empty glass above the corner of his mahogany desk, ready to shatter it into a makeshift weapon.

'Yes!' he asked, voice as deep and booming as he could.

The door to his office slowly opened. Danny stood to attention.

Jack poked his tiny head around with a puzzled expression, glassy-eyed with tiredness. 'Daddy?'

Danny let out a nervous laugh. Jack inched into the room sucking his thumb and clutching what Danny had started calling his 'manky blankey'. Jack wouldn't allow it anywhere near the washer. Clearly he'd heard the crowd noises in the footage.

'If you're good and go back to bed, Daddy will tell you another story. I'll be with you in a minute.' He didn't mind as he was fully awake again.

Jack disappeared on the promise.

Danny sighed and put the glass down.

He went back to the clip to examine it one more time. When he logged in again and clicked on the viewing history of SBStables, the black inset screen came up but this time with the message: User has removed this clip.

On the pathway beside the melee, Danny vividly recalled Gosworth in a blind panic as he greeted the returning runners with the bad news. To be that certain Campbell was already dead, the clerk must've already gone to check before the paramedics had surrounded the body. And yet, there wasn't even a spot of blood on his green racecourse fleece. He found it unsettling that Gosworth would make such a bold claim, even before the paramedics had finished working on the fallen victim.

None of it seemed to add up. And the clip had in no way satisfied the hollow feeling inside. Perhaps returning to the murder scene would help.

CHAPTER 3

Setting foot on Ely Park again, Danny felt his stomach go. He was more nervous than having a full book of rides on race-day though the anticipation felt more of dread than excitement.

Even if Keith Gosworth had curiously pulled a sickie just days after getting the job, Danny had the keys to the racetrack to let himself in.

The downcast skies reflected the mood on track; a far cry from the tumultuous crowds swarming there in the build up to Powder Keg's finest hour.

Danny knew people were part of the fabric of a racecourse. Without them, it felt a bit eerie and soulless, like an empty shopping mall.

He chose to take the longer scenic route round the front of the grandstand. Secretly he wanted to revisit where it happened.

As he paced by the blue and white police tape, a morbid curiosity made him glance over at the large dark pool of dried blood in front of the grid of holes marking out the bookies pitches of the now felled betting jungle. Forensics in white paper dust suits, facemasks and blue plastic gloves were taking photos and measuring up.

He glanced over at a few uniformed officers in bright yellow jackets lost in conversation near some more police tape stretched between the railings overlooking the track and the path offshoot, just down from where Gosworth had stopped the returning runners.

Inside the cordoned triangle, there were more of the forensic team on all fours, putting down white markers. All of them were apparently too engrossed in scouring and preserving the scene to see Danny walking in front of the tiered concrete of the viewing gallery and then round the side by the Tote betting shop and the bronze statue of the legendary mare The Whistler, who'd graced the first incarnation of the track all those years ago.

Danny regarded this place as his second home. He even had a copy of the original architect's plans somewhere in a drawer back at the yard's office.

The council had taken control of the racecourse as a public concern since previous owner and self-confessed murderer Ralph Samuel was spending time at Cardiff prison.

For a brief whisky-induced moment last night, Danny suspected Campbell's death was the work of Samuel or one of his contacts on the outside, as some twisted act of revenge for the loss of his beloved track. But why would he want a BHA chief dead? Samuel's downfall was all his own doing.

Up ahead, near the parade ring, Danny could see a serious face in a black suit. The officer was orchestrating the uniforms around him.

'Danny!' came from behind, in a strangled whisper.

Before Danny could turn, he felt a sharp tug of his black jacket sleeve and was yanked into the alcove of a fire exit door, sheltered from both sides.

It was good to see a familiar face, though Gosworth didn't seem as pleased to see him.

A few weeks back, Gosworth had been deployed there from within BHA inner circles to help turn around the struggling Ely Park. It was too soon for nicknames, though Danny suspected with Gosworth's type that day might never come. The clerk's face was a shade pinker and he was chewing gum with even more vigour than usual.

Given the clerk seemed to live on his nerves and was rarely seen standing still, Danny wondered how much he had to eat and drink to maintain that overhang. He would normally be seen around the racecourse in elasticated waterproofs, but was in a slimming pinstriped suit and tie this time. He still couldn't tame that white hair. It clearly wasn't a wig as there'd be no demand, even in the comedy range.

'Christ, Keith, when's the court case?' Danny asked, trying to cut the funereal atmosphere.

'What?!' Keith snapped, clearly in no mood to see the joke.

'The suit.' With the law swarming the place, Danny was left to assume Keith had dressed to impress. 'What are you doing here?'

'What am I doing here?!' Keith asked incredulously.

'Yeah.'

'Danny, this is a bloody murder scene. I'm here to help show police around. Make their life easy, so they can bugger off all the quicker.' He groaned as he pinched the bridge of his fat nose. 'Why did Campbell have to die now?'

'I'm sure Maria and Micky are saying the same,' Danny said. 'That doesn't explain why you're bricking it about the police.'

Keith paused as if considering the answer. 'We weren't the best of friends.'

'You and Campbell?'

'It's all in the past now, but you of all people know what the police can be like, they put two and two together…'

'I'm no fan of them,' Danny said, 'but I don't reckon you'll be a suspect just for not liking someone, otherwise half the population would be on the database.'

'One last time, why are you here?'

'Couldn't sleep much last night,' Danny said, rubbing his eyes, 'and anyway, since when has the racing consultant needed an excuse to be here?'

'You designed the track, Danny, you don't run it,' Gosworth said. 'So why the sleepless night?'

'Meg gave birth to a beautiful baby girl, just before Campbell died,' Danny said.

'Oh, sorry,' Keith replied flatly. 'I'd forgotten. Baby well? Weight okay? etc. etc.'

Danny opened his mouth to reply but was beaten to it.

'Good, good,' Keith said dismissively. 'Well done and all that.'

'Her name's Cerys by the way.'

It's only when the clerk offered a congratulatory hand that Danny noticed red scratches, like claw marks up the back of them.

'You should see her, she's a little angel.'

'All babies look alike don't they?'

'Well—'

'To more pressing matters,' Gosworth interrupted and then poked a head out from the well of the door, looking both ways. When he reeled his neck back in, he continued with, 'if the police ask questions, we were both on the path over there when Campbell fell, agree?'

'You might have been but all the runners were still out on the track waiting for the tail-enders to complete and for someone to tell us what the hell was going on.'

'But we did meet on that path, remember? You were still on Powder Keg and Micky hopped over the rails to get to his father.'

'Keith, why are you doing this?'

'To get our stories straight, so they tally on our statements.'

'Stories?' Danny asked in disbelief. 'I'm just going to tell them the truth.'

Gosworth paused as if sensing this wasn't helping his case.

'Why would you want the police to believe you were on that path when Campbell fell?'

'When I took this on, at council pay I might add, I didn't reckon on this happening at my first race meeting.'

'None of us did!'

'This place is struggling as it is without something like this. It will scare families away, our new core market. We'd only just spruced up the picnic area. I have a reputation to uphold.'

'What about the track's bloody reputation?' Danny snapped.

'I can see it in your eyes,' Gosworth hissed. 'You think I did it.'

'I hadn't thought that until now. Let's face it, I don't really know you and when you're acting like this—'

Gosworth grabbed Danny by the collar of his jacket. 'Like what?!'

Danny gave him a look. He smelt spearmint on Gosworth's warm breath.

Gosworth eased his grip, as if realising how this might look. Suddenly he was pretending to straighten the collar.

'That's better. Want to look your best for the police,' quipped Danny.

Gosworth stepped back to lean against the alcove wall and ran a calloused hand through that white bush on his head. 'It's just, I expected nothing worse than a faulty watering system, or a problem with the food vans paying up the rent but not this.'

'You knew this place was a problem track,' Danny said. 'The bigwigs of racing wouldn't have come otherwise.'

'And their party left one lighter,' Gosworth said and then frowned.

'Was he taken off in the racecourse ambulance?'

Gosworth nodded.

'So perhaps you were wrong and he was still alive.'

'He was in a body bag in the ambulance,' Gosworth replied. 'It's a sorry, god-awful state of affairs. I knew I should've taken early retirement.'

'A few more months of Ely Park and you might have to,' Danny said. 'Was it the bullet or the fall that finished him?'

'I saw him being let go.'

'Who let go?'

'It was hard to tell, I was on the ground without my specs,' Gosworth said. 'I wanted to be seen by the BHA mob to be customer friendly, so I was mingling with the punters down here.'

'So you're saying he died from the fall and not the bullet.'

'I didn't hear any gunfire,' Gosworth shrugged. 'Anyway, what difference does it make?'

'If he was shot it's murder,' Danny explained, 'if he fell it's a tragic accident.'

'Not if Campbell was pushed.'

Danny played along as if they weren't lies. In the online clip, he'd clearly heard a gunshot ring out from the PC speakers.

Gosworth held eye contact and didn't flinch when he talked. Either he was a superb liar, a psychopath or he was telling the truth. But could he honestly believe so many police and forensics would be deployed if this was an accidental fall?

'There was a waterfall of blood coming from Campbell when he was hanging up there. Are you saying he had a nosebleed? Cos I'm telling you Campbell's nose wasn't *that* big.'

'Don't make crass jokes of the dead,' Gosworth replied.

Danny stopped short of questioning why Ely Park's racing manager felt the need to blatantly lie about where he was and the cause of death as he suspected it would only lead to yet more lies.

As the pair stood there, the silence was piercing.

Danny broke it with, 'Don't let me stop you.'

'I'm quite happy to keep out of the way of the police,' Gosworth replied. 'My head is banging from all the questions, not to mention helping to organise the industrial-scale bagging up of phones and cameras from all the racegoers who'd filmed at the track for the police to cart away. That's yet another thing above and beyond my call of duty. You wouldn't believe how many see their life through a lens. Why they can't bloody watch it, remember it and if that memory fades relive it with a TV clip online, I don't know. The world hasn't overtaking me, it's bloody lapped me.'

'Not all,' Danny said, recalling the video footage he'd clicked on last night.

'What?'

'Not all the phones were handed over,' Danny replied. 'I've seen a clip of the moment.'

'Did you see everything?'

'I still don't know everything that happened, so how can I tell if I saw it all?' Danny said.

'Where is this clip?'

31

'It got taken down,' Danny said. He then heard deep voices growing larger from the parade ring somewhere off to the left. Perhaps the suited detective was coming round to order the forensics out the front. 'It won't look clever us two lurking here, now go.'

Danny turned and pushed the steel bar of the fire door. He was convinced Gosworth was hiding something and knew the best place to find it. Ely Park had already seen one rotten apple in charge. Danny wasn't prepared to let this place shut because of another.

With such a large police presence on track, he knew it was odds-on a few would be taking away evidence from the VIP suite. Danny reckoned if they were in Gosworth's office, he'd have to leave the way he came.

Danny headed for the third floor. He rushed down a wide corridor off a door marked: PRIVATE STAFF ONLY.

I'm the racing consultant, Danny reconciled.

At the end of the corridor, he knocked a door with a plastic nameplate: Keith Gosworth above Racing Manager and Clerk of the Course. It was one down from the cleaning storeroom.

The door wouldn't budge. He tried the key he'd been awarded for his consultancy work but, as he suspected, it wasn't of the skeleton variety.

He looked back down the long, dimly lit corridor. It was silent and empty.

Danny had better luck trying the storeroom. Among the stacks of toilet rolls and mops and litter pickers, Danny saw a clothes rack of moth-eaten tweed jackets and slightly frayed ties. He removed one of the coat hangers and set about fashioning it into a suitable hook. He returned to the corridor and swiftly picked the lock. With one last check to see the coast was clear, he turned and pushed into the office.

The pokey one-windowed room on the third floor was a far cry from the previous racing manager's office of Ralph Samuel located on the panoramic top floor where the corporate and VIP suite was now. Even the storeroom was larger and felt fresher than this room.

The morning sun was enough light as he rushed over to Keith's desk.

He guessed Gosworth would be some time yet assisting detectives on the ground but he still kept listening out for footsteps, picturing the clerk of the course steaming down the corridor. He didn't have any excuses ready and knew he'd be, at the very least, stripped of the keys and gallop rights if caught. It would also provide Gosworth with an excuse to point the finger of guilt away from him. He'd probably march him straight down to get cuffed.

Danny fished deep into the drawer. He guessed anything worth hiding would be there. Amongst piles of documents and forms, Danny could see two empty 75cl bottles of vodka beside a specs case and a hole-punch.

He'd only just got the job, Danny thought. He was seriously doubting whether Gosworth was the man to turn this place round. It explained why the clerk's breath was always minty fresh.

Danny opened a leather-bound diary in there. As he thumbed the pages, nothing had been put under today's date. But the previous five days, there'd been the same entry 'Campbell Galbraith is a complete—' the rest of the sentence was blocked out with ink. Danny looked closer and although he couldn't decipher the masked words, he guessed they weren't 'gentleman and scholar.'

With his breath and diary rants, Danny wondered what else Keith Gosworth was covering up. But there was nothing in the desk to pin a murder on the clerk. Many of his thoughts about rival trainers would also need censoring, he conceded. He guessed this was Gosworth's idea of a stress ball, perhaps he couldn't afford a shrink.

He continued to chance his luck by searching the top drawer of the desk. He pulled out a list of nine names.

Handwritten at the top was: *Welsh Champ Trial day guest list/seating plan.*

Danny guessed these were the VIPs. He knew the premium suite above his head could cater for more than double that. It seemed these nine guests were more than very important persons.

There was also a menu in the drawer, with fillet steak, veal, salmon and lobster among the offerings. Gosworth was really out to impress.

Among the guest list, there was a politician called Right Hon. George Wheater seated at the head of the table. The bookie Raymond Barton was also invited, presumably as a sponsor's perk.

Sat alongside on the table settings were Campbell and his wife Maria, whose horse Danny beat.

The balcony up there wasn't that big. Danny suspected all nine present would've had a clear view of the event and where the gunfire came from.

With increasing urgency Danny continued to delve, only looking up to check the door was still shut. He pulled out a rubber specs case. It felt flimsily empty and only when he shook it, out fell a USB memory stick.

He looked at the laptop on the desk but he knew the police might share Danny's suspicions of the new clerk and therefore decided against seeing what the memory stick contained as he'd leave an electronic fingerprint. He returned the stick as he didn't want to be removing possible evidence.

It was then he lost his nerve. He didn't want to risk being locked up in a police cell with Meg left holding the baby by packed bags at the hospital, more than ready to go.

Silently, he slipped away from the murder scene.

CHAPTER 4

Danny was secretly glad he'd prearranged this catch-up with Stony. He'd left Meg cossetting Cerys in the trainer's lodge. She was eagerly waiting to show off her first child to her excitable girlie friends from Rhymney.

'Sorry, you don't mind babes.'

'Don't be,' Danny said, as he hurriedly slipped on his trainers. He'd much rather leave them to it. Anyway, he had his own catching up to do with his oldest pal. Danny, with two children and dozens of horses to look after, was worried Stony would soon become a stranger.

He wondered how Stony, godfather to Campbell's son Micky, had reacted to the news from Ely Park.

Danny knew Stony and Campbell hadn't seen each other since they both put away their riding boots. Since then, the ex-jockeys had chosen very different paths and lost touch. Campbell had switched to the politics of the sport and risen to become chief executive of the ruling body, while Stony preferred to concentrate on his fifty pence patents and thirty pence Lucky 15s.

But for Danny, the best way to judge a man was who he'd prefer to sink a pint with and there was only one winner there.

Danny couldn't figure out why Stony had arranged to meet at his local bookies. Last time they'd seen each other he'd swapped punting for painting. He presumed it was for old times' sake. Danny didn't mind. Aside from Meg's arms, it was the one place he felt completely comfortable.

Danny turned into Greyfriars Road. Beneath the red sign of Raymond Barton's Bookmakers, Stony was loudly rattling the glass entrance.

'Since when were you back in the betting game?' Danny asked.

Stony peered through the glass and then turned. 'Oh, it's you.'

'Who were you expecting?'

35

'One of his little minions.'

'Whose minions?'

'Raymundo in there,' Stony said, 'and look at this.' He pointed at the closed sign on the window. 'I know he's in there.'

'But what happened to your brush and paints?' Danny said. 'I liked your early work.'

'Well, cutting a long story short.'

'If you would.'

'Some nude life model accused me of being a perv, said I was staring at her funny.'

'Staring at her what?'

'Her funny.'

'Were you?'

'No!' Stony protested.

'Do the face you made,' Danny requested.

Stony stepped back and then proceeded to widen his eyes and the curled tip of his tongue also made an appearance.

'Oh, I can sort of see what she means. When's the court case due?'

'Eh?!' Stony fumed and then nodded knowingly. 'Oh, I see. Bit of a joke to you is it?'

Danny sniggered. Stony rolled his eyes.

'I'm laughing with you, not at you.'

'But I'm not laughing,' Stony shrugged. 'That's what happens to my face when I concentrate. Ask him in there, I'm just the same when I'm studying form, and he *is* in there by the way, seen shadows moving.'

'So what happened?'

'Well, she said it unnerved her,' Stony continued. 'She's got a bloody nerve alright. Pervert?! She's the one happy to flaunt her bits to the world, cheeky mare. And by god, she'd got some cheek, especially when she sat down. And don't get me start on those pendulous t—'

'Too much detail,' Danny said. 'I wanna enjoy my pint.'

Stony fished in his baggy denims and removed a crumpled pink betting slip. 'This bastard owes me fifty notes and he knows

36

it, that's why the bloody crook is hiding in there. I thought betting was daylight robbery, but this is—'

'I don't think Barton would be hiding over fifty quid.'

'Ninety coming back to me if you include the stake, had a forty-win single on Powder Keg,' Stony said. 'Check the small print on that notice and you'll see what I mean.'

It was only then Danny noticed an A4 sheet of paper taped to the shop window.

It read: Dear Customer, This shop has sadly closed down. We are sorry for any inconvenience. Thank you for your support.

'Collect it at another shop.'

'I checked the branch down Newport Road, exactly the same there. He's gone bust and isn't going to cough up. He knew what he was doing taking this bet.'

Stony used his hand as a visor as he peered into the shop and then began to rattle the door again.

'Stand back,' Danny said.

'Don't bother picking the locks Danny, there's nothing in there. Even the bank of screens are just black holes now, see?'

Danny banged his fist on the glass. 'Raymond! This is the police, open up now.'

'He *can* see you,' Stony said.

'He doesn't know I'm not plain clothes.'

There was a few seconds of quiet before they heard two bolts being shot.

The door opened a fraction, enough for Danny to see two large eyes looking back. Seconds later the aftershave hit him.

'That's him,' Stony said, pointing at the large head peering out, beneath chocolate brown hair swept back. He was in a blue suit jacket with enamel cufflinks. 'I've seen a life size cardboard cut-out of him wearing the same near the counter. And I'll get his fat face on Crimewatch before I give up on this.' Stony waved his fist containing the crumpled betting slip.

'Are you really closing down?' Danny asked.

'I'm finished here, I'm out,' Raymond snarled. Danny reckoned he'd fit in well on the show Dragon's Den, but for the

37

fact his business had failed. He'd got the striking manly features and strong bones the cameras would lap up.

'Surprised those money-gobbling roulette machines alone couldn't keep this place going,' Danny said.

'Do you really want to know why I'm closing?'

'Yeah,' Danny said, 'my pal here deserves an explanation at least.'

'The government is passing a bill to restrict a shop this size to four machines,' Raymond said, angrily, 'and to rub salt in the wound, the Treasury will be slapping a twenty-bloody-per-cent charge on takings, that's on top of the ten point seven-five per cent racing levy, then add on the TV rights to show the racing, wages, energy bills. They've shafted the pubs now it's the bookies turn, really they're punishing the poor plebs.' Pointedly, his big eyes flitted between Danny and Stony.

Danny ignored the thinly veiled insult and said, 'Seems like your good thing has come to an end.'

'This added machines tax is just to appease the lefties moaning about addicts, debt and crime. But the government won't ever get rid of the gaming machines, because they do just fine out of them. The margins are so great, any profits lost from shops closing like mine will be offset by the ones left open now handing over this extra twenty per cent demanded by the Treasury to boost its coffers.'

'I'm sorry I left my violin at home, now,' Danny said.

'I'm not looking for sympathy,' Raymond replied. 'I'm just explaining why you're friend Smokey here no longer has a local bookie to go. I'm only sorry I didn't do this earlier.'

'Stony,' Danny corrected. 'It's Stony. I'm surprised you don't recognise him, he's been topping up your pension fund for decades.'

'Eh, I had some good wins in that time,' Stony interjected defensively.

'Stony, you're skint,' Danny said. 'You still wear your old riding goggles to the swimming baths.'

38

'They look good,' Stony said, 'and I only go cos it's supposed to be good for my hips.'

'Are we done?' Raymond asked sternly, glancing at his gold Rolex. 'I don't want to waste your time.'

'You do passive-aggressive well,' Danny said.

'I can do aggressive if you'd prefer,' Raymond snarled and went to slam the glass in their faces when Danny stuck a boot in as a makeshift doorstop. 'There's one thing more tragic than a loser and that's a sore loser.'

'Just pay the man and we'll go quietly,' Danny said.

'I haven't got the cash on me,' Raymond said.

'Not that old one,' Stony replied.

Danny could see Stony's hand was shaking and said, 'It's a bookies, go to the tills.'

'There are none,' Stony said, 'He's already stripped the whole shop. Funny there was no warning about all this when I put my money down.'

Raymond saw Danny step back and promptly shut the door.

'We're not bloody finished,' Stony ranted and rushed to the door but stopped when it swung open again.

Raymond reappeared with the life-sized cardboard cut-out of himself. Danny was surprised a frustrated punter hadn't yet punched its head off.

'The clearance guys left this behind,' Raymond said.

'Wonder why,' Danny asked sarcastically and then looked at the photo. 'It's been airbrushed more than a Banksy.'

'Perhaps it'll be worth as much, it's rare,' Raymond replied. He then handed it over awkwardly with his left hand, as if his right one was full. Probably a wad of notes, Danny thought. Raymond added, 'And it's yours Stoner.'

'Stony,' Danny corrected again, 'and it's only rare cos there'd be no demand for it.'

He then heard the scrape of cardboard on cobbles. When he turned, he looked on in disbelief as Stony was now struggling to drag the six-foot monstrosity. 'What the hell are you doing?'

Raymond was grinning.

'What's it look like? I'm taking it.'

'It's not worth the cardboard it's printed on,' Danny said, running a hand through his thick hair.

'That's still better than nothing.'

Danny looked at Raymond for some support, but there was no way he was going to back him up. The ex-bookie shut the door with another ring and a rattle of glass. Raymond then began to take down the bell above the door. It was hard to imagine he was a former winner of the Wales Business and Enterprise Award.

Danny quickly caught up with Stony and took hold of the feet end of Raymond.

Walking to the relocated Castle Keep, Danny asked, 'How well did you know Campbell really?'

Stony shrugged.

'But it was well enough for him to make you Micky's godfather.'

'I was the only one in the weighing room that said yes,' Stony said. 'You see, Campbell made enemies easier than friends. I'm never one to make enemies, so I was just a sympathetic ear for all his moans about other jockeys cutting him up in races, gave him encouragement when he'd pick up a niggling injury and when he'd bang on about the politics of the sport, I swear he could send a glass eye to sleep sometimes.'

'No danger of that anymore,' Danny said flatly.

'Terrible business that,' Stony said. 'It was a thriller of a race, and then the TV cuts to an ad break, leaving me clutching a forty quid betting slip, the suspense was killing me.'

'What was Campbell like?'

'Why are you so interested?' Stony replied.

'I'm racing consultant, it happened on my patch.'

'That's just a job title, not an actual job.'

'Looks good on my CV.'

'You've never had a CV.'

Danny couldn't come back from that. Instead, he asked, 'Was Keith Gosworth ever one of Campbell's enemies?'

'The new Ely Park man?'

Danny nodded.

'Nah, but then he was never a jockey,' Stony said. 'You think this Keith is a murderer then?'

Danny didn't reply.

'They don't have much luck with their recruiting down at Ely Park,' Stony continued. 'Two managers, two murderers. Mind, Ely Park's not exactly Royal Ascot.'

'We've sometimes got a dress code,' Danny said defensively.

'I've seen the sign: No string vests, including the ladies.' Stony laughed to himself.

'I didn't say he was a murderer,' Danny said, 'but I do know he's a liar.'

'It a shame though, I'd planned to make it a regular haunt, that place is the best thing to happen to this area. No one stares if you go racing on your own, different when you feel like going out for a meal.'

'Tell me to piss off,' Danny said, 'but has there ever been a lady in your life Stony?'

Stony rolled his eyes.

'No matter, not my business.'

'There's been a few, long time ago mind.'

'Dark horse, you,' Danny said.

'And one of them actually meant something,' Stony said. His eyes became misty, telling Danny he wasn't making this up to save macho pride. 'Janet was her name, lovely woman, met her in Newmarket. I think I liked her more than she liked me.'

'Why do you say that?'

'She left me,' Stony sighed. 'And do you know what her parting words were, "Even in sleep you annoy me".'

Danny looked across. 'Dare I ask?'

'Apparently I started to snore when I put on a few pounds,' he said. 'It was her good cooking.'

Danny saw some spark fizzle from Stony's eyes as quickly as it had arrived. 'She doesn't sound as nice as you say.'

41

'As I feared, I didn't deserve her, too good for a journeyman jockey.'

'And there hasn't been anyone since?' Danny asked.

'Alright, Dan Juan, we can't all be as fruity as you,' Stony said.

'I'm not gloating, I've made my share of mistakes in love,' Danny said. 'I just want you to be happy.'

'I'm too old and set in my ways to get back into that particular saddle. Being single so long, you become an exaggerated version of yourself. If I was annoying to Janet back then, I don't reckon I'd stand a chance now. Looks like Campbell beat me in love as well as life.'

'He put it about a bit did he?'

'It seems they were attracted more to the mean, moody types.'

Danny wondered if there was a scorned mistress behind Campbell's death.

'So you don't know Micky.'

'I lost touch with Campbell years back,' Stony said. 'Last time I met his lad was when he was a baby.'

'Did you fall out with Campbell?'

'He was moving in higher circles than me,' Stony said. 'Didn't Henry James once say "a friend in power is a friend lost"?'

'Have you been reading again,' Danny said.

'Only the local rag, quote of the day it was.'

'And you haven't seen Micky since then.'

'I'm sure he's turned out well and Maria can still give him support.'

'But if she's not around,' Danny said.

'Well, God help the boy if I'm all the support he'll have through life. I can barely boil an egg.'

'But you share the same passion for horses and racing,' Danny said. 'Don't you at least want to know who could do this to his father?'

'Not really. I mean it's sad, but what can any of us do about it?'

'So there's nothing else you can say about the man?'

'They used to call him Daddy in the weighing room,' Stony added, 'if that helps.'

Danny gave a look, 'Because he was the boss?'

'Nah.'

'Older than you?'

'He had long legs you see. He had to keep thin as a rake not to carry overweight. So when I saw a recent photo in the local rag, I wouldn't have recognised him. He'd clearly enjoyed the good life, looking at the size of him.'

Danny had even more sympathy for the redhead woman left to save the body from falling.

Stony then looked down at the stretched weave of his checked shirt. 'Mind, I'm one to talk. Do you know, these days I'd rather take off my trousers than my vest in public.'

'Don't tell that to the judge,' Danny replied.

He pushed the door of the refurbished Castle Keep pub, now opposite the Roman walls of the castle.

43

CHAPTER 5

WORCESTER RACECOURSE, 28th September.

Danny had been on track a few hours but his mind was still stuck at Ely Park.

With the help of a second handler called Jordi, who'd recently joined the yard from Mijas in Spain, their declared runner Seven Dollars – though known only by her pet name Tufty back at the yard – was slowly led round the parade ring.

Wanting the filly to look her best for the big day, Danny wiped white froth from the troubled youngster's bay neck.

Since being rescued, the diminutive five-year-old had quickly become a firm favourite with everyone at Silver Belle Stables, particularly Jack, who planned to ride her when he was old enough.

While the physical marks of neglect suffered at the hands of trainer Bert Mills' son Leo in the neighbouring Sunnyside Farm were now gone, the mental scars were proving harder to heal. He suspected those were memories both would rather forget. That's why he'd invited Jordi along as back-up in case she got upset and fractious from all the new and strange sights and smells of a racecourse introduction.

But seeing the recruit settle down and thrive had done more for the yard's morale than a big win. That made Meg yearn to take on more struggling runners in a bid to turn them around.

'Tell me our registered charity number again,' Danny would reply, only to be rewarded by a playful hit on the arm. He knew her heart was in the right place, but wasn't so sure about her business brain.

Not far away, Danny noticed Micky had finished receiving orders from his trainer near the verge of the grassy island covering most of the ring.

As Danny went by, he called over, 'Micky.'

Micky was now straightening his yellow and turquoise silks. Danny thought Micky couldn't look any unhappier but then the grieving jockey saw who was calling his name.

Tufty was still relaxed enough for Danny to allow Jordi to lead on.

'I'm so sorry, Micky. How are you coping with—' Danny stopped himself. It didn't sound right. But then, what would sound right to Micky at this time?

'Just keeping busy, so I don't think,' Micky replied, 'but it's bloody hard when people keep coming up saying sorry. What've they done to be sorry about, apart from saying sorry.'

'I just can't imagine what you're going through,' Danny sighed. 'He was proud of you, Micky. I still can't get over what happened. Have the police told you anything?'

'Like I said, I'm trying not to think about it,' Micky replied. 'Baby doing well?'

'Yeah,' Danny said and smiled. 'She's a darling. Mind, I don't say that at three in the morning when she's bawling her eyes out and I'm due up to send out the first lot in a few hours.' He quickly felt like he shouldn't be the one moaning. 'Never mind about me.'

The imposing figure of trainer Clive Kipper, who looked like a man mountain weaving among jockeys, placed a hand on Micky's rounded shoulder, making the jockey physically jerk free.

Danny suspected that nervous reaction was something far more than any pre-race jitters before this minor maiden hurdle. Micky's fear more likely stemmed from knowing the murderer was still at large.

Clive reacted by saying, 'Look, Micky, do you think this is a good idea?'

'Yeah,' Micky snapped.

'But I don't think you're ready,' Clive reasoned, arching bushy eyebrows.

'My job is all I have left, don't rob me of that, too!'

45

'Wrong! I offered you this spare ride Micky, thinking it might help. I now think differently,' Clive replied loudly. His large green eyes had turned cold. Danny suspected Clive's sympathy was quickly wearing thin.

Danny could see the TV camera not far away and, trying to cool the situation, told Micky, 'Clive here had nothing to do with what happened at Ely, if that's what you're implying. He hasn't robbed you of your father or your job. And whoever did do it, they won't come for you.'

'How the hell would you know?' Micky asked. 'No one knows who killed my father, least of all the police.'

'That's no excuse to start pointing the finger, particularly at a supporter like Clive.'

Clive winked at Danny for those kind words and then strong-armed Micky away to his mount. It looked like Tufty wasn't the one in need of a second handler.

Being a disciplinarian, Campbell would've surely frowned upon a public show of temperament, viewing it as a sign of weakness.

Hearing the bell, Danny went to mount Tufty.

Danny glanced over at the small white grandstand and then to the bookies pitched closer by, in a satellite betting ring between the burger and ice cream vans. They were doing more trade than the bookies – hardly surprising to Danny as this was a low-grade race full of unknown quantities.

Neither was he surprised to see twenty-to-one in flickering orange by Seven Dollars up on the electronic betting boards. She was unraced and paddock watchers would no doubt cross her off as lacking in size and scope. Meg had done her best but no amount of pleating, clipping and brushing could turn the looks of a lightly made jumper into a blue-blood thoroughbred of the Flat. But in Danny's eyes she looked a picture compared to the raggedy condition when they'd first met. A month or so back he'd overheard one of the stable lads say to another, 'seems you can't polish a turd after all.' He was now an ex-stable lad.

On the grass island, the roaming presenter for a racing TV channel was interviewing a man of similar build to Clive Kipper with black hair slicked to one side, wearing a tailored suit and blue-tinted shades.

From the speakers came, 'Can you all please give it up for our special guest, the Right Honourable George Wheater?'

There was a smattering of applause. Danny suspected more out of embarrassment to fill the silence. He clearly wasn't the MP for Worcester.

George Wheater. Danny stopped tugging on his gloves as he realised where he'd seen that name; on the seating plan found in Gosworth's desk.

He'd slipped out of race-mode and was now studying Wheater's every move. When he heard the presenter wrap up the interview, Danny saw the politician head straight over. Had he been caught staring?

Suddenly Danny wanted special dispensation to leave the parade ring and go down to the start early. *What the hell have I done now?*

Danny looked ahead, refusing to even acknowledge Wheater, who was now slowly walking the paddock in tandem. But it seemed he simply wasn't going to go away. Danny looked down. There was a mole on George's lined face too large to be called a beauty spot. The more Danny told himself to ignore it the more his eyes were drawn to it. Given politics was as much about image as policy these days, Danny wondered why he hadn't had it removed.

'What do you want?' Danny asked.

'Tell me, Danny, are you willing to throw this?' Wheater asked up to him.

Danny was too taken aback to respond immediately. A few steps on, he asked incredulously, 'What?!'

There was no way a politician in the public eye would so brazenly ask to cheat, Danny figured.

'You heard.'

47

Perhaps Wheater had been making use of the complimentary bar, though he hadn't meandered or stumbled across from the interview at the sponsor's podium.

Danny could only shrug it off as a misguided joke. 'I don't know whether I'm willing or not is going to make a difference.'

He was about to pinch back Tufty's big ears and whisper, 'She's not that good,' but Wheater was already returning to the sponsors.

That just happened! He had to replay the moment in his mind to make sure he hadn't misheard.

Why would he even joke about something like that? He must have one twisted sense of humour. Even if that was a proposition, where's the value in wanting a twenty-to-one rag beat? Wheater could hardly get rich laying it off on the betting exchanges, earning about a five per-cent return before fees.

When he looked over again, George looked like he was coming back for more. Danny was about to put him straight when Wheater ran a big hand down Tufty's gleaming neck, and thick mane. 'Congratulations, your groom has won a hundred pounds for best turned out.'

Danny suspected that would lift Meg's mood more than his own. Perhaps he should leave now before discovering the horse's limitations out on the track.

Filing out from the parade ring, Danny looked across at the row of powerful rails bookies – those more likely to cater for the hefty bets of high rollers handing over bundles of notes – with many of the high street chains represented. He noticed a gap where Raymond Barton once held a pitch there. It had probably already been auctioned off to pay the creditors, he presumed.

Cantering to post, Danny tried not to look down at Tufty's scratchy action. She simply wasn't stretching out on the ground, officially described as: good, good-to-soft in places. As he suspected, the horse would prefer more juice in the ground, but she was ready to run and needed some experience before the autumn campaign truly began.

With the River Severn just the other side of the curtain of trees lining the home-straight, Worcester was prone to flooding and was therefore restricted to mostly holding summer jumping fixtures. This was the third-last meeting of the year.

As the starter let them go for the two-mile maiden hurdle, Danny could soon tell his ground concerns were founded. By halfway, he was already toiling in tenth and even more concerning than that, he needed to squeeze her along to merely hold a position back there.

He was about to ease off and let Tufty trail home in her own good time when he felt her pick up the bridle on the sweep back into the straight. He guessed they'd met the good-to-soft patches.

Until then, the rescue filly had seemed to be holding something back. Perhaps she could now sense they were heading back to the racecourse stables and was eager to get there.

Danny raised his whip and gave Tufty a few swift reminders. They both were here to do a job. Seven Dollars responded by keeping on pleasingly into a remote fifth.

As they crossed the line, Danny was left with a positive overall impression of the debut. He came there with no expectations, no bubble to burst and would leave with a likely future winner. *Result!*

He leant forward and panted, 'You're definitely a keeper, girl.'

Returning Tufty to the stables, Danny spotted Micky slip into a gap in the trees behind the grandstand. As an ex-smoker, Danny knew the path led to a secluded riverside clearing where jockeys could sneak a quick ciggie between races, some to calm nerves, or to escape the mayhem of race-days, others to stave off cravings for nicotine or food.

He picked up his mobile from his kit bag in the weighing room to check for missed calls from Meg and then met up with Jordi, who'd put Tufty in one of the spare boxes to settle and cool down. He looked over to the opposite side of the stabling where Clive Kipper and Daisy Reed, who trained the runner-up and third respectively, were leading their horses away, accompanied by a blonde woman in an overall. They appeared to be heading for the sampling bay. Danny recognised her as a vet working for the BHA integrity unit.

Having finished in the frame, they were obliged to give urine and/or blood samples, sometimes hair, as a routine matter. The regulators of the sport were also targeting runners performing well above or below the expectations of the betting market. It was for the public to see racing run as a fair and level playing field for all competitors. With betting scandals now threatening most sports, here was racing's opportunity to take back some of the gambling revenue lost to them in recent years.

Having finished unplaced and run about to form, he reckoned Tufty would fly under the radar both with the stewards on course and at BHA Headquarters in High Holborn.

Danny was about to get changed in the jockeys' room but something was niggling at him. He didn't like leaving the track without clearing the air with Micky. He owed it to Stony.

'Won't be a sec,' Danny said to Jordi, who replied in a thick Spanish accent, 'Remember the traffic.'

'We'll beat rush hour I promise,' Danny replied.

As he past the BHA vet crossing his path, he asked, 'I'm good to go?'

She glanced at a clipboard and nodded.

Danny headed for the gap in the trees. He still didn't know what he was going to tell the youngster.

Although the words 'hang in there,' or 'time's a healer,' sounded naff in his head right then, it's probably what Danny had wanted to hear just after he'd lost his own father at a similar age, though he wouldn't have listened back then.

He followed a path of flattened dead grass and broken twigs on compacted earth, trampled by countless riding boots of the secret smokers among the weighing room.

He stepped into the small clearing. There were two breaks in the willows and bushes allowing windows out on the glittering dark waters of the slow, meandering River Severn.

Danny approached one and looked out to see a two-man rowing boat silently glide by almost unnoticed. He watched the rippling patterns fan out as their oars and bow broke the still waters. They wouldn't have noticed him even if he'd cheered them on.

As a kid, Danny spent hours beside his dad fishing on the riverbanks of the River Taff. Even now the sight of the water comforted him and refuelled his soul, like listening to the music of his youth or wolfing down home cooked food.

He glanced over to the riverbank opposite, checking the back gardens of the grand detached houses beyond another line of drooping willows. He then looked downriver to the footbridge spanning the Severn off to the left.

The serenity was broken by the snap of a twig. Danny turned on his heels. He swore he saw a shadow move in the dark beyond the leaves and branches. 'Micky? Is that you?'

Suddenly he didn't feel so alone there. Was it a smoker who wanted to keep it a secret?

It went deathly quiet. Not even the sound of birdsong.

It was only then Danny picked up on a whiff of smoke. Ever since quitting, even the smell nipped at the back of his throat.

When he saw the ghostly grey swirls rising from an ashtray's worth scattered on the ground his suspicions were piqued. He knelt. Among the cigarette butts, one still smouldered. Most of that ciggie was intact. Danny stamped it out before the dry grass there acted like tinder.

Had Micky left in a hurry?

He looked at his watch. There was still a good twenty minutes before the following race. Jockeys had to report to the weighing room for the next ride a minimum of fifteen minutes before the race. Micky would've had plenty of time to finish it. He certainly wouldn't have left it here to risk a fire with a packed racetrack and a wooden boathouse nearby.

Danny scanned the walls of vegetation forming this small clearing.

51

Perhaps he'd fancied a cooling dip in the river after riding out the finish to make second place but there was no pile of silks or riding boots anywhere.

He then questioned Concorde's state of mind. For months after witnessing his brother's brutal murder, Danny felt suicidal.

He surely wouldn't do something stupid, Danny reasoned, not with his whole life ahead, not Micky. But then he didn't sound himself in the parade ring. Perhaps he had jumped in the river but without the intention of swimming. It would explain why he'd left the ciggie and there was no sign of any discarded clothes.

Danny looked down the river bank. Below his feet was a mare's nest of thin gnarly roots tangled with weeds, leaves, reeds and some crumpled fag packets.

He glanced shiftily behind before lying on the earth and pushing his face to one of the holes made by the intertwining roots that stretched right down to dip their toes in the water. Through the gap, he could make out a shelf of silt by the water's edge several feet below.

He couldn't see any movement or manmade colours down there. If he'd fallen, surely the roots would've got in the way. He was about to return to the weighing room to get changed when he noticed patterns in the water just downstream from the root system.

It seemed something was disturbing the natural flow of water and sending ripples out into the river. He planted his face in another gap and suddenly saw a patch of colour. It was ruddy turquoise.

Danny pictured Micky in his turquoise and yellow quartered silks in the parade ring minutes earlier.

'Concorde?' Danny shouted. 'Are you okay, Concorde?'

Above the sound of rippling water, he swore he heard a groan. He got to his knees and snapped the poppers running down the body of his silks before peeling them off.

From the back of his breeches, he removed his mobile and called for an ambulance and fire brigade. They shouldn't take long, Danny thought, knowing there had to be two ambulances on track at any one time for race meetings in Britain.

He hurriedly tied one of the sleeves of his silks to the thickest root and then swung himself out. His heart started to go again from the fear of what he might find down there.

Hadn't the Galbraiths had enough bad luck for one week?

He abseiled as far as his silks would stretch and then dropped the rest. His riding boots splashed as they disappeared into the shallow waters of the river's edge. He fell forward to land on the silt shelf sheltered by the canopy of roots.

Danny looked to a mound on his left. It was a small body covered in wet mud. The arms were stretched out in front, as if he'd clawed his way out of the water and made it this far. His right boot was making the ripples in the water he'd noticed from the clearing.

He could see the patches of turquoise he'd also seen from above. When Danny pulled the face from the slop, the nose instantly identified him. *Micky!*

As he went to support Micky's head with a palm, he felt part of the skull was missing. Danny felt a peculiar falling sensation, like when reaching for a step that wasn't there. He blinked and sucked in air. He didn't want to faint backwards into deep running water.

Confusion quickly turned to horror as he realised the extent of the damage. He looked down for the missing bit of Mick's skull, but it had already sunk into the wet silt bed.

The body was limp and heavy. Danny feared the worst. But as he wiped silt from Micky's eyes, a red bubble appeared at the side of his mouth. Danny placed the back of his hand there and felt the tickle of moving air.

'Hang in there, lad!'

Who the hell would do this?

Unlike his father, Concorde was too quiet and unassuming to make enemies.

Neither was this about any jealous scorned lover. As far as he knew, Micky didn't even have a girlfriend. It was a compliment for a jockey to be told he'd got strong hands but in the weighing room Micky was reminded several times he'd got strong wrists. Danny wondered why the kid was the butt of so many jokes but guessed they knew he wouldn't bite back. He also suspected the other jockeys were jealous and resentful of Micky, who regularly got handed plum rides in his mother's colours. At the time, Danny thought it best for Micky to take it and grow a thicker skin. He wished he'd stepped in now.

'Micky!'

There was a splutter. Danny gently raised Micky's head in his arms and frantically scooped muck from his mouth. Even more worryingly, it came out blood red.

'Micky? Can you hear me, Micky?! It's Danny, you're safe now. Help is on its way.'

What the hell was keeping them? Could've pushed the ambulance over quicker, Danny fumed.

Micky's eyelids and lips parted. He then coughed up spatters of blood down his soiled silks. Danny suspected his lungs were filling with blood. He'd survived a fall into the river but his body was now drowning itself.

'I'm not going to leave you, Micky,' Danny said. 'Cos you're not going anywhere, do you hear? You're a fighter.'

Danny sat there in silence, counting the seconds as he gently cradled Micky. 'Did you fall down there and hit your head?' he asked, trying to elicit a response but nothing came back. He looked up at the roots. There was nothing sharp enough to make a hole that size in a skull.

He hoped to see the green of the paramedics beyond the roots.

'I'll … I'll be with Dad … again,' Micky suddenly croaked.

'Micky, stay with me,' Danny pleaded. 'Your dad would want you here. You've still got a life to live.'

Danny wasn't religious but now wasn't the time to question if there was an afterlife.

54

'Dad wants you to become champion jockey one day, we all do,' Danny said, 'find that fighting spirit you showed against me at Ely.'

Micky coughed and then groaned. 'I lost.'

'Micky! Micky! That's it, stay with me,' Danny said, tearfully laughing.

'Come closer,' Micky croaked.

Danny crouched lower.

'We all saw it,' Micky whispered.

'Who ... who saw it?'

'The nine,' Micky managed. 'Save the nine.'

'Nine?' Danny asked. 'Saw what?'

'Your killer.'

Danny immediately pictured the list of nine guests and the seating plan in the VIP suite at Ely Park.

If the Ely Park gunman was down on the ground – how could any, let alone all nine, see the killer from high up in the balcony, particularly with the race finish as a distraction.

Maybe Gosworth had in fact told the truth. Stony reckoned Campbell made enemies easier than friends. Perhaps he had been pushed and the killer was among the nine on the balcony.

Micky's overreaction to being touched pre-race suggested he might've foreseen this coming. Perhaps he'd been left looking over his shoulder for the killer. Maybe he already knew the identity of the killer. *We saw it.*

Danny could make only one glaring link between the Galbraith attacks. George Wheater was a guest at both meetings. Danny was beginning to think all was not right or honourable about that MP.

Danny broke from the reverie when his phone rang to the Champions film theme. He was about to switch it off when he saw the on-screen caller ID: Concorde.

Perhaps Micky had left his phone in the weighing room and it was one of the other jockeys on track. They could get help quicker, Danny thought.

But why are they ringing my phone? He knew Micky but they weren't best friends. He wasn't the natural first choice to check where Micky had gone.

Danny looked down at Micky's sickly white face and then pressed the green phone symbol.

'I'm watching you,' a whisper came down the line, slow and deliberate. Down there on the serene riverbank Danny had no trouble hearing every word.

He twisted enough to look back at the riverbank opposite and up to the windows in the large detached houses poking above the willows at the water's edge. He couldn't see anyone, or any movement, other than the floppy branches riding the breeze. There was only one person who knew where Danny was and where Micky was left to rot.

The bastard who did this must've nicked Micky's phone!

'Why do this?' Danny demanded. Waiting for an answer, he felt the rage building inside. 'Come down here and I swear I'll—' Danny moved and let Micky slip slightly along the makeshift headrest of his forearm.

'Calm yourself, you'll harm both of you.'

'Who the fuck is this?'

Danny heard laughter.

'Who are the nine?' Danny asked.

Suddenly Micky's young grimacing face relaxed to a freeze frame, as if he'd slipped off to someplace less painful. His head grew heavy and fell back over Danny's supporting arm.

Gooseflesh spread over Danny's bare forearm as he looked down. Micky groaned as he emptied his lungs one last time and his limp right arm splashed into the passing water.

Danny's insides felt raw. He moved his forearm, as if trying to shake some life back into the lad but he knew it was too late. His fingers felt for a pulse that wasn't there and then pulled down the blinds over those blank eyes.

'And then there were eight,' came down the line.

'You bastard!'

'Watch your words Danny, or you will be next.'

56

The killer had been watching and taunting Danny as he sat there on the riverbank cradling his dead friend.

'But Micky wasn't in the VIP suite, you sick fuck,' Danny raged into the phone. 'Why are you doing this? What've the Galbraiths done to deserve this?'

As he heard a splosh to his right, the line went dead. Black circles grew in the silvery surface of the water below the empty footbridge.

Micky's phone had now sunk to the bed of the Severn, along with any chance of tracing prints. The killer must've been watching from the bridge.

Shit, this can't be happening!

'What the bloody hell's going on, Micky?' But he might as well be talking to one of the tree roots.

He looked up again hoping to see the silhouette of the paramedics but saw nothing. He merely heard the liquid noise of lapping water around his knees above the patter of his racing heart.

Danny wondered why Micky had come to the riverbank. He felt sure he'd been killed here. There's no way the murderer could've carried a body anywhere near the bustling parade ring, stables or weighing room. Micky was certainly gullible enough to be lured here, perhaps by the persuasions of a conman or the promises of an attractive fan, though Danny had yet to be convinced jockeys had groupies.

Embarking on one of possibly the most dangerous careers, it was hard to comprehend his life would be cut short on the whim of some crazed killer. There was no way anyone could even invent a motive to kill the young lad in Danny's blood-soaked arms.

He removed his phone again to vent his fury on some unsuspecting emergency call centre worker but, having still to request for the police too, he knew how that recording would sound once finally discovered sat there covered in his friend's blood.

Danny recalled Micky's last words. *Your killer.*

His eyes suddenly darted from the top of the embankment, over to canoeists gliding out of sight round the bend, and back to the detached houses. Every swish of the drooping branches, twitch of the curtains, brush of the wind, distant cheer of the racegoers made him feel like his killer was still there, watching, waiting.

Now there are eight. Were Micky's final words a plea to save the eight still alive?

But Micky wasn't among the nine up in the VIP box. He was busy riding out the finish to the Welsh Champion Hurdle Trial at the time the gunfire rang out. Danny had several thousand cheering fans as a witness.

Parading, Danny recalled Micky flinching at a hand on his shoulder. Was it because he'd already seen the man at the racetrack he suspected of killing his father?

You will be next, the voice had threatened. Clearly Danny was also among the nine.

Danny suddenly felt the need to meet the one person who knew Campbell and Micky best. Maria Galbraith.

He heard something and looked up to see the shape of two paramedics on top of the riverbank looking down.

'Too late, he's dead!'

CHAPTER 6

Was this a mistake?

Danny wiped both palms down his loose-fit combats. He'd let Maria Galbraith believe he'd come to pay his respects, though his real motives were driven more by self-preservation than respect. He hoped she could shed some light on Micky's dying words.

Sitting in a lounge this size, he couldn't help feel small and, though alone there, he sensed an atmosphere as he waited for her return.

How long does it take to powder a nose?

He stood from the racing-green leather suite and looked over at the arched stone fireplace below a large gold mirror, fitting for such a grand Tudor manor nestled in the green commuter-belt haven of Oxshott in Surrey.

The place reeked of money. He wondered what the hell Campbell had invested in. Danny suddenly considered switching from the coalface of racing as a trainer and jockey to the backroom politics of the sport, but deep down he wouldn't swap being with horses for any amount of money. He loved watching them grow season on season, each a character, with their own preferences and foibles: some liked listening to a radio, others squealed if missing a gallop or being roughed out in the field at a regular time, some went quiet after a change in diet or bedding, some liked to meet prospective owners on stable tours, others shied away in their box.

Most of his current crop behaved, only a few had a naughty, disobedient streak. Danny cared for them all, but he would have his favourites, like Tufty. He guessed a teacher felt the same about each Year class.

Colouring the cream walls were oil paintings of racehorses in full stride with jockeys in Maria's black and orange silks and there were photos of trophy ceremonies on windowsills and side tables, but there were no family photos of Campbell or Micky.

On the mantelpiece there was, however, one showing four smiling adults standing holding drinks at some fancy do in a gilt frame and behind glass, bookended by two bronzes.

He stuck to the dark wood flooring for fear of soiling the vibrant Turkish rug as he circled the coffee table to take a closer look at the photo. In the mirror, he saw his face staring back and realised he badly needed a shave and a good night's sleep. He barely looked fit to be a handyman in a place like this.

Danny glanced over at the glass dome of a mantelpiece clock with its busy gold workings. Hearing Stony reminisce, he doubted it was Campbell's retirement gift from the other jockeys in the weighing room.

Next to the clock was a clear plastic bag. Inside, Danny could see an enamelled key ring showing Maria's silk colours, with Campbell Galbraith engraved in the silver border. It seemed the Galbraith racehorses were a joint venture, possibly to offset tax. There was a mobile phone, an expensive-looking pen and a leather wallet. They all appeared to be intact. Campbell clearly landed on his back. Maria must've picked up these possessions when she went to ID the body.

With two Galbraiths out of the way, Danny wondered if the killer was aiming to complete the set. Any fears she'd be under police protection had proved unfounded. She was all alone here when he arrived. Clearly the police didn't feel she was in as much danger as Danny suspected.

Danny looked over at the door leading to the hallway where Maria had left for the bathroom. He listened intently and hearing nothing except the tick of the clock, he hurriedly opened the bag and switched on the phone inside. Thankfully there was still some battery left. He felt his heart thump as he quickly thumbed down a contact list that was more like a phone directory. Power was about control. Campbell clearly needed to have as many onside to keep racing heading in the right direction. He noticed Raymond Barton's name as he scrolled down.

He stopped when he saw a mobile number with no name, just a full stop. Where there was a reason to hide, there was often something worth finding, Danny reasoned.

He heard the click of heels echo down the hall. He memorised the number, switched off the phone and resealed the bag. He dropped it back on the mantle and in the same movement, rested a hand on the glass dome of the clock. When Maria appeared in the doorway, he was thankful her focus was solely on balancing a tray with two glasses of wine. She rested the tray on the coffee table.

'I'd left the bottle in our… my bedroom. While I was up there, thought I'd slip into something more comfortable,' she said, glancing down at her silk dressing gown. 'You don't mind.'

'I see it's bespoke,' he said. 'Black with orange trim are your racing colours.'

'Campbell had a set made for me a few Christmases back.'

'What about this?' Danny said, gently patting the glass dome of the clock.

She looked up. 'What about it?'

'Shows you've both got good taste.'

'That's says more about your taste, it's horridly ostentatious,' she said, teasing her boyishly short russet hair. Her high cheekbones and flawless skin carried it off well. The minute he saw her hair colour and shapely body appear in the front door, he could tell it was those slender arms desperately locked around Campbell's legs in the online footage. Having barely held the tray steady, she had done well to delay her husband's death for those few seconds. 'But Campbell loved it. He liked seeing the precision of the timepiece. He said it was the only thing that worked harder than he did. I didn't argue with that. I always wanted to hollow the thing out and use the dome to keep my cakes fresh.'

Danny nearly blurted, 'You can now,' but quickly rediscovered his tact. 'Lovely place you've got.'

'I'm thinking of selling, too many memories,' she said.

'Is that why you've taken down photos of Campbell and Micky?'

She nodded. 'And there's only so many times you can derive pleasure from looking at the beauty of this place. There's a slight decrease in enjoyment each time until one day, it means nothing.'

'You're grieving,' he said. 'I've been there. You see no point in anything then something happens, might be a smile in the street, or a stranger picks up and hands you something you'd dropped, and then things ever so slightly, don't feel so bad.'

She downed the glass and poured a fresh one, seemingly less convinced.

'You shouldn't feel guilty,' Danny said. 'I saw you trying to save him when all the others had fled. They're the ones that should feel guilty, bunch of cowards. You gave your all when others ran for cover.'

'It made no difference.'

'He would've at least known for those few seconds there was someone looking out for him, someone who cared. That's all any human really wants.'

'He was already dead by then,' she snapped. 'But at the time, I didn't know that. His jacket had fallen down over his head and I could see no blood from above.' She turned her arms out to reveal a line of bruises up each one. 'That's why I got these, but turns out it was instant, the bullet had struck him between the eyes, which is a small blessing I suppose. He wouldn't have suffered, or even known a thing about it.'

Either Keith or Maria was lying about the cause of death.

'Was Campbell unhappy at all?' he asked. 'Suicidal thoughts, perhaps?'

'He didn't jump.'

'Clerk of Ely Park reckons so.'

'Ah, Keith Gosworth, trying to sully Campbell's good name, even in death,' she sighed and rolled her hazel eyes.

'What have the police told you?'

'Less than the media.'

'There's nothing in the papers,' Danny said. 'Just the usual ongoing enquiries and open lines of investigation.'

'Precisely.'

'Has the autopsy already taken place?'

'Not yet,' she replied and gave him a look. 'But the toxicology reports said he wasn't off his face on drink or drugs if that's what you're implying.'

'Did that surprise you?'

'No, he liked a social drink or three, but he wasn't a drunk,' she said and then put her wine down.

'Was he depressed at all?'

'He'd just been prescribed Prozac which I later learned can increase risks of suicide in the early stages of use,' she said. 'But it wasn't suicide if that's where you're going.'

'But if he was taking—'

'He'd been prescribed them, but had yet to start taking them. He was a stubborn sod at times and, despite my best efforts, was steadfastly refusing to rely on pills for his lows.'

'Did he leave a note?'

'No, but most don't,' she replied, 'you don't have to leave a note to commit suicide. I fear the answers have died with him, unless you can magic him alive from coffin B5 in Cardiff morgue.'

'So you've been left in the dark.'

'I do know he didn't commit suicide! He didn't shoot himself or jump. He wouldn't, alright with that?'

'I'm just trying to work out what happened.'

'Why? You didn't even know him.'

'I believe the person who killed your husband and your son also wants me dead.'

'That explains why you wanted to believe it was suicide. I've been reliably informed they are separate murders, so you can sleep easy, there's no serial killer coming to get you.'

'I'd still like to know more about your husband.'

'You were a friend of Micky,' she said.

63

'I was his biggest supporter in the weighing room,' Danny said, though that wasn't saying much.

'Then ask away,' she said. 'It's comforting to meet someone who helped my son.'

Danny looked again at the mantelpiece.

'I know, I know, it's too early to start, but I need this right now,' she said, taking more of a gulp than a sip. 'I'm sure a jockey like you will lecture me on how the body is a temple.'

'I wasn't looking at the time,' Danny said and picked up the framed photo.

When he took a closer look at the picture, he saw there were three men in tuxes and a woman in a blue gown. They were standing in front of a big circular table covered in a white cloth and laid out with silver cutlery and cut-glass decanters, and the back wall was mirrored. They were all holding champagne flutes and a smile for the camera. Danny could now put a name to all of the faces. From left to right there was Raymond Barton, Maria Galbraith, George Wheater and Campbell Galbraith.

Given their flushed cheeks, glassy eyes and relaxed, smiley faces, Danny presumed this was taken some way into the evening.

Danny showed it to Maria. 'Better to think of the happier times.'

'People are ordered to smile for photos,' she replied. 'During some of our saddest times, in the photos we're all still smiling. They show a snapshot in time but sometimes a picture doesn't tell a thousand words. Life isn't one long jolly. And that was the case for the five of us invited there.'

'Was his work getting him down?'

'He knew better than to bore me with talk of work all the time. Campbell was obsessed about leaving a legacy from his time as ruler of racing'

Bet she didn't complain when the fat pay cheques rolled in, Danny thought.

'He was always working then.'

'There were three in this marriage.'

'I'm sorry.'

'I wasn't,' she said. 'Unlike most red-blooded males, racing was his mistress.'

'Was he working here?' Danny asked, looking down at the photo in her hands.

'More like networking, it's the Lesters,' she said. 'Racing's equivalent to the Oscars.'

'Did anyone win anything?'

'Ray and George were there to give out awards, and Campbell did a speech saying the future of racing was so bright they'd be handing out shades by the door. A few giggles eventually came but I think they had found the tumbleweed-silence funny.'

'Just curious how they managed not only to get a politician, a bookie and racing's ruler in the same room, but also to have them get along.'

Horse racing was often criticised and held back by having too many factions all battling for their own interests – mainly money and power – in the sport. The bookies want more race fixtures to increase shop turnover, while the jockeys, trainers and owners all want better prize money and the rulers want racing to thrive and stay clean.

Danny suspected Campbell was as unpopular in that ceremony as he was as a jockey. It was proving harder than he thought to find a prime suspect for the Campbell killer who now apparently wanted Danny dead.

And it wasn't that he'd met a dead end, there were in fact too many with a motive – it would be impossible to narrow it down. Unlike Maria, he felt certain the two murdered Galbraiths shared a killer. But by adding Micky to the mix, the list of suspects would grow not shrink. The Galbraiths were a powerful family in racing. Danny knew money and influence can breed jealousy as well as top racehorses. Micky invariably got plum rides on the best horses among Maria's successful string, not to mention Campbell calling in favours to snag outside bookings.

This would make him a target for jealous rivals in the weighing room struggling to get any rides.

Danny studied the photo even closer. He could see George's arm was behind Maria's back but his hand hadn't made it as far as her hip. He wondered whether it had stopped for a rest on her arse. 'How well did you know George?'

'Well enough to know he was a serial flirt,' she said. 'But I never saw him that way, if that's what you're implying. He had a wandering hand. Not long after that was taken, I remember his wet breath as he slurred into my ear that he'd gone there commando just for me.'

'Did that do it for you?'

She shook her head. 'God no! My first thought was, he'll need his trousers dry-cleaned too.'

'Bet he's used to women going weak to the knees at that line,' he said. 'Suppose he didn't take the rejection well.'

'I had Campbell Galbraith, ruler of the second most popular sport in Britain,' she said, 'why would I want an MP, even if he was Minister for Gambling?'

Guess that explained why George was at the racetracks and the awards ceremony, Danny thought.

'When was this taken?'

'Last month.'

Danny recalled George's brazen proposal to fix the race at Worcester. 'Was George an owner, like you?'

She shook her head. 'It would've been raised in conversation that night and I've only seen him a few times in the parade ring as a guest.'

'Do you think Campbell was in any trouble?'

'Why would you think that?'

'He was shot dead in broad daylight, singled out.' he replied. 'This wasn't a random killing by some trigger-happy loon.'

'I don't believe he was in trouble, he didn't have any gambling debts.'

66

'How can you be sure they weren't settling up with Raymond Barton?'

'He told me he'd be on ethically shaky ground if he won money on the sport he governed. And I could see how much was in our joint account.'

'And there was no other woman you say.'

'It's a bit late for marriage counselling don't you think,' she snapped. 'I think you'd better leave.'

'So he was faithful.'

'Look, he came home late some days but I didn't complain about that.'

'You didn't like him around the house?'

'I knew the overtime helped pay for all this,' she said, hand gesturing airily like the royal wave. It gave Danny an excuse to scan the room again.

'There must've been plenty of late nights,' Danny said, unless he had a bit on the side and was making money some other way.

Danny was aware of George being present at both murder scenes. 'Did George talk to Campbell at any point that evening?'

'They were in deep conversation for too long, so I made myself scarce.'

'What were they were talking about?'

'Who knows what they were plotting,' she said, 'but the fact I didn't get to hear a word of it makes me believe they weren't making plans for a round of golf or a meal. It's only when Raymond got Campbell alone a few large drinks later things got a bit livelier. Something had played on Campbell's mind ever since that night. He grew even more distant from me.'

Danny wondered if Raymond was trying to recover a gambling debt to stall the closure of his business. Maria believed Campbell didn't gamble. But gamblers rarely boasted about losses, particularly to their other halves. 'Would they normally get along?'

'At the top, you can't fail to make enemies in some faction or other. You can't please all of the people *any* of the time, he'd moan to me after a particularly bad day.'

'Was Keith Gosworth among his enemies?'

'They fell out when the pair ran for the top job at the BHA a few years back,' she replied. 'Campbell won, Keith lost.'

That explained the self-censored entries in Keith's diary, Danny thought. He pictured the clerk hastily scribbling them out for fear he'd become a prime suspect.

'But Keith wasn't gracious in defeat,' she added. 'In fact he didn't accept the result at all. Said the recruiting panel were paid off – utter nonsense I might add. When things finally settled down between them, Campbell found Keith a job at Ely Park.'

'So Campbell didn't hold a grudge then,' Danny said.

'Some at the BHA regarded being posted at Wales' newest track akin to be being banished to the Gulag,' she said, 'so I don't think he was extending the olive branch.'

Danny felt wounded, as if the insult was being aimed at his family.

'He would do anything to secure racing's future. He cared more about his colleagues and peers in the sport than he did about me. He told me things like, "you look a right state, woman," and "start acting your age".'

'Well, for what it's worth, I think he was wrong, you've got nothing to worry about on the looks front,' Danny complimented, mindful he'd come here for answers.

As she dabbed her wet eyes and nose with tissue, she blurted, 'Your wife is one lucky woman.'

'Have you got a friend that could support you?'

She smiled as she filled another glass to the rim. 'Say hello to my friend. Cheers, Danny boy. Chin-chin.'

'I'd go easy on that stuff,' Danny said.

'Why shouldn't I get wasted?'

'Your husband and your son have both been killed just days apart,' Danny said. 'I'm no detective but the fact they're both Galbraiths puts you in danger. You need to stay alert.'

'I'm grateful for you looking out for me, really I am, but you don't even know me,' she said. 'So take that imaginary deerstalker off, and let the police do their jobs, without some amateur sleuth getting in the way.' Her large eyes fixed on him. 'Tell me, why are you really here?'

'Micky's final words.'

Suddenly her face didn't look so relaxed.

'I held him as he passed away, peacefully,' Danny said diplomatically.

'Tell me, what were they?'

Danny opened his mouth to tell her the truth when she added, 'Did he mention me? Did he say that he loved me?'

'When I sat there with Micky, his last words were—'

'That he loved me,' she interrupted, as if feeding him the lines she wanted to hear. She nibbled her bottom lip, nodding slightly in anticipation.

Danny forced a comforting smile. He could almost taste the desperation. He felt a duty to protect her feelings. Sometimes honesty wasn't the best policy, he reasoned, if the truth only led to a lifetime of pain and disappointment. Anyway, he felt sure Micky would've expressed his love had he time and hadn't had something more pressing to share.

'Of course,' he lied.

She smiled.

'But after that he told me to "save the nine". Does that mean anything to you?'

She sat there in silence staring to someplace beyond the fireplace, as if trying to decipher the meaning behind those words.

'He said we saw it,' Danny added.

'Saw what?'

'My killer.'

'But you're—'

'Alive, I know,' Danny replied and shrugged. 'That's what I'm here about.'

'What do *you* think my boy was trying to say?'

69

'There were nine guests up in the Ely Park box where Campbell... passed away,' Danny said, 'but you'd know that, you were one of the nine.'

'I didn't know that,' she slurred. 'People come and go from those places, refilling glasses, popping down to the betting ring to soak up the atmosphere. We're not snobs you know, sometimes it's good to go mingling with the ordinary folk down there.'

Not snobbish at all, Danny huffed.

He felt he was no nearer to knowing the real Campbell behind the public face. He looked again at the framed awards photo. 'Can I borrow this?'

'Be my guest, you can keep it if you really want,' she said.

'I couldn't.'

'I insist.'

'But don't you want it as a reminder?' Danny said.

'There are others,' she replied, 'you don't get to be ruler of racing if you're camera shy.'

'You must've been proud how Campbell reached the top in both sides of the sport, as a jockey and a leader.'

'Not as proud as I was of our Micky,' she said. 'Tell me Danny, how the hell has this happened?'

She put her now empty glass on the woodblock flooring and began to bawl her eyes out.

Danny looked over at the door leading to the hallway. He didn't know how to handle this and wanted to get away, perhaps come back when she was more stable and sober. 'I'm sorry again, I'll leave now. I shouldn't have come, it's too soon.'

She recovered enough to catch her breath. Still sobbing, she garbled, 'No. Don't be sorry.'

Danny went over and sat awkwardly on the arm of the chair, as if ready to do a runner if her mood swung again.

'Down on the riverbank, you being with him when he left us,' she said. She reached out and placed a hand on Danny's thigh. He didn't move the hand or his thigh. He couldn't let Maria

70

feel the whole world was against her. 'That gives me some solace and peace.'

'I only wished I could've done more.'

'Knowing Micky wasn't alone in his final moments is enough,' she said. Danny's eyes sought the floor. He noticed red lippy on the rim of the wine glass when she added, 'Did he say my name specifically?'

'I really must be going, horses won't feed themselves.'

'He did, didn't he?'

Danny paused. 'I think so.'

'What were his exact words?' she asked. 'I'll cherish them.'

'I don't remember exactly,' Danny said, curling a lip. 'But he said he loved you and thanked you for everything.'

She paused, as if to reflect. 'Did he call me by a special name?'

'Um,' Danny said, wishing he hadn't begun to spin a web of lies. 'Might've done, tell me what it is?'

'Lady M,' she said.

'Yep, he did.'

'He didn't have a special name for me,' she said. 'Now, what were his exact words? I'm a grown woman, I can take the truth.'

'Look, he didn't say much at all. I just held him up as we waited for the emergency services to finally find us.'

He didn't dare reveal the truth about Micky's condition. She was in bits as it was.

'Did Micky ever talk about me?' Danny asked.

She shrugged.

'It's just I now know he had my number on his mobile.'

'How would you know that?'

Danny stopped short of revealing that the killer called him on Micky's looted phone from the footbridge as he sat on the riverbank. 'He called me.'

She stalled as if choosing her words. 'Your name never came up, but that doesn't mean he didn't think about you.'

Danny pursed his lips.

'What was it about?' she asked.

'What?'

'The phone call,' she replied, 'if you don't mind sharing, what did he want to talk to you about?'

Danny was now left to consider his answer. 'I didn't answer it.'

He then studied her face. Either she didn't believe him or she didn't like the fact he'd rejected her dead son.

Keen to change the subject, Danny went over to the two bronze statues of leaping racehorses on the mantelpiece. One of the bases had a brass nameplate engraved with Guilt Trip. Danny recognised the name. He'd written it out on betting slips to allow his dad time to get showered and changed from a shift down the pit and then rush down the bookies before race time. Danny recalled the chaser racked up a six-timer and was earning his father a second income until the moment he crashed out at the third last fence in the Midlands National at Uttoxeter. The horse was never seen again and neither was the wad of notes that was the betting bank. At the time he didn't know it was owned by the Galbraith family. His dad had blown the lot and had to cancel the Christmas hamper payments. He made Danny swear not to say a word to mam.

'Your drink,' she said, lifting the second glass.

'I did say I was driving.'

'You don't mind if I refresh mine,' she said.

'Have mine, I haven't touched it.'

She raised the glass and then downed it in one. A burp escaped her full lips and she sniggered. 'Not very "lady of the manor" of me, I'm afraid.' Her head started to bob. From the fireplace, Danny found it hard to tell whether she was sobbing or laughing. She patted the leather beside her.

'I'd really best be off.'

'Please stay,' she said and came over. He couldn't work out whether she was trying to walk sexily, or if it was the drink.

She finished off the wine and then loosened the belt on her silk dressing gown.

A mix of shock and embarrassment made Danny look away as she flashed her skimpy black knickers and bra. He seriously wondered if that was her first bottle of wine. He couldn't have avoided seeing a fit and pert body for a woman of fortyish, with skin as flawless as her face except for a red scar, presumably from a C-section.

'Perhaps I should go,' Danny said, feeling his cheeks burn. He then swallowed. Shouldn't it be her feeling awkward here, Danny thought – she was the one in next to nothing. He put it down to trying not to think about her son or husband. He suspected he'd be in a padded cell if anything happened to Meg, Jack or Cerys.

'Don't you like what you see?'

'I don't think that's really relevant,' Danny said, looking up at the exposed beams on the ceiling. 'Can you just put it away now? My neck's getting stiff.'

'I love a euphemism,' she said.

'That wasn't one!' Danny said. 'This is so wrong.'

'Yet it feels so right,' she replied, wrapping an arm round his waist. Danny tried to back away but he was already up against the fireplace. He swallowed as her fingers walked slowly down his trim torso. He knew where they were heading and stepped to one side. 'I'm a new father for Christ's sake!'

'You think I'm ugly,' she said and frowned.

'It's not that,' Danny said. 'It's more the fact I'm a happily married man who's only just met you while you are recently widowed and clearly not thinking right.'

'I'm sorry,' she said, and quickly covered up as if realising her mistake. She sat back down and started to weep gently. 'You don't have to tell me I'm ugly, Campbell said as much.'

Danny grimaced. By now he'd completely lost sight of his comfort zone. He simply didn't know how to deal with such raw and uncontrollable emotions. He'd come here for answers, not to upset her or embarrass himself. 'I can't believe he'd say that.'

'He didn't have to,' she said. 'We stopped having sex months ago. For an ex-jockey he wasn't very good with his hands. In the end, he wouldn't even touch me.'

'That doesn't mean you should pounce on the nearest man,' Danny said. 'You'll only end up more hurt.'

'I'm sorry… the drink,' she slurred, 'it's gone straight to my head.'

'We'll blame it on that,' he said as he headed for the hallway.

'I'm sad and lonely,' she called after. 'At least pity me.'

Danny did pity her, but didn't think that was actually what she was after.

He left with a creak of the heavy, ornately carved oak door and stepped out into dazzling sunshine.

Crunching down the Galbraith gravel driveway, Danny dialled the nameless contact lifted from Campbell's phone.

Danny heard the rings stop. 'Hello?'

There was a brief silence before a deep male voice said, 'How did you get this number?'

'I was a good friend of Campbell,' Danny replied.

'What did he tell you?'

'Everything,' Danny bluffed. He wanted the mystery contact to speak without barriers.

There was another silence, broken again by the voice, 'Have you changed your mind?'

Danny frowned. Who the hell did he think was calling? It seemed neither knew who the other was. This could end badly, Danny thought.

The voice added, 'Well? Are you on board?'

Fearing he was already a dead man walking, Danny was desperate for answers. 'Yes, I'm in.'

Keep your friends close and enemies even closer.

It was too late to ask for a name, Danny thought, seeing as I apparently knew 'everything'.

'Good,' the voice said firmly, 'it's time we met.'

74

CHAPTER 7

Danny could hear a whirring.

Shaded by a tree on this bustling central London road, he was busy spying on the steady stream of suits with briefcases. They were passing through a glass door etched with a large frosted seventy-five at the foot of a red-brick Georgian five-storey building on High Holborn, better known as the home of the British Horseracing Authority. He had pictured Campbell making his daily trips into BHA's nerve centre. He wondered if the killer trod the same path.

He knew the BHA was concerned with promoting and regulating British racing from here. In 2006, it had largely taken over these duties from the Jockey Club which now concentrated on the running of its estates, including fifteen of the biggest racetracks and the National Stud. Ely Park wasn't among them.

As a full-time jockey, he'd had the displeasure of visiting there to discover the outcome of an appeal on a ban. Not knowing the meaning of this latest calling made him even more nervous this time.

He'd counted eight suits. There must be a big meeting of minds scheduled, Danny reckoned and then wondered whether he'd been invited.

Seeing the large frame and big head of a man heading for number seventy-five, he looked even closer. Raymond Barton? What the hell was he doing here? He was dressed as smartly as the rest in the same blue suit seen in Stony's cardboard cut-out and was shouldering a man bag. Danny wondered how many tubs of hair gel a year it took to maintain that slimy look.

Like the others, he was sucked in by the black hole of the open door.

Seemed like he'd fallen on his feet again, Danny thought begrudgingly. Just days after his business had collapsed Raymond must've landed another job, though the ex-bookie hardly stood for the fairness and integrity watchwords of the BHA.

'Get in the car,' came a voice, the same as Campbell's nameless contact.

It was only when he looked down that realised that a silver Audi A8 had rolled up in front of him. It was the driver door's blackened window that he'd heard whir opened.

'In,' the voice came again from the passenger seat. 'Now.'

Danny opened the rear door on the driver's side and slid over the black leather trim. When he shut the door, there was a click of the locking system.

'Will we be joining the others in the BHA?' Danny asked, but was met by silence as the car joined the flow of noisy traffic. 'Even Raymond Barton is there.'

'Raymond who?' the passenger said.

'The failed bookie,' Danny said. He pictured the BHA chief's contact list. 'You both had a common friend in Campbell Galbraith. Where are we going?'

'No more words. We'll be there soon enough.'

Danny stared through the grey of the tinted windows. He felt his legs start to go. Without realising, he'd lost control of the situation. His mother always told him not to get into a stranger's car. All these years later, Danny wished he'd heeded those forgotten words. When the passenger twisted in his seat to look Danny in the eye, he realised this was no stranger.

George Wheater!

Danny hid his surprise. After all, he apparently knew 'everything'.

'Good to see you again Danny, now sit back and enjoy the ride.'

George then opened the glove compartment. Danny caught a glimpse of a handgun in there.

'Can you drop me somewhere?' Danny panicked.

George twisted again. 'What's wrong?'

'All of this,' Danny said. 'I want out.'

'You're already in,' George said. In the rear-view mirror Danny saw George's eyes narrow. 'Too late to jump ship now.'

When George looked up at that mirror, Danny's eyes shied away.

Outside, he saw road signs for Dorking, Leatherhead and Brighton. They had left the City southward.

The buildings had shrunk in size and frequency, and the suburban roads were less frenetic.

Up ahead, Danny saw the traffic lights turn amber. He felt the car slow. Now was his chance.

As they crept to the car in front, Danny yanked on the door lever. As he feared, he was locked in. He began to yell at the passers-by weighed down by shopping bags on the pavement. No one even turned an inquisitive head.

George laughed. 'See no evil, hear no evil. The windows are blacked out and soundproofed, so important ministerial matters aren't lip-read or overheard, you understand.'

Danny removed his phone and banged on the glass.

'And did I miss out they're also bullet proof?'

It didn't stop Danny continue to bang out of sheer frustration, more with himself than anyone else. How could he have let it get this far? He knew the risk and yet still went ahead. It seemed going after the killer out of self-preservation had in fact put his life in more danger. He began to bounce on his knees hoping to rock the car as his only way of communicating with the outside world, but he knew the suspension would be too advanced.

He switched the phone on and began to punch the nine button.

'What will you tell them?' George asked. 'That you're being kidnapped. By who? A cabinet minister. You'll be laughed off the line.'

Danny turned off the phone and resumed banging his fists on the window but he knew it was futile. They'd left the suburbs and were now out in remote countryside.

Options running low, he looped an arm round the driver's neck with hands linking up at the side of the headrest. He yanked back. The car skidded to a stop throwing Danny forward against the driver's seat, catching his head on the metal strut of the head rest.

He fell down into the leg well and groaned. He felt motion sickness but he knew the car had now stopped.

'You asked for that,' George said, face poking between the seats.

Both George and the driver got out and covered either rear door, probably to block his escape. They didn't realise Danny wasn't in a state to make a run for it. He shook his head again. He'd felt the same after taking a heavy fall from a chaser on summer ground.

Danny was dragged by the driver to the rear of the Audi parked up in a country layby. The driver was as big as Raymond with cropped hair and tattoo depicting a 1er creeping up his neck. He'd removed his driver's hat and shades. Danny was like a ragdoll in his strong hands.

Danny caught a distorted reflection of his frightened face and ruffled hair in the car's gleaming silver paintwork. 'Where are you taking me?'

George joined them there, gripping the hand gun. 'Not far. Call it a constituency clinic.'

The boot door silently glided open with a bleep of a key card.

'Where?!'

George kept the gun trained on Danny's chest as his hands and ankles were hog-tied with silver tape by the driver.

Danny started to yell but was only heard by the scattering birds from the trees. He was soon silenced by a strip of tape over his mouth.

'Some place quieter,' George replied. 'For us.'

Danny was bundled into the boot. When the lid came down, his ears popped. He waited for his eyes to slowly adjust but there simply wasn't any light to work with in there.

His head was still banging and he felt sick as he lay on his back, staring into the blackness. He couldn't tell if he'd gone blind from the bash on the head.

He winced from the sharp objects digging into his back and shoulders. It felt like treading barefoot on the pins of a plug. He also smelt rubber. He guessed they'd left the spare tyre in there.

He tried to catch the gaffer tape against the cold of the metal beneath him by wriggling but he couldn't feel any sharp edges and his arms were weak with fear.

He rocked slightly as the car's engine revved up. They were on the move again.

Several minutes later, the purr of the engine died. He then heard footsteps. Danny lay there as if playing dead. As the boot lid disappeared, he squinted into at the blinding white of the sky above.

As Danny was pulled from there, he could see they were back among civilisation. They'd parked up in a dark alley. Litter was dancing on the funnelled breeze.

'Where are we?'

'Away from the cameras.'

Danny guessed Wheater was referring to CCTV not the paps.

He was forcibly turned by the sidekick and then felt something aggravate his sore back.

'It's loaded and has a silencer,' George said. 'Start running and you won't get very far.'

With a penknife, George slashed the tape round Danny's ankles. He was dragged round a tall red-brick wall and through an iron gate, then pushed through a small backyard cluttered by wooden crates and cardboard food boxes piled high.

Steam rose in ghostly swirls from a flue in the brickwork to the rear of the neighbouring property. The sweet smell of bacon was also carried on the breeze, wetting his dry mouth and lips. He guessed there was a greasy spoon cafe next door.

He was forced through a battered metal door at the back and then down a narrow corridor to a door marked 'Staff Room'. Danny noticed polystyrene packing balls on the tiled floor. He was led into a small windowless room with a sink and kitchen

79

cupboards and a chrome kettle. There was damp up the walls and the air felt as cold as outside. He guessed this was at the back of a shop that had stood empty for quite some time. It was like the staff room at his school but without the stench of stale smoke.

He was pushed down on one of two chairs either side of a plastic table covered in brown rings.

'Why here?'

George sat down opposite while the driver remained standing between Danny and the door. 'Listen.'

Danny paused. 'I don't hear anything.'

'Precisely,' George said. 'I feel most comfortable conducting sensitive business here, like a football team playing at home. It was a breakfast café. When something similar set up next door, this place shut.'

Danny had heard smell comprised ninety per cent of taste. It was easy to sniff out the real reason why it shut. He saw rodent droppings in the corner. Perhaps one had died under the floorboards.

'It's in both our interests that we work well together.'

'Then can you start by loosening the rest of the tape,' Danny said. 'I can't feel my hands.'

George went over and as he cut Danny free, whispered, 'But know this, let me down and you'll end up like the Galbraiths.'

Danny stretched his white fingers. 'Is that why Campbell was executed publicly? He'd let you down?'

George smiled again as he returned to the seat opposite and started idly carving lines in the table surface with the flick knife. 'You could say he let me down.'

'I'm guessing you own the place, if you feel comfortable here.'

'I let it,' George replied. 'It's a good investment. My property portfolio now matches my share portfolio.'

'Haven't you got enough?'

'One can never have enough.'

The disarming smile and charm were clearly reserved for the cameras.

'So why is it lying empty?' Danny asked. 'If you can never have enough.'

'This best serves as a recruiting office.'

'Recruiting for what?' Danny asked. 'Another driver?'

'I have a driver, Roy here,' George said. 'Where I go, he goes.'

'Lucky he's your driver then,' Danny remarked.

George smiled. 'I think we could make a good team, Daniel.'

'Danny.'

'Danny it is,' George said. 'Pleasantries over.'

George placed the cylinder of a silencer on his side of the table.

'Are you a man of the world, Danny?'

'This world, or your underworld?'

'Do you know what this is for?'

'It's a silencer,' Danny replied. He knew playing innocent wouldn't fool these guys. They probably knew what he'd had for breakfast.

'And conveniently, it doesn't just silence gunfire,' George said.

'I wouldn't ever fess up about any of this,' Danny said. 'I'm no grass. I got out of prison in one piece.'

'Yet without the gun, this silencer is useless,' George continued. 'A bit like our arrangement.'

'What arrangement?'

'So you want to know why you are here,' George said. He stood and went over to the sink cupboard. There, he carefully removed a brown paper package. He rested it on the table by the silencer.

The parcel was about the size of a paint box he'd seen round Stony's house and on the paper wrapping there was D.R. of G. penned in black marker.

81

'Danny Rawlings of Glamorgan,' Danny guessed. 'When did you write that?'

'After you called me,' George replied.

'But I never mentioned my name on the phone,' Danny said.

'I tested the water in Worcester parade ring, remember?' Danny could hardly forget the proposition to throw the race. 'I asked around for your number and when it flashed up on my mobile screen,' George said. 'I always knew you'd come. Once a criminal, always a criminal.'

'But who put my name forward?'

'Someone with links to the BHA,' George replied. 'I knew then you could be trusted.'

Danny didn't know anyone that worked at the BHA. He then recalled Maria say Keith Gosworth ran against Campbell for the top job. But he'd only known Gosworth a few weeks, hardly enough time to justify a glowing reference. 'Was it the new clerk of the course at Ely?'

George shook his head.

'That's all you knew before dragging me here, I was trusted.'

'And that you knew Campbell.'

'But I never said that,' Danny replied.

'You didn't need to tell me, I knew already.'

Danny had never met Campbell. George wasn't as clued up as he reckoned.

'You see, only Campbell knew that number you called,' George continued. 'Now he's dead, he must have trusted you enough to share the number with you when he was alive. He trusted you, then I trust you.'

Danny kept quiet how he'd obtained the number from Campbell's possessions bag.

'You shouldn't have,' Danny said as his palms skated over the rectangular parcel. 'What is it?'

'Call it an introductory gift.'

'I've already got an alarm clock.'

'Open it.'

Danny ripped off the brown paper to reveal the chequers of a wooden chess box with shiny metal hinges.

'You really shouldn't have.' Danny swallowed. 'What am I joining? Some kind of chess cult?'

'Look after it like a priceless antique.'

'I'm guessing it isn't, so what's this really about?'

George slid a cheap-looking mobile over the linoleum surface. 'Keep this fully charged and you'll find out in good time.'

'This isn't going to be something I want to hear, or you'd tell me right now. You do know I'll back out of this if I want.'

From his black woollen coat, George produced a folded sheet of paper. 'That's why I've come prepared.'

'What is that?' Danny said with some trepidation.

'A form.'

'I'm not bloody signing for this,' Danny said. 'No way am I having my name linked if ever this shit gets out.'

George unfolded the sheet. 'No need, it's already signed, all part of the service. I had a copy made via a friend at the Passport Office. It's not what you know, but who you know.'

'That's forgery. It won't stand up.'

'And that's your word against mine,' George said. 'Why would they believe an ex-con small-timer racehorse trainer over an esteemed member of the cabinet?'

'What am I supposed to have signed?'

'Nothing,' George said, 'If you follow my instructions, you will in fact be rewarded.'

'And if I don't?'

George waved the sheet in his hand. 'This is a request by you to the BHA to terminate your trainer's licence with immediate effect.'

'I'll go there and deny I sent it,' Danny said.

'Then I'll go after you,' George replied, 'and I'll use your eyeballs as pin cushions.'

'I didn't have you down as the sewing type.'

83

'I'm not.'

George's black eyes had the fiery intent of a greyhound in the traps hearing the electric buzz of the approaching hare. Danny knew this was no empty threat.

'I know you're a risk taker, Danny,' George said, 'you wouldn't be in racing otherwise, so why the face?'

'I fear for my life, my family needs me.'

'If you don't fear death, you lead a much fuller life,' George said.

'You lead a much shorter one.'

George laughed. 'I think *we* could definitely work.'

'Tell me what all this is about or I'm walking,' Danny said and placed his hands on the chess box.

'It's too late for that,' George said.

'You can't kill me,' Danny said. 'Public figure like you, they'll slaughter you and your party if they even link you with an unexplained death. You can't cover all your tracks.' Danny picked up the box. 'Probably doesn't even contain any pieces.' He rattled the box.

'Put it down!' George barked.

Danny was shocked into doing so.

George lunged forward. Danny thought he was about to push the gift closer. But it was only then he saw a flash of the knife buried in George's balled fist. The blade arced down and buried in the webbed skin between first finger and thumb, pinning Danny to the wood of the chess box.

'Shit!' Danny yelped as a bolt of pain shot up his arm. Instinct made him try to pull his hand from the danger but it was going nowhere. 'Get it out!'

He saw a moat of blood growing from his hand.

George still held the knife there, as if enjoying this. 'Did I say you could take it?'

'You bloody implied it,' Danny said, biting back the pain.

'In future, actually listen to my instructions. Don't do anything until I say so.'

84

George stayed there perfectly still, eyes fixed on Danny's contorted face.

'Please!' Danny pleaded.

'Or next time, it won't be your hand.'

He swore George twisted the knife as he removed it.

As Danny lifted his hand up to stem the flow, he felt warm blood tickle down his forearm.

'Go run some cold water over it,' George said. 'I've paid the water rates.'

'With gifts like that, wouldn't want to visit you on Christmas morning,' Danny said. He walked silently to the sink under the watchful eye of Roy.

He planned to call the police as soon as he'd escaped from there. He couldn't allow a psycho like that walking the streets, let alone running the country.

'And if you ever feel like grassing me up,' George said. 'They have nothing on me.'

Danny let the icy water flow over his hand. He now knew which way George's moral compass pointed.

He turned to see George tug at his leather gloves. 'No finger prints, no phone calls, no digital traces. Let's be clear, Danny, I always win.'

'I'm sure the police will dig up something.'

'Only your body,' George replied. 'They wouldn't even dare start looking into my life.'

Danny had no intention of going along with whatever George had planned but he wanted to at least give the impression he was. 'How will I be rewarded?'

'We'll discuss this on that phone when I trust you will deliver.'

'I look after horses,' Danny said, 'Most of my relationships are based on trust. Shouldn't I be asking you that question, you're the bloody politician.'

'Trust is earned, much like profit.'

Surely the police would've checked out the nameless contact before sealing up the possessions bag on Maria's mantelpiece, Danny thought. They probably assumed the BHA chief would know the new Minister for Gambling as part of the job. But surely having a minister on your speed-dial was something to show off, not hide behind a full-stop. Why didn't that set off alarm bells with the police, Danny thought, unless they were in on it.

'Were you friends with Barton?' Danny asked.

'We have yet to meet.'

'I've got a photo that says you're lying,' Danny said. 'Trust is a two-way street.'

'What photo?' Roy asked.

'He speaks as well as drives then,' Danny said. 'It was taken at an awards ceremony.'

'We may have shared a photo, but not a conversation. Campbell had accosted me for most of that evening. You know what he's like when starting on racing, a man possessed.'

Maria had said something similar about her husband. George clearly knew Campbell well enough.

'Did you fall out with Campbell?' Danny asked.

'Why would I want Campbell dead?' George asked, tilting his head slightly. 'I'm guessing this is what you're really asking. You tell me.'

Frustratingly Danny couldn't find an answer. 'I'd have suspected you less if you'd just admitted you'd met, even been friends. The fact the BHA chief and the Minister for Gambling had never spoken seems odder.'

'I've been too busy working hard,' George said.

'Like your boss Hugo Forster,' Danny replied dismissively, 'caught out drinking and gigging.'

'That was all staged,' George said. 'It was an attempt to make the PM seem less stuffy and more accessible to the younger vote. In a way it humanised him. They could see elements of themselves in him. Though I don't think it will do much to increase the fan-base of Kiss The Trouble.'

'So he doesn't like the band.'

'God no, more of a Brahms man I heard.'

86

'That exclusive in the red top didn't win me over.'

'You're hardly young, Danny,' George replied. The realisation hurt Danny, probably because it was a truth he didn't want to face. 'Anyway, I don't think anything would change your attitude towards us at Westminster.'

'Did you go to the gig?'

'Like I said, I've been busy working on two bills integral to guarantee future income streams from gambling revenues, namely the new machine tax and racing levy. Failure would put my job on the line before I'd barely warmed my seat at the Department of Culture, Media and Sport,' George explained. 'Campbell was on a one-man bloody crusade to get the bill in place for racing to reap the rewards.'

Danny recalled Raymond Barton outside the Greyfriars shop, moaning about the introduction of a limit to the number of those slot machines per shop and a twenty per cent charge on the profit from them, adding to the levy taken from all bets placed on racing. Danny knew racing was dependent on this twelve per cent levy as every penny went straight back into the sport to fund prize money and the admin costs. The smaller the total amount staked on racing, the less went back into sport.

Danny had seen the crowds around those slot machines on the bookie floor. He knew first hand they ate into the slice of the punter's pound bet on racing. Lured by the colourful flashing lights, catchy tunes and instant returns of those machines, suddenly the prospect of a seller at a rainy Catterick would seem less enticing to many wanting to gamble their last few quid.

Maria and George reckoned Campbell was obsessed. He'd be frothing at the mouth to get the machine tax bill voted through to reverse the slide in racing's income. Putting a limit on the number of machines in each shop and then slapping a charge on those remaining would surely strengthen racing's place in the bookies'.

The introduction of a tax on those machines would also see an increase in revenue for the Treasury while reducing the number of machines in each shop would see the government heralded by charities and concerned citizens for its efforts to cut public for efforts to cut problem gambling, debt and crime.

George had no reason for wanting Campbell to stop his crusade. They both wanted the bill to pass. Danny could see no conflict of interest there, certainly no motive for murder.

'We speak soon,' George said. 'And Danny, your wife mustn't know any of this.'

Chessboard under one arm, Danny was dumped on a remote country lane to find his own way home.

As he walked the snaking road, Danny searched the internet for George Wheater on his phone. There was an article in some City finance magazine. It was basically an opportunity for Wheater to show off his wealth and bask in his own success.

Back in the empty shop, George had boasted of a share portfolio, but he failed to reveal that last year, according to the magazine, bought a thirty per cent stake in a start-up company called Lucky Linda Enterprises. In the interview, George predicted great things from the company. He said he'd 'backed a winner there.' Was he trying to talk up the share price?

Searching the company revealed their software developers were about to roll out a series of new games to put in those gaming machines. In their promo, thirty-five-thousand of the total of one hundred and forty thousand casino slot machines in UK were now in bookies, returning about forty-seven thousand profit a year per machine, often accounting for eighty per cent of overall shop turnover.

Suddenly Danny could now see why George secretly didn't want this bill passing. He didn't want the machines to become less profitable and less prevalent. The share price in the software company would crash on news of a cut in the lucrative supply contract to fill those slot machines with games. He reckoned George would feel shame and anger from a failed investment. *'I always win.'*

But would George really kill to save an investment? Danny looked down at the dried blood on his hand.

He was convinced he'd got his man on side. He then looked at the chessboard. He was less certain about what else he'd taken from the meeting, other than he'd been duped into possibly signing his career away.

CHAPTER 8

'The king is dead,' Danny said.

He then boomed an evil laugh as he waved the ebonised piece in Jack's face.

'Don't scare him,' Meg said.

'I'm teaching him the rules,' Danny replied. 'Isn't that right, son?'

'I don't think you'd catch a Grand Master doing that when they won.'

'He knows it's only a game,' Danny reasoned. 'It's when this piece can't move out of being in Check. What's it called again?'

'Checkmate!' Jack screamed.

'That's right,' Danny said. He wasn't convinced any of it had sunk in. He suspected Jack liked an excuse to shout.

'Don't you think it's a bit complicated for him,' she said.

'I'm not saying it's simple, took me four sessions to learn the basic rules from my roommate as a stable lad in Lambourn.'

George's gift had been laid out on the wooden table in the centre of the lounge. Two halves of the box had swung open on brass hinges, joining up to form the playing surface, now stood on four black rubber feet with the chess pieces already in place. It turned out to be a complete set with two spare pawns, which he left in the smaller wooden container on the floor.

Danny studied the chessboard. The chequered playing surface of mahogany was inlayed with a lighter wood. It had a rough finish and the hinges squeaked.

Definitely looks more like a chess set than a priceless antique, he reckoned. So why did it warrant his kidnap, bribery and stabbing?

Initially he feared he'd become embroiled in some sinister match of moves and countermoves, perhaps with the victims as pawns, though he counted only eight of them.

Danny felt sure George was no deranged killer looking to satisfy a bloodlust. He was all about the money. He was equally sure this was not just some introductory gift like all those over-fifty life policy firms in the ad breaks during racing on the TV.

One by one Danny examined the lacquered pieces. They were equal size and each felt light in his palms. He was tempted to split one to make sure bags of cocaine hadn't been smuggled in and he'd unwittingly become a mule in George's cartel.

Jack had finished racing around the room.

'Perhaps he shouldn't have had that second slice of cake,' he said.

Before he was off again, Danny tried distraction tactics by showing him something new. At that age, most things were. 'Shall we play a game then?'

Jack picked up one of the knights and chanted horsey as he proceeded to march the piece around the chequered board until he'd made sure all the others had been toppled.

'Hmm,' Danny said. 'One way of playing it I guess. Remember what I said about the way the knight moves. That wasn't really an L shape, Jack, and they can only take one piece at a time.'

'Horsey wins.'

'It'll be more fun if you learn the proper rules, so we can play each other, not the board. You see, unlike the stables out there, there's more to this game than... horseys.'

'Isn't he a bit young for that?' Meg said. 'He's only just started school. You're not going to turn into a competitive dad.'

'I've seen them on the box playing fluent Beethoven or whatever on piano at Jack's age. Life is a competition Meg, survival of the fittest,' Danny explained. 'If we bring them up thinking, oh well, losing's fine, there's no way he'll make it as a jo—'

Danny stopped himself. He knew how much Meg hated him channelling Jack's future career path.

'He's five, Danny, let him enjoy life before all that competitive nonsense comes in, being a grown up is overrated, I wish I was back his age.'

'But then think of all the years ahead of you at Rhymney High,' Danny said.

Meg fell silent.

Jack flicked over the final rook and laughed.

'Why don't you just play Subbuteo?' she suggested. 'He'd like that. Pretend he's playing for Cardiff City.'

'I want him to use his mind, not his finger and thumb,' Danny said. 'I wasted too many years messing about and getting into trouble. If I can get him into this stuff early, he'll be several steps ahead of where I was. At least it's better than sewing.'

'At least that's a proper life skill.'

'Just get the jockey's valet to repair his silks,' Danny said, 'that's if he chooses to be a jockey and I'm in no way suggesting—'

'Stop digging, Danny,' she said. 'And don't rib him about the sewing. He asked me earlier if it's okay for him to do it. When he showed his teacher a pattern, his friends called him a girl. If he's going to get teased it may as well be for a life skill like sewing.'

'Chess teaches tactics,' Danny replied. 'It will help him to react to an opponent's moves and change the game plan in an instant.'

'That wouldn't be race tactics,' Meg said, tilting her head and raising a pencilled eyebrow.

Danny knew it would be helpful in many walks of life and that just so happened to include race-riding. As Stony told him before going out for his first ride all those years ago, 'there are no indicators or brake lights on a horse, so once the stalls part always expect the unexpected.'

Danny concluded, 'Chess it is, then.'

'No!' Jack cried and flipped the board over, sending it crashing to the hardwood floor. The chess pieces went everywhere, apart from the knight still in Jack's hand.

Danny reacted by diving to shield the cot on the floor.

'Jack! One of them could've hit your little sister and badly hurt her,' Danny fumed, with a wagging finger. 'Do you want that?!'

Jack stood there quietly sniffling, showing his bottom lip.

'Go sit on the naughty step until I allow you back in.'

Meg said, 'Keep it down, Danny, or you'll be the one that sets Cerys off again.'

Jack threw the knight at the door and stormed off, arms still crossed, leaving Danny to clear up the mess he'd made.

'Don't undermine me like that again Meg, he's got to learn right from wrong.'

'He's five,' she said, 'I dread to think what you were like when you were his age.' She got up from kneeling by the cot. 'What's really wrong?'

'Nothing.'

'Can't be nothing, cos this isn't the Danny I fell in love with.'

'I'm under some pressure right now, that's all.'

'The only person that can put you under pressure is yourself. Isn't that what you told me?'

She clearly hadn't met George Wheater. He consciously put on a mask. He didn't want her thinking something was really wrong and asking awkward questions.

'This chess board was given me to look after,' Danny explained in a softer tone as he began to pick up the pieces, hoping none had flown someplace impossible to find. 'If it's broken or any of the pieces are missing, it's me that has to tell the owner.'

'Then why did you give it to Jack if it's valuable?' Meg asked.

Danny didn't answer.

Meg got up from the sofa. 'Time for a coffee methinks. Want one?'

'My nerves are shot as it is.'

Not long after she left the room, Danny heard a loud smash from the kitchen. He then heard a muffled, 'Jack stay on the naughty step.'

Danny got to his feet and shouted after her, 'What's he done now?' There was no immediate reply. 'Meg? Answer me.'

Danny rushed for the kitchen door when Meg shouted back, 'It's just me, again.'

Relief made Danny smile. He was glad for a shred of normality.

She eventually returned balancing a steaming Union Jack mug in both hands.

'Have you been spinning plates again?'

'Eh, cheeky,' she said and smiled. 'Don't mock the afflicted, I'm dyspraxic.'

'That's just a fancy way of saying clumsy,' he replied. 'I'm amazed you don't fall off the horses.'

'That's the weird thing,' she said and blew steam from her mug. 'When I'm on a horse or a dance floor I seem to lose it.'

'I always lose it on the dance floor.'

'You were okay in the first dance at our wedding.'

'That's a slow dance,' Danny explained. 'You just have to stand there and sway gently. I honed that skill drinking down The Red Dragon.'

He began to check over the cracked chessboard, trying to find a reason why he shouldn't feel bad for breaking it. It didn't have much age to it. 'Would you say this was worth anything?'

She looked over her ballroom mag. 'Not in that state. Why don't you get it valued?'

'I'm not flogging it.'

'Then why ask?'

'Someone reckoned it might be priceless.'

'I'd get a second opinion,' she said. 'I know as much about antique chess boards as you but even I can see that looks like a cheap import you'd find down the market.'

It was then he recalled George's blade-wielding reaction to him shaking the box. He held it to his ear and when he gently shook it again, he heard a rattle. 'It's as if something has dislodged inside.'

'A spare piece?'

'Dunno,' Danny replied and searched the walnut writing cabinet in the corner where he'd hidden Maria's photo of the awards do. He returned with a knife and glue.

He prised open the crack enough to see there was a narrow cavity between the chessboard playing surface and the inner wall of the box. It was lined with green felt. Danny knew there was no point in making the effort to cover the inside of a box unless it was to cushion something else inside there.

'I'll just take it to the office, there's more room.' But really he didn't want Meg to find out whatever was inside.

To see what was causing the rattle, Danny had to dismantle one half of the box. Once all four side panels had been removed, the false wall of the box came away in his hands to reveal the felted secret compartment. Inside, there were four plastic test tubes secured in place by wire ties. He could now see why George had overreacted to him shaking the box back in the empty shop.

He untied the tube on the left. When he carefully removed the rubber bung, a sugary sweet scented cloud was released into the room. The liquid was gloopier than water, like one of those sickly alcopops Meg liked to down with her friends when they first started going out.

Although it neither smelled nor looked like steroids, he had a feeling this wouldn't be going in the yard's Medical Records Book in the desk drawer by his leg.

Danny was lost in a maze of thoughts as he stared at the broken chess board and the four tubes.

George's cheap phone burst into life.

Danny flinched and held his chest. Jesus!

'Are you alone?' came down the line.

Danny recognised George's guttural voice and answered with, 'I swear I never touched your gift.'

'Well, it's time you did,' George replied. 'There's a cavity between the walls in one half of the box. Inside, you will find the real gift. There are plastic tubes filled with a potent equine cocktail of sugars and steroids.'

That explained the cloudiness. 'So it's drugs.'

'I prefer performance-enhancing stimulants,' George said. 'The horse gets an energy hit from the concentrated glucose solution and the stamina-boosting anabolic steroids help counter tiredness towards the business end of the race. A perfect tonic for a jumper needing to get its career back on track and your Head Hunter fits that profile perfectly.'

Danny frowned. He didn't want his most promising chase prospect caught up in a drugs scandal. 'But none of this explains the chess box.'

'Let's just say Her Majesty's customs are less appreciative of the R&D gone into this king of all energy drinks.'

'In other words, it's illegal.'

'But ironically it's been more rigorously trialled than most human medicines bought online,' George replied, 'boasting proven beneficial results over time in a region where racing is… less well regulated than ours.'

'Beneficial to the punters in on it rather than the horse,' Danny said. 'How the hell do you imagine we'll get away with doping horses in this country? We've got the most stringent testing in the world.'

'With power comes influence,' George replied, 'let me deal with that side of things.'

'You're telling me you can avoid getting sampled after winning the race. It'll take some bottle leading a horse like Head Hunter to the sampling bay knowing he bleeds steroids and pisses glucose. His results will read off the charts. You keep banging on about whether you trust me. I don't trust you.'

'Samples may be taken, but they won't be tested. His results won't be read.'

'I know cutbacks mean not all finishing in the money are tested, but a horse like Head Hunter tailed off when last seen,'

Danny said. 'If they don't random test me on track, the stewards at High Holborn are bound to order a test, or at least ask me to explain the massively improved form.'

'Blame it on the better ground or a change in training routine, or he liked the flatter track, or just say you cannot explain it, that's often enough for those amateurs to accept and take no further action,' George said.

'What if I back out?'

'I have the signed form ready for posting to the trainers' licensing committee.'

Micky's dead eyes and white face smeared with blood came back to haunt Danny as he weighed up the risks and rewards. The risks of getting caught and barred from racing for life. The rewards of potentially entrapping the Galbraith killer and saving the lives of the nine.

'If you want to up anabolic levels why don't you just fill the tubes with steroids?'

'There is only one purer source to boost the anabolic rate than steroids and that is carbohydrates. The steroids have been mixed into a sugar solution with a secret ratio to induce a career-best performance. It's taken orally rather than risking needle marks in the skin. I take it Head Hunter has a sweet tooth.'

'Yeah, several.' After a successful gallop, the gelding would snaffle up the mints quicker than Jack.

'That's good news as he will be our first target horse.'

'And that same solution is in all four tubes?'

'Who said there were four tubes?'

Silently Danny cursed. He cringed as he lied, 'I'd prised open the box as you were speaking, I'm that eager to get this thing started.'

'Then you'll be glad to hear that we begin tomorrow.'

'What?'

'So we watch this comeback spin,' Danny presumed, 'and then we land the gamble next time out.'

'The target race is the three-fifteen at Ely Park tomorrow.'

'But he'll need the run.'

97

'The steroids will bolster stamina reserves when the horse begins to tire from a lack of race-fitness.'

'I don't think he'll win if we strap an outdoor motor to him,' Danny said, making his excuses already. 'His successes have been over hurdles, he hasn't even run over fences.'

'But he won well in an Irish point-to-point before joining you and quotes in the press suggested you felt he was more of a chasing type.'

George had clearly done his research.

'That doesn't mean he won't make mistakes on his debut over regulation fences.'

'Add one whole tube to Head Hunter's water at the racecourse stabling in the hour before race time and he could win with me on, this stuff is rocket fuel.'

'Can't I dope the horse in the yard?'

'We don't want Head Hunter peaking too early and playing up in the van,' George said. 'Just be bloody sure not to be seen, roaming TV reporters or racecourse security get everywhere these days. And above all, keep calm. We don't want you drenched in sweat, looking like a panicked killer on the run.'

Takes one to know one, Danny thought.

'Just think, next time we speak I will be congratulating you on a job well done.'

'But—'

The call had already been cut.

Danny slumped back on his leather swivel chair.

Head Hunter had finished tailed off after winning his first two hurdle starts with something in hand. To this day, Danny was mystified by the flop and put it down to the vagaries of racing. *Horses aren't machines.* But he still decided to play the long game and put the gelding away for the summer as a precaution to let him grow into himself rather than risking a quick turnout in a bid to restore lost reputation back in the spring.

Secretly he still had every belief he could become a successor to Salamanca. He had the same deep chestnut colouring, and a similar size and scope as the former stable star, now enjoying his premature retirement in the lower field due to tendon trouble.

Drawing upon his past as a form analyst, Danny rated Head Hunter at about one hundred and twenty-five in the handicap system. Officially the BHA handicappers had allotted him a mark of just one hundred and ten which meant, if Danny was proved right, the gelding would effectively carry fifteen pounds less of lead weight in the saddle than his true ability warranted in tomorrow's novices' handicap chase.

Even so, he wasn't fully wound up for this belated comeback and would probably come on for the outing. Whatever boosters were in that tube, he suspected it still wouldn't be enough to carry him home in front on this occasion.

Danny looked over at the TV screen showing a grid of CCTV pictures within each box of the old stabling quarters. Danny watched box sixteen. Head Hunter was standing statue-still staring at the breezeblocks of the side wall near the water container and feeder ball. He wasn't even aware he was set to make his chasing debut tomorrow, let alone what was staked on the outcome. The five-year-old was blessed with the placid temperament and worker attitude of one beyond his years. *Old head on young shoulders that one.*

Danny looked down at the remains of the chess box and the four full tubes. He knew there was an air vent big enough and low enough to stash it away with ease. Head Hunter was the ideal companion as he wouldn't kick out or make a noise when Danny carried out some 'repair work' on the vent grille.

Right then Danny could only see two options: administer the drugs and likely win the race but risk being caught by the BHA and banned from racing for life, or try to win the race on merit drugs-free and risk putting his actual life on the line as payback for the resulting gambling losses.

Danny had no trouble narrowing it down to one option. He uncoiled the wire tying two of the tubes to the felt and crept downstairs. He heard the muffled noises of the TV in the lounge.

It sounded like a kids' show. Meg and Jack would always watch together on the sofa.

Danny turned at the bottom of the stairs and could see the kitchen was empty. He quietly padded across the slate floor and removed the bung from one of the plastic tubes. He rested the other on the draining board. He poured the contents down the sink.

From the cupboard above the fridge, Danny took down Jack's lemon squash. He poured a generous measure into the tube and then diluted with water. Against the light from the window overlooking the stables, Danny compared the colouration and consistency of the solution in both tubes. It turned out the measure wasn't generous enough, so he poured some more down the sink and topped it up with some more cordial.

Perfect match, Danny thought.

He glanced over at the door leading to the lounge. If he was caught right then, he had nothing to explain this away.

Danny wedged the bung in tight and quickly returned to his office. He rewired the tubes to the back of the chessboard and then set about gluing the sides back on. He exited the Lodge by the front door.

He greeted Head Hunter, who barely stirred. He turned on a radio hooked to the wall near the feeder sprouting with a beard of hay. He wanted something to mask the noises.

He unscrewed the vent grille and slotted the stash inside the cavity.

Danny started to fasten the vent back in place. His heart was racing and his shaking fingers fumbled with one of the screws. He felt something similar when he'd hid his secret stash of tobacco from the other prison inmates.

'What are you doing down there?'

Danny leapt to his feet and pointed the screwdriver.

'Bloody hell, Danny, it's me,' Meg said, standing in the mouth of the stable door. 'Who were you expecting?'

'Don't do that,' Danny said. 'It's dark, I'm stressed.'

'Is there a problem with the vents?'

'No,' Danny replied without thinking.

'Why are you down there then?'

'There's no problem because I've just unblocked it. Just some straw being kicked up by this one.'

'I don't know, Danny, what would we all do without you?'

Danny feared she'd find out soon enough if tomorrow veered off plan.

'I thought I heard you sneaking out,' she said. 'I was worried you were seeing your other woman.'

Danny smiled.

'Can you hear that?' she asked.

Danny listened. 'No.'

'There's a clicking sound.'

'Perhaps the council are finally cutting back some of those overhanging hedges on the country road,' Danny said. 'I swear if I get one more scratch down that horse box I'll—'

'No it's coming from this,' she interjected and unclipped the baby monitor from her waist.

Danny began to brush Head Hunter down. He wanted him to be at least looking the part for his big day at Ely Park.

She opened the stable door and came in to comb a hand down Head Hunter's mane.

'Oh yeah, I can hear it now you're closer,' Danny said.

'No it's got louder,' she said. 'It wouldn't be radiation after that fracking scare.'

'Not unless the baby monitor is really a Geiger counter in disguise. It's probably static.'

A metallic cry came from the monitor.

'And that's definitely a baby,' she said. 'Your turn.'

CHAPTER 9

TUESDAY, 7.42 A.M.

Danny was loosening the first screw of the vent when he was distracted by the silhouette of Jordi's head against the morning light of the half-open stable door.

'Mr Rawlings, persons here,' the lad said.

'I wasn't expecting any owners this morning.'

'Not owners.'

'Who are they then?'

Jordi shook his head. 'Definitely not owners.'

'Police?'

Jordi looked off to his side and then backed away from the door.

Danny heard a voice grow larger. 'BHA Integrity Unit.'

With his last turn of the screwdriver, Danny fastened the vent secure again. He slipped the tool down the back pocket of his combats and flipped his sweater over the protruding handle. He quickly took a sidestep and casually put a hand on Head Hunter's broad neck.

A narrow face shaded by a blue peak cap and shades appeared alongside Jordi in the stable door. He was shadowed by a taller bearded colleague in similar uniform. They looked more like FBI than BHA.

Danny tried to act casual but it probably looked like a catalogue pose. 'I'll take it from here, Jordi.'

He didn't want the inevitable gossiping if any of this got out.

The man seemingly in charge entered the box, flashing laminated ID. 'We're vets working for the BHA. We're here to take a look around.'

Why this one?

'You know there are fifteen other boxes in this stabling block,' Danny said.

'Here is as good a place to start,' the vet said. The taller man remained outside and was ordered, 'Go check the rest.'

'They couldn't afford a stamp for the letter then,' Danny huffed, 'an email would've been nice.'

'Mr Rawlings, this is a random spot check. If you haven't done anything wrong, there's simply no need to look as worried as you do right now.' He then smiled in Danny's face.

Fucking jobsworth, Danny thought, as he smiled back.

The vet kicked up some of the hay on the floor.

Danny sneezed. 'It's good quality bedding, changed daily. Nothing but the best for my lot.'

There was no way was he going to let them add neglect to the list of charges.

'I'm not interested if your horses live like kings,' the BHA vet replied. 'I only care if they're clean.'

'They're hosed down regularly, even thinking of getting a pool.'

'Clean of drugs,' the vet replied.

'You can have a look in our medical records book,' Danny replied. 'Medicines and treatments are logged there, it's all in order.'

The vet no longer appeared to be listening.

It was then Danny noticed a clear plastic wire curling between the back of his ear and his blue collar. Danny suspected the vet wasn't hard of hearing. The earpiece more likely allowed this drugs bust to be orchestrated from High Holborn. Danny hoped the vet wouldn't have anything to report back.

The man knelt by the vent.

Danny swallowed. *This can't be happening!*

His heart began to beat faster than when he'd completed the Grand National. He watched intently as the vet's fingers touched the stone floor as if he'd spotted something. Danny breathed out. *Anywhere but the air vent.*

The vet examined a white powder now covering his fingertips.

'It's not drugs if you're thinking.'

The vet smelt his fingers. 'What is it then?'

Danny glanced over at the damaged plaster round the edges of the hastily replaced grille. It was clear the vent had been recently removed. Pointing that out to the vet might help explain away the powder but he feared that would merely delay the guilty verdict. 'I don't know what it is.'

'Have you got a screwdriver Mr Rawlings?'

'Nope, sorry.'

'What's in your back pocket?'

'What?'

'I saw something in your back pocket as I moved round the box.'

Danny removed the tool and handed it over. He wasn't even fooling himself when he offered up, 'How did that get there?'

The vet removed the grille and then the chess box from the cavity the size of one breezeblock.

'You like to play the horse at chess.'

'I haven't told him the rules.'

'This isn't a joke, Mr Rawlings.'

George gave his word this wouldn't happen. He said he'd take care of that side of things. *Bloody politicians!*

Danny said, 'I'll just be a minute.'

The vet looked around. 'Don't go far.'

'You know where I live if I try do a runner.'

The vet didn't take that in the spirit it was intended.

Nerves were making Danny say the wrong thing. He rushed to a quiet shady spot in the bushes behind the stabling before he made this any worse. He dialled for George, confident this classified as an 'emergency'.

Answer! At least answer!

'Not you again.'

'Yes, me again,' Danny snapped. 'I thought you'd said drug testing wouldn't be a thing.'

'After the races I said, not at the yard.'

104

'Thanks for not bothering to mention that small print,' Danny said. 'He's already got into the air vent.'

'So?'

'That's where I hid your... gift!'

'It's yours now,' George replied.

'So how the hell do I bat this one away?' Danny asked.

'I'll leave that with you,' George replied.

'You're the politician,' Danny said, holding his forehead. 'You must have a bloody degree in wriggling out of awkward places.'

He felt like running to the next valley.

'Show the same bottle and guile as you do out on the track.'

'That's where the result of one race is at stake. My entire career is on the line here.'

'So make sure you don't fuck up.'

The line went dead.

'George? George?!'

Danny took a calming breath before returning to Head Hunter's stable.

In there, he found the vet kneeling in front of the felt inner wall of the chess box displaying the four tubes of cloudy liquid.

'What have we here?' he asked. 'Do you have anything to declare, Mr Rawlings?'

'I swear I've never seen it before in my life, probably stashed away by the previous owner here.'

'You say the boxes are cleaned daily,' the vet said, 'then can you explain why dust from the damaged plasterwork on the floor by the air vent hadn't been swept away.'

'The vent has only just been repaired.'

'Mr Rawlings, if what you say is true, someone in your yard has removed that grille within the past twenty-four hours.'

'It was me,' Danny said. There was no way he would use one of the stable hands as a scapegoat.

'Did you put this in there?'

'Yes.'

'I will take one of these back to the labs for sampling.'

'Do I have a choice?' Danny asked.

'Afraid not, that would be as good as an admission of guilt, like if you refused to take a breathalyser test by the road.'

Danny knew his career hinged on the vet picking the tube he'd refilled with lemon. He hoped he'd got the concentration right, so the misty colouring of the tampered tube wasn't set apart from the others.

As the vet's hand hovered over the choice of tubes, Danny knew it was only a one in four chance to save the yard. He didn't like those odds.

'Shall I help you there,' Danny said and began to untie the tube containing the lemon squash on the left.

The BHA vet swatted his hand away and then gave him a look. 'That's if you want to be found guilty of tampering with evidence? Now stay back.' He then pointed to a corner of the stable.

'Sorry, I've never had a drugs raid. Who was it that tipped you off?'

'This was a random spot check, not a raid.'

He was left wondering how he'd got in this deep. He was then haunted again by Micky's dying words, 'We saw it... your killer.'

Micky used his final precious breath to share this. Danny believed every word. He knew lives were at stake and he simply couldn't walk away.

Danny stared at the tube full to the bung with lemon in the left tube, as if hoping to discover he had telekinetic powers. The vet went for the tube furthest right and began to untie the wire. He now wished he'd tried reverse psychology and gone for that one instead.

His last sliver of hope rested with the cocktail being free of any substances on the lengthy banned list published by the BHA. But he recalled George mention anabolic steroids which would surely be the first drug tested for.

Danny pleaded, 'Note that they're full to the stoppers. None of that has touched my horses' lips. You can't do me for possession. That's like calling me a murderer for possessing a kitchen knife.'

'We'll see what the samples contain before we *do* you.'

'Don't you want to take blood or hair samples from the rest of the string,' Danny said. He knew they were all clean and might shine some light on this being a one-off mistake.

'This find is more than enough for now.'

'I guess the new chief is taking a harder line on drug misuse,' Danny said but it fell on deaf ears. Probably too busy listening to them cheering down that earpiece.

'I'm done here,' the vet said. 'We have all we need, Mr Rawlings. You'll hear again from us soon enough.'

'Did you ever meet Campbell Galbraith?' Danny asked.

The vet shrugged.

'You know – the BHA chief. Your boss. The one shot from the balcony of Ely Park.'

'He was pushed,' a voice came from behind.

Danny turned to see the bearded vet in the stable door.

'Where did you hear that from, Keith Gosworth?'

'Overheard a detective at the integrity unit,' the man said. 'It's the latest line of investigation being work on.'

'Pushed?'

Perhaps the bullet had in fact been a decoy to scatter the crowd. Maybe the pool of blood inside the cordon by the betting ring was from impact injuries.

Maybe it was a racegoer who'd fainted from seeing all that blood falling from the skies. He pictured Micky running to the scene. He wondered who in fact he'd seen lying there, or whether he'd been pushed back by the paramedics.

From behind the railing, Danny recalled looking up to see the VIP box had emptied. No surprise there, Danny thought, as they'd be sitting ducks for a gunman on the loose. Might Campbell have actually been on the ground checking the running of the track's facilities? That's why the BHA representatives were

107

there, according to Gosworth. Perhaps the hanging man in the clip was merely a drunk who'd cut his face on the glass? He didn't know why Campbell would fake his death. Unless Raymond was after gambling losses.

'But that wasn't from us,' the BHA vet in the door said. 'They're looking for any excuse to downsize staff.'

A muffled tinny tune came from Danny's jacket where he'd left the cheap phone. He didn't need to see the caller ID to know who was calling back.

'Is that in any way connected to this?' the main vet asked and then motioned to take the call.

'No, it can wait,' Danny said.

'So can I,' the vet said and opened his palm for the phone.

'Don't you need some warrant,' Danny replied. The ringing stopped. 'It's gone to messaging anyway. I'll deal with it later.'

The vet stood there staring.

'Are we done?' Danny asked.

The vet placed the tube into a sealable bag and removed his plastic gloves. 'Are *we* done?' he then asked his bearded colleague who nodded.

Am I still here?

'We're done, for now,' the main vet confirmed. He then brushed between Danny and Head Hunter. 'We'll see ourselves out.'

The stable was quiet again. Danny rested a hand on Head Hunter's strong shoulder. 'What the hell have I done, boy? If I don't get enough on Wheater before this goes public, *I'll* be the one that ripped racing's reputation to shreds.'

Danny removed the cheap phone and was now more than ready to return the missed call. He had to let George know that he'd been found out. He then realised drug test results for both A and B samples would take weeks to return a positive result, affording him enough time to pin the Galbraith murders on George. He slipped the phone back in his pocket.

Head Hunter turned to chomp on some hay in the feeder.

The BHA vets had left Danny alone with a backlog of thoughts.

Danny knew the game was now up. His heart sank. He thought of all he'd been through over the years to keep the yard afloat: the countless early mornings on the cold gallops, the nervy visits to the bank to get extensions to loans and overdrafts, the endless journeys halfway across the country's jammed roads just to see the only runner fall at the first fence, the facing up to the retirements and injuries of stable stars. After all the tough times, it felt such a waste that the yard could close on one stupid decision to go after Wheater.

He felt it best to keep busy. He had to be in a bullish mood for the race. He finished grooming Head Hunter and gathered up the racing saddle and bridle from the tack room.

Van safely loaded up, Danny left Meg making Jack and Cerys giggle and headed straight for the racetrack.

He put the tampered tube of lemon cordial in the glove compartment.

On the way, Danny was calling upon the van mirrors more than usual. He'd spotted a silver Audi following from a distance. He didn't need to see the driver or passenger to know who was in the car. George wasn't kidding when he said they were thorough.

Danny was glad he'd taken the fake tube. It appeared they were tracking his every move and would know before the race result if Head Hunter was running clean.

The horse walked down the van's ramp as cool as a seasoned hack but inexplicably started to kick out on the way to the racecourse stables. Danny struggled to keep hold of the reins. This wasn't like him, he thought. It's as if he could sense something strange was brewing.

'Come on boy, it's time to earn your keep.'

CHAPTER 10

Danny saw the Welsh flag was flying half-mast above the grandstand where it had happened.

He then noticed a very different atmosphere. He sensed it was a lot more subdued, as if the regulars among the crowd had a hangover from the horrors of the previous meeting there. With the killer still at large, perhaps the racegoers feared a repeat. There was visibly increased security to act as a deterrent to the killer and an assurance to the punters. Danny believed it was a waste of money the track couldn't afford. It wasn't some random killing. The gunman had wanted Campbell Galbraith dead.

From the entrance to the stabling Danny looked back as a respectful and sympathetic ripple of applause greeted Maria as she entered the parade ring in readiness to present a prize for the opening race in honour of her departed husband and son.

He finished tacking up Head Hunter. He hoped the big strapping chestnut five-year-old could bounce back from the flop last spring. He tightened the girth strap to a snug fit, comfy yet secure. He ran a hand over the gelding's barrel, but couldn't feel a ribcage. Carrying some condition, he feared the horse was sure to come on for this run.

Danny glanced at his watch. There was now an hour to go before the only race that mattered. According to George, it was time to administer the solution.

He was distracted by movement outside the stable door. Across the courtyard, Roy was stood there arms crossed like a nightclub bouncer.

Danny suspected he wasn't going anywhere until he'd witnessed the deed being done. Aside from driving duties, he was clearly being paid overtime to be George's eyes on the ground.

He hadn't planned using the liquid but he was suddenly being pressured into it. He was now glad he'd swapped the steroid cocktail for harmless lemon cordial.

Like a stage magician, Danny theatrically removed the tube from his jacket as he wanted this to at least be seen to be done. He showed Roy the full tube and then emptied the liquid into the water container. He then looked across to give the thumbs up, though he'd rather have shown two fingers. He needn't have bothered; Roy had already vanished. He'd clearly already seen enough to report back to his boss.

The lemon squash was hardly going to help make a difference, even if carbs were apparently the purest form of anabolic stimulant. The only way he was going to get out of this alive, and still with a career, was to win on Head Hunter drugs free.

Leaving the pre-parade ring, Danny caught a glimpse of a TV screen in the corporate tent. Head Hunter's odds remained steady at eight-to-one. While that implied the bookies were receiving a steady flow of money for Danny's mount, it wasn't nearly the gamble he'd anticipated.

Clearly the money from George and his cohorts hadn't reached the on-course betting market, Danny reckoned, unless the concoction in that tube was in fact to dope the horse to get beat.

Danny recalled George's brazen request in the Worcester parade ring. If he was prepared to scrape a tiny percentage gain by laying off a twenty-five-to-one rag on the exchanges that day, he would certainly be interested in a guaranteed eight-to-one loser here to earn about twelve per cent profit, better than the interest in any bank.

Danny couldn't tell if George was bluffing. He suddenly didn't know what was being asked of him or the horse. At least if the stewards on course or those watching TV screens at BHA nerve centre asked whether he was told to throw the race, Danny could honestly plead ignorance.

Circling both parade ring and down at the start, Danny discovered it wasn't that easy to just look and act normal. Every action and word suddenly seemed self-aware and somehow false.

111

Head Hunter was walking on springs after the drugs raid and a bumpy ride in the horse van. His placid temperament was being severely tested.

Right then Danny hoped George was watching on from afar. It certainly looked like he'd laced the water with steroids and glucose.

When the tape rose, Danny didn't need to coax Head Hunter forward. Within a few raking strides, the chestnut was fighting for his head galloping at pace towards the first barrier of tightly woven birch. Danny knew the horse under him lacked the fencing experience to tackle a regulation fence at such a breakneck speed. He yanked the reins to act as a handbrake but the half-ton of greenness beneath was fully lit up and wouldn't have slowed if he'd dropped an anchor.

Closing in fast on the daunting five-foot wall, Danny wanted to shut his eyes. He had no time to offer assurances or instructions from the saddle. It was up to Head Hunter to get over in some shape or fashion. But the horse spooked a few strides before. Danny tightened his knees around the barrel of the horse and his grip on the reins, bracing himself for being shunted forward by the jolting impact.

Ears pricked, Head Hunter appeared to spot the orange take-off board in time and the turf fell away beneath them. There was a brush of dead leaves as the gelding's belly skimmed the top of the fence but he landed assuredly, with both enthusiasm and jockey still intact. Danny had to flex his biceps and clench his gloved hands if he was restraining an unbroken yearling. He was running far too fresh and would surely pay for expending so much energy at these early stages, particularly after a six-month layoff since the Sandown flop.

Danny wished there was some way to tell Head Hunter there was a lap to go and he would regret showing off with these flighty antics.

Passing the stands, Danny was haunted by a flash of gunfire and the dangling body up in the stands.

112

Listening to the horse's wind, Head Hunter was blowing hard. Crossing the finish line first time round, Danny already had a bad feeling about their prospects.

Turning into the back straight, Danny asked Head Hunter to use his stride, but the gelding couldn't let himself down on the drying ground. It felt like they were running with shoelaces tied together. Galloping over the valleys, Danny knew the horse had the legs but he suspected the youngster felt some jarring here and was reticent to use them.

He met the first two fences down the back with care, clearing them without incident though making no gains on the market leaders a good five lengths ahead. Clearing the second of two fences down there, Danny was thankful just to be in contention.

Banking left at the farthest point from the stands, there was then a long run down the side of the track. Danny's strong arms began to row. Head Hunter had gone from doing too much to doing too little in the space of two fences. Exiting the back, he was still treading water. Danny could imagine George's face turn pinker with every shortening stride. Perhaps the gelding was flattered by his previous wins and the latest Sandown flop was in fact the truest reflection of his ability.

Being sat on a half-brother to Nebula, who finished third covering just over four miles and twenty seven fences in Ayr's Scottish Grand National, Danny knew stamina wasn't a concern on breeding alone. But today was more a question of fitness.

Danny liked to leave a bit of work to do on horses making a seasonal return, so they benefit from the run and ease in for fruitful winter campaign. He hated having to ask Head Hunter to leave everything out there on the track in a bid to save the yard and his life.

As they closed in on the third last fence – the first in the home straight – he felt Head Hunter still had something to give. Another persuader with the air-cushioned whip and Head Hunter found some more. By now they were both running on fumes. He

113

felt the burn as he stretched his arms, legs and lungs so not to disappoint his ride and more importantly, George Wheater.

Closing in on the final fence, Danny knew only a perfect jump would do. Head Hunter attacked this fence with the same vigour as on the first lap. He left the ground and they soared through the air. Head Hunter's bent forelegs were tucked neatly against his ribs and fearing they would buckle on impact with the drying ground, Danny pulled back on the reins. He needn't have bothered as Head Hunter's strong tendons absorbed the impact with ease.

Danny growled, 'Get them, boy! They're ours.'

He could see the leading pair was beginning to falter, paying for setting such a proper end-to-end gallop. Danny looked between Head Hunter's pricked ears to see the leader Spare Feelings edging left and the second Dream To Dare veering right. They'd parted like the Red Sea. *Here's our chance!*

Head down he pushed and shoved, again and again. He glanced up to see the leaders grow larger, but so was the red circle of the finishing post. Three lengths down... two lengths... a length.

Danny looked across to see the lollypop stick. Shit!

The speakers bellowed, 'Spare Feelings has got home all right, from Dream To Dare a length back and a neck to Head Hunter in a flying third. Another thriller here at Ely Park.'

He was pleased for the horse but was worried for himself. He knew there'd be other days for this dark prospect for chasing but he wondered whether he could say the same for himself. He hoped they'd done enough to fool George into believing the drugs had been consumed.

His sides hurt as he desperately tried to catch his breath. He rid his mouth of bile. This don't get any easier with age, he thought.

They'd performed above market expectations, he reasoned, but then pictured George slowly turning the flick-knife and saying, 'I always win.' He shivered.

Perhaps he'd backed Head Hunter each-way. An eight-to-one finishing second at place terms of one-fifth the odds would still claw back the win part of the stake which had lost and a sixty per-cent profit. But George didn't seem like an each-way kind of guy.

Danny slowly guided Head Hunter down the asphalt path to the paddocks behind the stands. Normally he would ignore the sea of blank faces either side of the rails. He'd only pay attention if some drunk heckled, 'give up part-timer,' or 'my nan could've won on that and she's dead'.

But knowing Campbell's fate, Danny's alert blue eyes were flicking from face to face. His heart was still thumping.

Suddenly a loud crack filled the air. Instinct made Danny crouch low in the saddle. There was another. It sounded like they came from all angles. He looked to where it was loudest and saw a loud speaker pinned to the wall of the stands opposite The Whistler statue.

'Sorry about that, just some static,' came the MC, who looked like a holiday camp reject, standing by the winner's circle. 'But there was nothing static about that finish.'

Danny saved face by staying down and hugging Head Hunter's thick neck. He looked over to see a young couple holding their chests and sharing relieved smiles. He wasn't the only one there on edge.

As they came into view from around the side of the stands, Danny saw Maria dabbing her eyes. Nearby, above a ripple of polite applause, the MC continued, 'I'd like you all to welcome back in our winner of the K.L. Davies Building Contractors Novices' Handicap Chase... Spare Feelings!'

Danny had lost the race on a clean horse. He'd betrayed George's trust.

Showered and changed, he sat in the weighing room, staring at the cheap phone. He was tempted to switch it off. He knew he had to cross the River Taff on the way home. He could so easily chuck the phone away, like the killer had from the

Worcester footbridge. But, like turning to drink, he knew the same troubles would still be there in the morning.

Safely in the van ready to leave, he wondered where George had watched the race. He looked over at the side of the grandstand from where he'd parked up. Perhaps he was in there, Danny thought, and quickly fired up the engine.

As he slowly turned from a tight fit between horse carriers the sound of the cheap phone made him brake hard and kill the engine. Removing the phone, he felt his heart work harder and his cheeks burn. It felt like Satan was calling.

Danny's thumb hovered over the green phone symbol. The last thing he needed right then was a proper bollocking for the ride and angry threats on his life from a sore loser. But if he just let the call go to messaging, it would only add to the bad blood between them, like ignoring the final demand on a debt.

Danny saw Clive Kipper lead one of his by the van. He acknowledged the big man with a wave and a nod but was glad to see them walk on by.

He couldn't put it off any longer.

'Let's face the music,' he muttered as he pressed the phone. He felt the best form of defence was attack and began with, 'I did warn you he'd need the run but you wouldn't listen. He did bloody well to fill third thanks to your gift. I wouldn't have bet on it with counterfeit money myself, drugged or clean.'

'And neither did I,' came down the line.

'What?'

'It was a trial.'

'What?!'

'The drugs raid at the yard was to test your loyalty when put under extreme pressure. Head Hunter was chosen to see if you're willing to put forward a horse no matter your concerns and grievances. I also have it on good authority the gift was administered on time.'

Danny had assumed the BHA raid was the response to a tip off from a whistle-blower among George's inner circle.

Danny hadn't realised it was in fact George's inner circle carrying out the drugs bust.

He recalled the odds had remained steady at eight-to-one in the minutes before the race. 'No money was lost.'

'This time.'

'So did I pass?'

'With flying colours.'

'But the horse lost.'

'A stronger candidate will be chosen when we go live,' George explained, 'but be warned, the trial ends here. Everything that happens from now on is not a drill but real life.'

'What now?'

'You go home, keep this phone charged and don't do anything until I say so,' George said.

Danny felt the scar on the webbing of his hand. 'Wouldn't dream of it.'

He then returned to Silver Belle Stables feeling he'd had a stay of execution.

CHAPTER 11

TUESDAY 7.52 P.M.

'It's gone.'

'What has?' Meg looked over her copy of *Horse and Hound*.

'There was a photo, in here,' Danny replied, standing by an open drawer of the writing cabinet in the corner of the lounge.

'I put the snaps of Cerys in our room,' she said. 'I like to look at them when I can't sleep.'

'Not them.'

'What photos then?'

Danny would find it easier to describe the photo showing strangers at an awards ceremony than to explain why it was in their lounge.

'Just racing stuff, it was framed and behind glass. Have you been in here?' He looked down at opened envelopes, bills, bank statements; basically everything with their address on they hadn't time to shred. He began rummaging in there again. 'It has to be here.'

'Don't keep going back,' she said. 'It's not going to magically reappear just because you can imagine it there.'

Danny straightened. 'Where were you when the vets came?'

'Upstairs, with the kids.'

'Did you hear anything down here, any banging, footsteps?'

'I heard the backdoor, but I just presumed you'd finished getting Head Hunter ready.'

'I hadn't finished,' Danny replied, though he didn't reveal why he hadn't finished. That he'd been held up trying to explain away a stash of steroids in the air vent of Head Hunter's box.

'So… who was it?' she asked and then visibly shivered. 'Forget that, this is freaking me out, I don't want to know. This is our nest, I want to feel safe here.'

'It seems he wasn't in here for you or the kids,' Danny said. 'It's that photo he wanted.'

'What would a vet want with a photo of yours?'

'They weren't vets.'

'Danny, what is this really about?'

'Probably nothing,' Danny said. 'Don't worry.'

Danny had nothing concrete to go to the police with except for the gun in the glove compartment and even that was probably licensed for protecting a minister. He feared there might be reprisals for Head Hunter's failure. George had held back the truth when his men came to the yard, so why should Danny believe him about it being just a trial run.

Suddenly Danny wasn't happy with the kids sleeping at Silver Belle Stables. He took them round to his mum's place for a few days until George cooled down. His mum seemed as pleased to see them as Danny was to leave them there. Jack was always excited to go round Granny's.

When he returned, Meg had brewed a cuppa and was warming herself cross-legged by a crackling and hissing fire. 'You forgot to take the baby monitor.'

'Mum's already got one,' he explained, 'and anyway, that one needs replacing.'

'It hasn't clicked once since I joined you in Head Hunter's stable,' she said, 'you wouldn't know the thing's sat there until Cerys kicks off.'

Danny picked up the baby monitor and rushed from the lounge.

'Where are you going now?' Her question was met by the clap of the kitchen door.

Danny turned on the baby monitor as he headed for box sixteen. Inside Head Hunter was stood quietly. His inquisitive eyes followed Danny as he quietly entered and bolted the stable door behind him.

He flicked on the night lamp. There was the clicking again. As he closed in on the air vent, it sounded like a cat on lino.

In the half-light, Danny removed the grille and the remains of the chess box. His fingers skated over both the mahogany and the felt sides. He studied the wire holding the remaining three tubes in place. He then looked closer at the solutions to see if anything solid had settled at the bottom of the tubes.

When Danny turned to check the four black feet at each corner of the walls framing the felt side, he noticed one was a fraction larger. He'd normally have put that down to the quality of the maker but this one felt cooler and smoother than the others. The metal foot, not much bigger than an Aspirin tablet, wobbled out like a milk tooth. He left the monitor by the open vent and walked to the stable door with the find. The clicking stopped.

He recalled the vet searching for evidence wore an earpiece. He now knew luck had nothing to do with them chancing upon the hidden stash. He looked down at the tracking device in his palm.

He thought about flushing it down the toilet but George would soon guess it wasn't Danny rushing towards the sewage plant on his GPS map. And washing it down the sink would send it straight to the waterworks. Putting a sledgehammer to it would simply make the locator blip disappear. George would immediately suspect Danny's loyalty. He didn't want another reason to be killed off. Instead, he slipped it into a zipped pocket inside his jacket until he found a way to make it work in his favour.

Back in the lounge, he put the baby monitor to his chest. He smiled as he heard the crackle again.

'You didn't mention you were radioactive in our wedding vows.'

'We're being tracked.'

'What?'

'I found a tracking device in box sixteen.'

'By who?'

'The same people who took the photo.'

120

'Are you saying some spy crept in here while I was up there with the kids?' she asked, eyes wide. 'But you were with those guys all the time.'

'One of them left almost immediately to check the rest of the yard, I didn't reckon on him including the Lodge,' Danny stopped himself from saying too much.

'But the door was locked. I checked the latch.'

'Not the kitchen door at the back,' Danny said. He could see the fear in her blue eyes. 'They didn't trash the place or nick anything valuable.'

'That's what's worrying me, Danny,' she said. 'If they weren't here for the property, what the hell were they after? The Lodge is our home, it's not part of our business. So why the hell is the BHA snooping in here and removing photos?'

'They weren't the BHA,' Danny explained. 'And trust me, the way they searched the stables, if they were after you, they'd have found you.'

'Don't tell me that,' she screamed. 'I feel scared enough, we're in the middle of nowhere. The nearest family are the Millses up at Sunnyside Farm and they're like something out of that Deliverance film we saw the other night. What if they come back?'

Danny joined Meg on the sheepskin rug in front of the orange of the hearth fire. His warming cheeks tingled.

He spotted a tear sparkle like a tiny diamond as it trickled down her cheek.

'There's something wrong,' he said. 'I can tell.'

'No shit, Sherlock,' she said.

'What is it?'

'We're good aren't we, Danny?' she suddenly blurted out.

He sat up and held her glowing face in his strong hands. He glanced down at her enticingly full lips and then back up to her almost hypnotically blue eyes glistening in the light of the fire. 'Why are you asking that?'

'It's just you seem a bit... serious, lately.'

121

'These early weeks are going to push us both,' he said. Danny couldn't tell her the whole truth. 'It won't be a party looking after two kids and dozens of flighty horses, each with different attitudes.'

She forced a smile and sniffled. 'Look at me, I'd better grow up quick, I'm a mother now.'

'You were before – Jack sees you as Mammy Meg.'

'You know what I mean.'

'I fell in love with you because of you, not someone else. I even love that you're the clumsiness person I've ever met, banging into everything and dropping plates.' She flashed a more natural smile. 'But most of all I love you for accepting me for who I am and what I do. Not many would put up with this kind of life.'

'I don't put up with it,' she interrupted, 'I love it. And I love you.'

'And I'd make you employee of the month every month if you weren't my wife.' He paused to kiss her. 'Just don't ever change, not for me, not for Jack, not for Cerys.'

'Oh, Danny, I'd do anything for you.'

That gave Danny an idea. 'Anything?'

She nodded.

Danny fell back on the rug and lay there silently, staring up at the white plaster and oak beams.

'What are you thinking about?' she asked as she lay down beside him.

'Who wanted Campbell Galbraith dead?'

'Not now, Danny,' she said, 'Bad things happen. Let's not spoil the mood.'

'It's possible just two people know the answer: the killer and Campbell.'

'You won't get any answers out of either of them, especially Campbell,' she said.

I wouldn't bet on that, he thought.

He got up off the rug. She looked up and took his hand. He led her to the hall and she began to climb the stairs. Danny pulled her back.

'What? Downstairs?' she asked.

'No,' Danny said, and led her to the coat-stand next to the Welsh dresser in the hallway. He began to put on his jacket.

'Not outside, I needed several dock leaves last time, remember?' she said, 'And I don't want to get hypothermia, I'm trying to get back my fitness for the ride on Powder Keg in the Welsh Champion.'

'We're not having sex,' Danny explained. 'I'm taking you out. Okay?'

'Okay.'

'Get some layers on,' Danny said and glanced at his watch.

He waited for her to tug on a coat and woollen mittens.

'Where are we going?' she asked. 'Is it that new Italian opened in town? I love nice surprises.'

He knew it would be a surprise but wasn't so sure about the 'nice' part.

CHAPTER 12

'When you said a surprise, I didn't bloody expect this much of a surprise.' Meg crossed her fleeced arms and turned up the car heater.

'I never said it would be a pleasant surprise,' Danny replied as he stared through the glass doors of the coldly lit reception to Cardiff Morgue.

'Did you mean a word of that Hugh Grant speech in front of the fire?'

'Every letter of it,' Danny replied. 'Now cheer up.'

'Cheer up?!' she said and flicked him on the ear.

'That's it, let it all out, I need you to be in a happy flirty mood.'

'Why should I? We're not in a Michelin-starred restaurant, we're at a mortuary. My bestie Lis was moaning that her man took her to the speedway.' She shook her head. 'Come on, Danny, I know you bang on about being a rubbish romantic – but a mortuary?'

'It's a morgue, where they store bodies waiting for autopsy by a coroner. A mortuary is more for bodies awaiting burial.'

'Morgue, mortuary, house of the bloody dead, what difference does it make? God, Danny, you really know how to treat a girl.'

Maria had mentioned Campbell's body was in container B5 awaiting an autopsy. Danny guessed security would be as low as the demand for decaying corpses. He reckoned a quick in-and-out job could resolve this and point police in the right direction where the coroner couldn't.

'You know the thing that hurts most,' she said, 'it's not that I'm stuck in an empty *morgue* car park in the middle of night, it's the fact you lied to me. Don't you want Jack and Cerys to know right from wrong, to tell the truth, to look up to you?'

'I never lied,' Danny said. 'And if we don't do this, they might not have a daddy to look up to.' He could hear George's voice say, 'Your wife mustn't know any of this.' He reckoned it was time she did. 'Campbell's killer is after me, among eight others, seven if you include Micky.'

'After you?'

'He wants us dead.'

'Are you shitting me?'

'No,' he replied. 'Micky's last words weren't "tell mum I love her". He told me to save the others.'

'I don't believe this,' she said and palms slapped the dashboard. 'Why you? Can't you just let the police sort it?'

'I'm one of the nine.'

'So you're going to break in there.'

'Not exactly.'

'Finally, some sense.'

'We are.'

'What?!'

'Well, I am, with some help from you.'

'We're not in mission-bloody-impossible.'

'No,' Danny replied. 'Getting our hands on police files for the investigation would be impossible. They weren't even saying a word to the press.'

She looked away and huffed, breath steaming up the passenger window.

'But it's a crime!'

'Against who?' Danny asked. 'The bodies in there aren't going to care.'

'The relatives might.'

'Look, if you're not up to it, I'll go it alone, take my chances. I used to do this for a living.'

'And how will that make me feel if you get caught,' she said. 'No. I'll have to do this, but you owe me big time.'

'You sure, now?'

'Don't tempt me to back out, Danny.'

'Right, you see the fat bald guy manning the front desk,' Danny said, 'I need him to be putty in your hands, you'll be my decoy. It shouldn't be difficult, a man with a face and figure like that won't have had any attention from a beautiful young lady in a long time, if ever. He'll be as grateful as he is stunned.'

'It's too late for flattery now,' she said. 'So you want me to chat him up?'

'Just smile and laugh at his jokes.'

'Won't he wonder why I'm there at this hour?' she said and glanced at the clock on the dashboard. 9.43 P.M.

'Just act drunk and pretend you got lost on the way back from an office party, ask for directions, get him to ring a taxi, anything to distract him while I get to the door leading to the storage facility beyond the desk.'

'Not even a weekly meal out from here to Christmas could pay me back for this,' she said. Her leg started to shake. 'I'm rubbish at flirting. I'd always be the one walking home alone after clubbing. What do I get out of this?'

'How about a guarantee the burglar won't be back?'

'How can going in there stop that happening?'

'I don't know for sure yet, but I'm certain the answer is lying in there,' Danny said, 'in container B5.'

'This is beyond ghoulish,' she said. 'It'll give me nightmares.'

'At least then you'll know you're sleeping,' Danny said. 'You've been staring at the photos of Cerys every night since they came knocking.'

He straightened and they both stared through the windscreen, listening to the hum of distant traffic.

'Come on, then,' she said and then emptied her lungs. 'Let's do this.'

Danny kissed her on the cheek. 'I'll make it up to you, I swear.'

'The things I do,' she said and pulled down the sun-visor with a vanity mirror. She began to apply some lippy and her hands frizzed up her blond curls.

'I don't think that's necessary.'

'If you want a job done properly,' she said and gave a look. 'And is that jealousy I see? Remember all this is your idea.'

Danny shook his head. He was glad the receptionist looked the way he did.

He turned the car heater off and said, 'Remember what I told you, and once I'm clear, don't hang about, you leave. He might call the police if you become a nuisance.'

They crept up to the glass door. The receptionist's work station was framed by a three-sided counter jutting into the room.

Beyond, Danny could make out windowless swing doors below a brown sign.

Meg pushed the glass entrance door but it wouldn't budge. She looked across at Danny, now crouching in the bushes to one side. He shook his head again and whispered, 'I don't exist.'

Meg knocked the glass. She then peered into reception and pointed at her watch.

Danny heard the rattle of keys and the door disappear. 'Can I come in? I'm catching the death out here.'

Smile, Meg, Danny pleaded. Smile.

'I'm lost you see.' There was a painful pause. 'Please.' She tilted her head and batted her eyelashes.

She then stepped in saying, 'Oh, thanks, babe.'

Danny edged out enough to see the receptionist was returning to the sanctuary of his desk. Danny stealthily moved to shadow Meg in there and then ducked as he heard the air-cushioned swivel chair hiss almost out of protest as the receptionist dropped his weight down.

Shielded by a solid front to the desk, Danny crept around her legs. It was up to Meg now.

'I'm impressed by the shininess of your head,' Meg said, 'Tell me, do you polish or is it… natural?'

'What?' the receptionist said.

Danny would've replied the same.

He'd often laugh off her claims she'd struggled to pull in nightclubs and he was her first true love. He didn't believe how a girl so pretty and bright could possibly fail? He was now a believer. Shiny head?!

At least ask his name, Danny thought.

She continued to dig by saying, 'Can I pat it?'

Can I pat it! Danny groaned. *What is this, Benny Hill?*

'Are you drunk, missy?' the receptionist asked.

'That would be telling.'

'So… tell me.'

Danny could hear she wasn't winning him over. But he still had to somehow get past her to the double doors beyond the reception before she was asked to leave.

He was now crouching perfectly still by her buckled suede boots in the shadow of the desk.

'Then, how about you tell me why you're here in a morgue at this hour preferably with an answer somewhere in your reply?'

He seemed like more of a jobsworth than Danny had hoped. He saw her feet were fidgety. She was struggling here.

Danny needed the receptionist facing away from his planned route from the cover of the desk to the door in the far wall.

Crouched silently just beyond her feet, he had no way of communicating this. She daren't look down for long enough and he couldn't make a noise.

He softly pressed an index finger against her black legging just above the boot. Instinctively she moved her leg, but then quickly planted her foot back on the floor once realising what must have touched her. When his finger pressed again, there was no reaction from her. He was about to write 'leave' up her calf but then opted for 'go'. It was quicker for him and easier for her to decipher.

As soon as he completed circling the 'o', she started to slur, 'I will tell you why I'm here, but I'll express myself in the form of song.'

'No, you won't,' grunted from the other side of the desk.

'Let's see,' she said and then belted out a song Danny didn't recognise, probably something from the last decade. He tended to stick to the songs of his teens and early twenties. Either way, he felt sure he wouldn't recognise this rendition even if he had heard the original. He knew she was no Adele but he'd heard her sing softly to horses while tacking up some mornings and that was easier on the ear than this.

'I can't take any more,' the receptionist growled. 'You're pissed and I'm pissed off.'

Bravely she kept singing. Danny heard the creak of the hatch in the desk's side wall. It seemed like he was leaving his station to remove her from the building.

Danny darted for cover from by her legs to round the far side of the desk.

She stopped the singing to say, 'Don't touch me, I've got legs.'

'Then try using them,' he growled, 'that is, if you're not too drunk.'

Danny then heard the clap four feet walking away from where he sat. He peeked around the desk corner to see them facing the glass entrance. He heard the jangle of keys. He saw her looking at him in the reflection of the glass. She started singing again. Danny heard the glass door open and her reflection disappear. Seconds later he felt the rush of cool air.

Now was his chance.

As he ran for the swing doors, the squeak of his trainers on the shiny floor was drowned out by Meg's second verse.

Still crouching, he made for the swing doors on the far wall and shouldered his way through. He reached back and used a hand to guide the door silently shut.

Peering back through a crack in the door, he could no longer see Meg. He could've done with a similarly smart sidekick back in his days as a housebreaker. Perhaps then he wouldn't have ended up in prison. Her job here was done. When he heard the receptionist double-locking the front entrance, Danny knew his job had only got even harder.

As he turned and sprinted down the grey rubber-tiled floor of a corridor, motion-sensor strip lights came on. He was glad that the reception door was windowless.

Danny glanced up at more brown signs on the white walls, following arrows to the B wing of the storage facility. He paced up a flight of stairs and took a right and then a left.

At the end of another corridor, Danny rattled the door with frosted glass windows. He checked the walls for sensors or alarms and wasn't surprised to see them bare. There was nothing but decomposing bodies in there.

He looked back down the corridor and saw the end light turn off, and then the next. Soon the corridor would be black again. Danny turned, removed his trusty wire hook and began to work the lock. There was now only one strip light on.

Click.

Danny pushed past the swing doors and flicked on the lights in there. He could see what looked like an examination room with three shiny steel tables. They were behind a glass wall, making a room within a room. Danny had to look elsewhere for the bodies. He followed the glass round to a refrigeration wall, holding a bank of cold chambers that stretched to the end wall where there was a window. Danny searched for B5.

He shivered though it wasn't cold on this side of the metal hatches. As a kid, even graveyards unnerved him. He'd actually turn up for Double Maths when his classmates chose Rhymney graveyard to have a smoke. But he found the strength when visiting the headstones of his dad and his brother in later years.

He hoped the autopsy had yet to be carried out on Campbell's body and that he hadn't been moved on for burial or cremation.

He twisted a metal lever on the door marked B5. The tray glided open on rails to reveal a mounded white sheet.

He took a calming breath and tried to think about what he needed to learn from the cadaver.

How and why were you killed Campbell? What did you see? Danny hoped the answers hadn't died with him. If that was

130

the case, he suspected he'd also be ending up here sooner than he'd hoped.

He carefully removed the sheet. It was definitely Campbell. The protruding nose, swollen belly and long legs told him that. The skin had already turned grey and blotchy.

Danny felt his stomach turn. His hand shot to his face. He didn't want to spew DNA over the murder victim.

One look at Campbell's face told Danny he wasn't pushed. There was a crusty black hole in the middle of his grey forehead.

It seemed Maria was telling the truth. Campbell was already deadweight in her arms before she could hold on no longer.

Keith Gosworth had claimed it was a push that sent Campbell here in a body bag. He had lied. Why?

At least Campbell hadn't suffered. He wouldn't have known anything about it. One second he was watching the finish to the big race and the next...

Without a ruler or a measuring tape, he put his hands either side of the entry hole and pushed his fingers together, using them as a measure. He could see the wound was in the centre. George was clearly as handy with a gun as he was with that flick knife.

When he lifted the head, he saw a larger hole in the crown of Campbell's scalp. Against the grey of a bald spot, he could easily make out it was another bullet wound.

The flabby arms were broken and twisted out of shape. Working his way down to the right hand, Danny noticed a white fishbone scar between Campbell's middle and index fingers. This injury had at least partly healed; it was older than the rest.

When he touched the scar, his fingertip left an impression in the cold, rubbery flesh.

He compared it with the red gash on his right hand he'd picked up in the staff room of the empty shop.

Had Campbell been gifted a chessboard too?

131

As he lowered the bloated hand, he heard a clap of boots grow louder from the corridor outside. When he looked over at the door, he saw a brightening light through the frosted windows.

Shit!

He pushed B5 to click shut. He then began to pull open other chambers until he found an empty. The first two were occupied by similarly large bodies. The footsteps grew even louder and then stopped.

He pulled the B7 chamber and seeing the steel of the tray, he lay back on to it with head nearest the refrigerator wall. His hands then pawed the steel ceiling to shut himself in until he heard the clunk of a lock.

Danny stayed perfectly still, arms crossed, like a vampire in wait. Outside the storage wall, he heard the bang of the swinging doors.

Nearer, he heard a loud click and then felt waves of chilled air brushing over his face.

He was among the dead and was being treated as one of them. Suddenly he felt panic fill his limbs, but there was barely room to twitch in this steel coffin. He suddenly reckoned Meg's candlelit dinner seemed the better idea.

He knew there must be some kind of lock mechanism near his feet. He tried to prise off a shoe using his other and perhaps then work a lever with his toes. But he'd been on cheap flights with more legroom. He guessed the usual occupant needn't worry about deep-vein thrombosis. With inches to move either side, he had little choice but stay perfectly still, as he listen to the footsteps pace up and down the refrigeration wall.

He fished for his trusty wire hook and tried to flick it to the feet end of the cold chamber. Right then, he wished he'd taken up Meg's advice to practice Subbuteo with Jack.

In the blackness, he couldn't guarantee any contact let alone a clean one. He flicked the wire and heard it slide but not for long.

His fingers explored the smooth steel as far as he could stretch by the thigh of his combats. He reckoned it had ended in no man's land by his knee or shin.

He cursed to himself.

He was already shivering. This clearly wasn't signposted as the refrigerator wall for nothing. They'd need to store bodies awaiting autopsy at sub-zero temperatures to halt the rate of decomposition.

By morning, he would be as dead as those around him. Save them carting me here, he thought morbidly.

Better be found out than dead, he reasoned, and kicked a heel on the metal hatch door. The sound bounced off the metal walls. It sounded like he was living in a kettle drum. The pacing outside stopped.

The silence was filled by Danny stamping the door again.

There was a clunk of a lock and light began to pour in there. He was slowly revealed to the waist but when he moved his leaden feet, the tray stopped. In the room Danny heard a screech of rubber and then a thud.

Danny pulled up the hood of his tracksuit and then palmed the steel roof of the coffin. He glided the rest of the way out and, as soon as his head was back in the room, he sprang up from the tray.

He jumped out to see the receptionist also getting to his feet and then snatching the torch he'd clearly just dropped. He made a crucifix with his fingers.

'Alright, mate,' Danny said, trying to humanise himself and thaw the atmosphere. 'Can't fault the air con, but I've stayed in roomier.'

'So help me God,' the receptionist whispered. The bald man looked paler than Danny had remembered from the car, as if he'd seen a ghost.

His jaw had slackened but no sounds were coming from his mouth.

133

'It's okay, I'm not a ghost or an undead, I was never dead,' Danny said. 'I just got trapped in there by mistake. A dare that went too far.'

As if assured by this, the receptionist took a tentative step forward. He then called into his radio receiver clipped to the breast pocket of his shirt, 'Security, I need back up here, intruder in B wing, got him trapped, come quick!'

'Roger that. On my way. Over,' replied a crackly voice.

'You don't need back up, pal, I'll leave peacefully, no harm done, nothing taken, nothing damaged.'

'You won't mind telling that to the police then.'

Danny knew he could outrun the big man but that wasn't much use when he was blocking the way to the only door out of there.

The receptionist was pointing the torch as if it was a weapon. In the half-light, Danny could make out the fat above his left eyelid begin to twitch.

Danny span and sprinted for the window he'd seen in the back wall. In one swift move he'd unlocked the window and shunted it up enough to slip through but not enough for the receptionist to haul him back in.

He heard the receptionist bark into the radio, 'Security! Get to the lawn out front, he's getting away!'

Danny recalled climbing just one flight of stairs. He knew that a fall from the first floor on to turf would be no worse than being fired from a two-mile chaser at a fence. At least he didn't have to worry about a kick from horses in behind. Carefully, Danny swivelled on the sill and then dropped to hang there by the fingers in the dark, facing the red brickwork and, with arms and legs stretched to shorten the fall. When he saw a flash of light, he looked off to the left. There was a floating white dot growing larger. It was splashing light over the long strip of grass and up the brickwork where he hung. The security guard had clearly heard the receptionist.

How the hell could he talk himself out of this?

134

An arm stretched through the gap in the window and grabbed one of his hands. Danny shook it off and then swung once before recapturing the sill with both hands. He couldn't drop as the guard below was too near.

Suddenly there were a couple of flashes of light up the bricks. Danny feared the guard had spotted him up there. But when he looked to his left the guard was walking off to the line of trees and bushes bordering the lawn directly behind. Danny turned his neck enough to see the flashes were coming from headlamps beyond the trees. He heard the rustle of leaves and snap of twigs. He guessed the guard had step into the undergrowth to check for a getaway car.

He heard the rev of the engine and a skid of rubber. Meg was clearly being thorough in her role as a decoy. It was now or never. He lifted the tip of his boots to grip a groove of mortar between the brick, like balancing a toe in the stirrups, and then relaxed his limbs as if drunk. He then let go with his hands and pushed off with his feet, mimicking a backstroke swimmer starting a race.

He saw the grass come spinning towards him.

He rolled on impact and lay there until the stars above stopped moving. He then scrambled to his feet and limped the fifty yards to the end of the tree line and the gateposts of the exit. He decided he could run off the pain in his ankle. As he made his way out, he saw his own hooded silhouette stretched out ahead in the pool of white light shining from behind. He knew the guard was chasing and not wanting his face to be seen by another witness, resisted the temptation to look back.

By now the car was gone from the road. He was disappointed there was no easy getaway but relieved she'd escaped. She'd already gone beyond the call of duty.

Safely clear of the area, he kept running into the blackness and didn't stop until he reached a taxi rank in Cardiff's centre, near the New Theatre at the top end of Greyfriars Road.

Leaving Cardiff for the valleys in the back of a cab, he felt he'd never come away from a break-in job with so little yet so much.

At Silver Belle Lodge, he noticed his red Mazda 6 was back safely in the drive. That meant Meg had also made it home. He still felt the adrenalin as he crept up the stairs and then played a form of silent hopscotch along the landing to avoid the several loose boards, though he felt he needn't have bothered. Having aided and abetted that night, she was probably as awake as he was, in their room right then.

He unlocked his office. The work had only just begun.

CHAPTER 13

In his office, Danny switched on the laptop and went to the filing cabinet.

He delved deep in there for the rolled up copy of the original architect's plan of both the stands and the new racetrack at Ely Park.

He then pulled out the bottle of single malt whisky from the locked desk drawer. He gulped back enough to numb the pain in his throbbing right ankle and to stop his hands from shaking. Later, he planned to slap some of Meg's hand cream on his grazed palms.

He heard movement on the landing and then on the stairs. Meg was on the move. She was clearly giving him the silent treatment. He glanced at the clock on the office desk. 12.26 A.M. He knew she was never angry for long or held grudges. He would wait until she'd calmed down, so relief could again become the overriding emotion.

He flattened out the plans to cover his desk and called upon makeshift paperweights, including his laptop, to prevent each corner of the map from springing back. Danny sank lower when he saw the sheer expanse in front of the stands and even larger area of green racetrack where the killer could have been positioned.

Where were you?

Danny remained convinced that even in death Campbell would provide the answers.

He felt numbness as the alcohol joined his bloodstream.

Think, Danny, think!

He kept being haunted by Campbell's grey face and the black bullet hole between even darker eyelids. He recalled the wound in the thick frontal bone of the skull's forehead was smaller than on the crown of the head. He suspected the bullet would cause greater trauma on exit. The gun must've been fired from the front and not from behind in the VIP suite.

The entry wound was also a lot lower on the head than the exit. The steep upward flight-path of the bullet suggested it was fired from below in the public enclosures fronting the stands rather than a flatter trajectory associated with a long-range shot from the far side of the track and the housing estate beyond.

Both wounds were central, consistent with Campbell facing his killer head on, though the BHA chief didn't know it at the time.

Since the Galbraiths owned one of the duelling leaders, Danny was equally certain Campbell's eyes would have been flitting between Powder Keg and Maids A Milking to get perspective as to who was leading on the run for the line.

Danny knew the killer was facing Campbell, who in turn was facing the horses. But he couldn't simply draw a single line from the balcony to the horses to find the killer as he didn't know where Campbell was stood on the balcony or which horse he was watching at the moment he died.

Danny recalled hearing the loud bang two strides after the final hurdle. At that moment, the leaders were level and about four horse-widths apart. He marked each horse on the hurdles track with a pencilled X.

Danny put an X at either end of the balcony to cover the entire width and then joined up the X for Maids A Milking with the left side and Powder Keg with the right.

He then shaded the strip between the parallel lines he'd made. That area covered every conceivable straight line between Campbell and the horses where the killer could've fired the bullet that perfectly dissected the brain.

Danny felt flat. It remained a disappointingly large area, including several bookies pitches in the betting ring, a few benches on the picnic lawn, part of the disabled viewing area, and most of the final fence of the chase course on the outside of the hurdles track.

Danny recalled a steeplechase had yet to be run on the racecard. With all eyes on the finish of the feature race, the killer could've used the five feet of birch as a barrier to hide up and as a makeshift tripod, resting the barrel of the gun on top of the tightly packed bristles.

Danny had an idea. He picked up the laptop and let the map curl back into a roll.

He went to revisit the footage of the race's aftermath. He knew it was blurry and shaky, as if taken by a drunk at a wedding, but he felt it might help place Campbell on the balcony. He could then put just one X on the grandstand and from there draw two lines fanning out to the two horses Campbell was most likely watching when he died. This triangle would eliminate a great swathe of the strip he'd already shaded.

In hope more than expectation he clicked on the video sharing website to see if any new clips had been uploaded. Only one result came back from the search and that was the page that once contained the original twenty-seven second clip. Danny stared at the black inset screen. He began to read down the line of usernames below. He was among them. There were nine.

His face moved closer to the screen. He studied the names, more intently this time, and instantly recognised SBStables as his own.

The second was almost as familiar: 'concorde21.'

Danny recalled Micky's twenty-first birthday a few months back. He'd shaken up a bottle of champagne and soaked the birthday boy in the weighing room.

Micky's last words entered his head. 'Save the nine… we all saw it… your killer.'

'It' was the clip, not the killer.

Danny now had a better idea why it had been removed. The gunman was captured somewhere in the twenty-seven seconds of footage.

Danny drew upon his photographic memory to recall what he'd seen the first time. It was hopeless. He had been so focused on looking out for Campbell while moaning about the quality of the camerawork that he hadn't bothered to look out for anything else. If he hadn't seen it, there was no chance of him recalling it.

139

He jotted the usernames down before they mysteriously went the same way as the clip. Aside from Micky, he didn't know who they were or where they lived but he suspected another one would be dying soon. Danny needed to track George's every move and called him on the cheap phone.

'I told you nothing doing for now,' George began with. 'The next target horse is being lined up with another trainer.'

'How many of us are there?'

'The less you know the less you'll need to lie if all this hits the fan and we're left covered in shit.'

'I need to talk.'

'Remember the form signing your career away,' George said firmly. 'It's stamped and ready to go.'

'I don't mean talk to the police, I haven't got cold feet.'

The line went silent. Danny opened his mouth but George beat him to it. 'Meet me at the Chieveley services just after junction thirteen off the M4. Do you know it?'

'I have to drive the horse van to tracks all over the country when the travelling head lad is off,' Danny explained.

'I'll expect you there on time, say three.'

'In the afternoon.'

'A.M.,' George said, 'I work around the clock, my time is money.'

Danny signed off. He knew that services was out of the way for Westminster and George's constituency in Surrey. It might well be work, but not linked to his day job.

Unless there was a mistress involved, Danny reckoned George was on the way to eliminate another of the nine witnesses.

That night, Danny didn't protest at being banished to the spare room as payback for the morgue date. It allowed him an opportunity to slip away quietly in the night without more questions asked.

CHAPTER 14

Up ahead, Danny spotted the silver ministerial Audi fill a parking space near the pyramid-shaped roof of the motorway services. Inside he could see the shape of George's head. He was alone in the car.

Danny dropped to first gear and crept forward until sandwiched between two large trucks with trailers in the lorry park. Curtains had been pulled in both their cabins. Danny was confident he wouldn't be reported and moved on. He waited there.

3.08 A.M. George put a phone to his ear.

Danny's cheap phone rang. George was too far away to hear that but could possibly catch some silvery light from the phone's screen in one of his rear view mirrors.

Danny chucked the mobile in the glove compartment and sank lower in his seat.

Lights off, Danny inched the car a little closer. Nosing out from the cover of the trucks, he suddenly felt more exposed. From there, he saw George get out and pace lengths of the Audi, checking his wrist every few strides.

3.24 A.M. Against the glow of the services cafe, he saw the considerable silhouette of George climb back into the car and heard the engine firing up. Danny had clearly tested George's patience too far. The car sped away.

Danny pursued from a safe distance. Hunting the hunter, he no longer felt like the prey.

Danny touched ninety on the clock as he chased George down the motorway until both left at junction seven. He soon realised it was easier to pursue a car for hours on a motorway where a driver's mind can switch to cruise control and see the same cars for miles on end. Now on an A-road Danny knew more mirrors would be checked. He felt conspicuous, particularly at this time of night. Occasionally, he'd slack off and allow George to leave his sight at junctions, roundabouts and traffic lights.

As George turned into what looked like a business park, Danny pulled up at the side of the main road to give the Audi a head start. He flicked off the lights as he turned into the estate. He could see George's Audi had parked up by an innocuous box of a building. The lit sign on the side suggested it was a Specialist Hardware Supplier. There were bars over the few first floor windows and a metal-plated front door with an intercom. George pressed the buzzer and then entered.

From a distance, Danny watched and waited. His eyes never left the Audi. He knew George could leave the building by a discreet back door but he couldn't leave the industrial park on foot.

When Danny saw George reappear, there was a brown package under his arm. George unlocked the boot and placed the parcel in there.

Danny pulled up the hood on his tracksuit top and left the Mazda behind. In the dark, he silently walked over to the Audi. As George got back into driver's side, Danny dropped to his knees and circled the car to the passenger side, close enough to be hidden by the blind spot in the wing mirror.

He crouched with ear to the cool of the metal, waiting for the seat belt to lock.

Click.

Danny flung open the door and jumped in. Before George could react, Danny pulled down the glove compartment and produced the gun he'd seen when last in there.

George lunged forward but was yanked back by the seatbelt.

Danny put the gun to George's head and leant over to kill the cabin light. He knew someone must be on a nightshift to hand over the parcel and didn't want to shine a light on his presence there.

'You're making one hell of a mistake,' George growled, shifting uneasily in the black leather seat.

142

'What's in the boot?'

'Nothing.'

'Don't mess with me, George. I saw you put something in there,' Danny said. He buried the gun hard into George's fleshy temple, loose skin wrinkled up. 'Slowly, we're both going to get out of the car. I'm going to hide this gun in my jacket pocket. If you try to run, I will shoot. As you know, when you've killed the once it only gets easier.'

Danny and George went to the back of the Audi. George pressed the fob and opened up the boot door.

Danny looked down at the parcel in there. 'B.N. of L,' Danny read aloud the black ink on brown paper. 'Who is B.N.? And where is L? Is this destined for the trainer of the next target horse?'

'As with spy agencies, I believe in a top-down, compartmentalised approach. Everyone knows their job but have no clue what the others do.'

'What is that place, a lab?' Danny asked but got no immediate answer. 'Looking at the levels of security, I'm guessing it's not just hardware they deal in.'

George replied, 'That business is just a front to cover a drop off point for shipments.'

'I'm guessing it's not your regular sorting office.'

'Like the sign says, it's a bit more specialist.'

Danny looked down into the boot. Any blood stains he'd left had been scrubbed and the smell of rubber had also gone. 'Pick it up.'

George picked up the parcel he'd just put there.

Danny ran a hand over the prickly carpet covering the floor of the boot. There was nothing in there. Danny felt the bruises on his back. He hadn't imagined it.

'Have you had a blowout since we last met?'

'No.'

'Are you sure?'

'For god sakes man, I think I'd know.'

'So there was never a spare tyre kept here.'

143

George shrugged and then looked at his watch again.

'Back inside,' Danny whispered.

They both returned to the front seats; George holding the parcel, Danny holding the gun in his pocket.

'Now open it,' Danny ordered.

'This isn't for you.'

Danny showed the gun. 'Open it.'

George began to peel off the layers of paper. Danny flashed on the cabin light long enough to see the contents. 'Why always a chessboard?'

'It's easier to smuggle drugs into the country without being seized by customs.'

'What's inside?'

George opened up the chess box.

'Pull off the lid.'

George removed his knife.

'You so much as twitch, so will my trigger finger,' Danny warned.

George prised the lid open to reveal an empty cavity. There were no test tubes, no felt board, no wire clips.

'Looks like you've been short changed this time,' Danny said.

George slid off the lid to the smaller box and removed two canisters nestled in a sea of polystyrene beads, neither much bigger than an aerosol. He weighed one in his palm. 'Light as a feather and odourless too, more reason for the customs officials to let it go.'

'You're planning on gassing the horses,' Danny said, incredulously.

'In moderation, inhaling this won't harm the horses,' George said.

'They've proved that as part of the R&D have they.' Danny tried to keep calm, but it was proving hard.

'They've shown the xenon and argon in these samplers can boost red blood cells in athletes, allowing greater performance stamina,' George said. 'And unlike liquids, they are untraceable in post-race and in-training samples and, even if they were, noble gasses aren't on the banned list of substances.'

'That didn't answer my question.'

'It's not been tested in the real world, only labs.'

'So we'll be the real guinea pigs, me and this... B.N. of L.'

George unravelled plastic tubing also in the chess box. 'This will be inserted into the nasal canal of the targeted horse, like a regular endoscopy, to improve the rate of absorption into the horse's bloodstream.'

Danny didn't reveal he wasn't a qualified vet as he had no intention of using this paraphernalia. He'd rather be hunted down by the killer than risk the health of his horses.

'Where were you off to?' Danny asked.

'What?'

'Kill another of the nine witnesses to your crime at Ely Park. Don't waste any more lives. The police are on to you. It's over.'

'I don't know what you mean.'

'Don't give me that,' Danny snarled and pushed the gun back on George's head. 'You called me from the footbridge as I held my dying friend. You said I was one of the nine and I was going to end up like Micky. I now know who the nine are and I know why they're in the firing line. You fear they saw your face in the crowd footage after the race. You had to get to them before the police did.'

'You're shaking,' George said. He was trying to seize some power back.

'So are you.'

'I'm not the one with the gun.'

'For a change,' Danny replied.

'It could go off by accident in the hands of an amateur.'

'What's wrong? You're happy to blow heads off, unless it's your own. Now, where do they live?' Danny asked.

'How the hell should I know?'

'You have to find them to kill them one by one,' Danny said, 'and you won't tell me because I'll be in your way.'

'I won't because I don't know who they are or where they live, nor do I care.'

'Bullshit,' Danny snapped. 'One of them is Micky Galbraith, the first of the nine to die. I also witnessed the footage and you know me.'

'I thought I'd met some loons in the House,' George muttered. 'Are you on something?'

Danny shook his head. 'But I'm on to something.'

'No, you are not,' George snapped. 'You're going after the wrong man!'

'Prove me wrong,' Danny snarled and pressed the gun harder against his temple.

'Put that thing down and I will.'

Danny didn't move. 'No more lies.'

'Nothing but the truth, so help me God.'

Slowly, Danny pulled the gun from George's throbbing temple though he made sure to keep it trained firmly on the belted man.

George breathed out. 'I mentioned that I'd been working on two bills that will transform gambling income streams: the machine tax and racing levy. One is a sweetener for the Treasury, the other for racing. The government wanted both voted through asap.'

'But the new regulation means you're also limiting the number of slot machines in each shop,' Danny said, recalling the grievances aired by Barton as he locked up for the final time.

'Any loss in revenue from restricting the number of machines will be more than offset by the twenty per cent charge we're also introducing. The government wants this bill to help balance its books and improve its perceived image in tackling problem gambling associated with some of these high-stake machines.'

'Not everyone in the government,' Danny said.

'What are you insinuating?'

'I've seen the article reporting you'd invested in a software development company ready to roll out a new range of games to fill those machines. You knew Campbell was a powerful man with an endless contact list and a desire to pass the bill, he needed to be stopped.'

'When was the article?'

'February I think.'

'I took office as Minister for Gambling in April. The post didn't exist before then. It's a newly created position within the department – you see, betting is big business these days. And by then, I had sold the shares as, like you, I knew it would be seen as a conflict of interest. Shame, because I could've made a killing, no pun intended.'

'Why didn't that show up in the news search?'

'Probably because it wasn't deemed as newsworthy, an MP selling shares before getting promoted to a new job,' George said and smiled. 'Hacks are in it to shock and provoke a reaction, the stories then go viral, feeding the revelations with oxygen and helping to sell more newspapers. And in any case, Campbell had no interest in passing the bill, all money from the machine tax went to the Treasury, not a penny went to benefit racing. And why would he want a reduction in those machines? They're vital to keep struggling high street bookies open. Even with a twenty per cent tax slapped on the profit they bring, bookies are still eighty per cent better off than before they spread from arcades and casinos into bookies. If the gaming machines go, in time so will many of the bookies. Like it or not, the bookie is racing's shop window. Sport is a product. How can you sell that product if you have no shop? It's a catch twenty-two situation: can't live with the machines, can't live without them.'

'That just leaves the second bill,' Danny said. George nodded. 'But the racing levy is already there. The BHA charges just over ten per cent of all bets placed on British racing by Brits. Without it, racing would fall and I'd be out of a job. Why would Campbell be campaigning for something that exists?'

'This bill is an extension to the one already in place,' George said. 'When the racing levy was first introduced years ago, many of the big bookies fled from these shores to avoid paying it, moving to foreign havens, along with their call centres and online businesses. These bookies are immensely successful and it's easy to see why when some could pay just six hundred grand in taxes on a three hundred million profit out there. And it wasn't just racing's pot drained by the bookies deserting the UK. These firms had tremendous spending power and attracted the best number crunchers and risk assessors from the City, not just from trading offices of other bookies, but also lawyers, insurance brokers, even accountants. They all suffered from the brain drain of this mass exodus as their best workers were attracted by the pay and the sun.'

'So Campbell was championing businesses all over.'

'But he was doing this solely for racing's good,' George replied. 'He was obsessed with the sport. Campbell was on a one-man mission to make it happen, turn around racing's fortunes and thereby become a hero in the eyes of his peers as, unlike the gaming machines tax, every penny of the racing levy goes to fund the sport. The clue is in the name. Maria, poor girl, was left a racing widow long before she was widowed.'

Danny recalled Maria say, 'Campbell was obsessed about leaving a legacy from his time as ruler of racing.' He now reckoned he'd found the third person in the marriage mentioned by Maria.

George continued, 'With this new bill, we close a loophole to ensure bookies based abroad paid for the privilege of taking bets on British racing by punters living in the UK. This will help level up the playing field for those who remained and paid up all these years. It opens up a whole new income stream to help fund racing moving forward. Every faction of racing wants increased prize money: trainers, jockeys, owners and even punters, as the bigger money will attract the best from abroad.'

'I can see why Campbell wanted to get it passed.'

148

'And the government wants racing to succeed and be self-sufficient. It provides crucial employment throughout our nation, it's a draw for tourism, a big part of British culture. Westminster wants racing to stand on its own two feet. Eventually, the levy will then be abolished and racing will run as a profitable business,' George replied.

Danny asked, 'Why would anyone want Campbell dead for that? He deserved a medal not a bullet.'

'There's only one loser from this legislation getting the green light.'

'Foreign-based bookies.'

George nodded. 'You got it.'

'It's about time they did something. I feel for the poor sods that stayed loyal to this country and paid the levy here, like Raymond Barton. It was the gaming tax from those machines added to the levy that made his business collapse.'

'Did it?'

'He wanted out,' Danny answered, 'I heard it straight from the horse's mouth at his empty Greyfriars Road branch.'

Suddenly Danny pictured the silver plate he'd picked up for Powder Keg winning the Welsh Champion Hurdle Trial. The sponsor in that engraving was *Bet with RBOnline for the Best Value.*

Danny always thought it odd Barton had sponsored the big race just days before quitting. 'Raymond Barton hadn't wanted out of the industry, he wanted out of the country.'

George turned to say, 'At the awards that night, Ray had loose lips from all the champagne and told me he'd ploughed all his wealth into the move, relocating staff and offices to the continent, plus recruiting for the call centre and online techie bods. All to make his business pay by evading the charges, only to then discover the racing levy was about to follow him over there like a bad smell. A few drinks later, I caught him begging Campbell to quit his campaigning.'

'No wonder Campbell and Raymond were stood at opposite ends in Maria's photo,' Danny heard himself say. 'I'm guessing the BHA chief refused to change his position.'

' "Served him right," Campbell told me. "Barton was turning his back on the sport that still gave him the majority of his betting turnover," ' George recounted.

'And that effectively signed Campbell's death warrant. He had to stop this influential campaigner for the racing bill. Raymond Barton publicly executed Campbell Galbraith.'

'A few weeks later Campbell was dead. Presumably Ray wanted Campbell to suffer the same public humiliation he was going through. He'd spent most of his life building that business. If he wasn't such a shit, part of me could feel sorry for him.'

'Perhaps the shot was fired from beneath the umbrella of Barton's Ely Park pitch in the betting ring.'

George shook his head. 'Barton had already sold his pitch.'

Danny recalled the gap in the bookies pitches at Worcester. 'I never liked the bloke either but he'd be pretty messed up after losing it all.'

'He was that evening,' George said, 'Barton saved the best for last where he threw a punch at a waiter who'd refused him another drink and then spun to slur the words "You'll pay for this" right in Campbell's face.'

'I can't believe Campbell was willing to make enemies, risk his job and his reputation all for the sake of one Commons vote ?'

'Campbell wasn't afraid of making enemies for what he believed in. That Commons vote was all he'd worked for,' George replied. 'And sounding out opinions, it looked like going down to the wire.'

'But I thought you said it would benefit the government.'

'It's surprising how many had investments and were on the board of directors in these bookies. A "no" would also mean a vote of no confidence in Campbell's position at the head of the

BHA, he'd lose his job and any chance of becoming a hero among the racing community. In the end, he didn't want it, he needed it.'

Danny recalled where he'd got George's number off Campbell's phone in the possessions bag. 'That's where you came in.'

George nodded.

'More by accident than design, I discovered we could scratch each other's backs.'

'So he was your man on the inside,' Danny suggested. 'And what better man than the chief executive at the BHA. But you're not even a whip. You couldn't rally MPs to guarantee the bill gets the nod.'

'It all started when I approached a lab technician at the integrity unit, though he turned out to be more of a lab rat.'

'What did you offer?'

'I didn't get a chance,' George replied. 'It's only when he shopped me to Campbell that we discovered both of us had something the other wanted. He saw me as a chance to manipulate the impending vote on the racing levy. I saw him as a chance to drug horses to win races risk-free and elevate my power and standing in the Commons. It was a win-win for both of us.'

'You bastard.'

'Since the expenses scandal, some of us have had to find an alternative means to top up our pathetic public pay – just to get by, you understand.'

'So you swap one form of cheating for another.'

'Campbell in turn threatened the lab guy with his job if he didn't play ball.'

'And that's why I shouldn't be worried about samples being taken,' Danny said. 'There's me thinking all horses were tested.'

'In an ideal world maybe, but cutbacks at the BHA mean not all are. As a punter, you'd expect all horses finishing in the prize money would be checked, along with the favourites that flop and the outsiders that wildly exceed market expectations, but this isn't an ideal world.'

'So why bother asking Campbell to intervene? You might get away with the odd doping here and there.'

'I'd prefer to remove all risk,' George said. 'Campbell intercepted samples from certain trainers in certain races at the integrity department. No questions were asked at the labs, he was their boss of bosses.'

'And those certain trainers just happened to be working for your betting ring, including me. I think they should rename their integrity unit,' Danny said.

'The unit is world class. That's why I had to resort to these lengths, but like any institution it only takes one bad egg to spoil an omelette.'

Danny said, 'So you wanted Campbell alive to keep this scam going.'

'Precisely, we didn't want him dead but we did want his hands tied to this. He was in it until we wanted to cut the strings.'

'But without your key man controlling the lab rat, there's a greater chance of a winning sample being tested at the integrity unit,' Danny said. George looked down at the canisters in the chess box. 'So that's why you're experimenting with untraceable gasses.'

'When you came calling, I asked a friend at the Met to run a police check and saw you'd got form in the courts as well as on the tracks. I knew you'd be willing to take a risk and break a law. That's why I tested the water by asking you to throw the race at Worcester parade ring. I wanted to see your instant reaction. I could tell you weren't shocked or horrified by the proposition,' George replied and turned to look Danny in the eye.

'That's because I brushed it off as a joke.'

'As it turns out, I chose wisely. When we raided the yard, you stood firm and didn't name names.'

'Shouldn't we go to the police?'

George said, 'It has to be you that proves Barton's guilt to save the nine.'

'Surely you've also got the contacts and power to send him down.'

'He has something on me, or should that be someone,' George replied and lit a cigarette. 'Too famous to forget, too important to be named. It ties my hands I'm afraid.'

'What something?'

'It's classified,' George said and blew a smoke cloud. 'Let's just say, if he found out I was behind his arrest and conviction, it could risk destabilising the country.'

Danny suddenly wondered what the hell he'd gotten himself into. He combed fingers through his brown hair. *This can't be happening!*

'Where has Ray set up base abroad?'

'The new gambling capital of Europe.'

'Monaco?'

'Gibraltar,' George answered.

'Las Vegas on the rocks,' Danny replied.

'Except it's the bookies flooding there, not the gamblers,' George said. 'But I know right now he's back in the country.'

'To kill another one of the nine,' Danny thought aloud.

'Well it's not to stop the bill or save his business here, he's sadly too late on both counts.'

'But to track someone, you need to find them first,' Danny said. 'Barton will have surely flogged his house in Cardiff to free up funds.'

'Perhaps you should find the potential victims.'

'I don't know who the others are, only that Micky and I are among the nine. Anyway, how the hell do you know for sure Barton's back in the country?'

George fished in the silk lining of his woollen coat. He removed his wallet and from within, a card with writing inked on one side. 'Copy these details down and then download the app here on to your phone.'

'What does it do?' Danny asked.

'It locates planted tracker devices with GPS.'

George then removed a smartphone from his coat and pressed the screen a few times. He handed it over for Danny, who saw a map of Britain scattered with several flashing dots on the

153

screen. There was one over Cardiff and another next to an X somewhere near where they were parked up. Danny recalled he'd put the tracker in his coat pocket.

'Is this legal?'

George smiled as he stared at the windscreen and then leant forward to wipe a stain off the glass but it was on the outside. 'You don't strike me as someone who is concerned by the answer to that. Remember, this man is a killer and he wants you dead.'

Danny removed his phone, went to the app store, downloaded the GPS locator software and filled in George's log-in details. On the back of the card there was an address, with ink yet to completely dry.

'What's this?'

'Raymond's new pad,' George said. 'I penned it down while I waited for your no-show at the services, thought you'd be wanting it after our little talk.'

Danny memorised the villa's address and then touched the screen with the flashing dot over Cardiff. A bubble appeared with the letters R.B. 'Barton is in Cardiff.'

'Perhaps you dodged a bullet coming here.'

'Why are you doing this?'

'I knew Campbell,' George said. 'He was a good man. I want the creature that did this to him found.'

'So you want me to do your dirty work.'

'I'm not the marked man, Danny. Now leave. I have a busy day ahead. Don't call me for a while, there'll be a gap before the next horse while things cool down and it won't be trained by you.'

'How many trainers are on board?'

'Just three others,' George said and blew another smoke cloud.

Danny coughed. George lowered the window slightly but stopped short of flicking the cigarette out.

'Who are they?'

'I work top down. Everyone only knows their own job, separate cogs in a wheel. The more cogs in a machine, the more chance it will break down. It's for your own good.'

'And yours,' Danny replied.

'It's unlocked,' George said and glanced at the door. 'Anytime you start to get cold feet, Danny, it's not just me you'll have let down; there are twenty others banking on you to deliver winners. Remember what I said – it's now real life not a trial, and people get hurt in real life.'

Danny returned the gun to the glove compartment. 'You won't need this.'

'Good,' George said. 'Glad we understand each other.'

As Danny climbed from the car he pulled his sleeve down over his hand and pulled the tracker out with his other. He pointed at the stain on the windscreen. He leant over the bonnet and while rubbing the glass with his sleeve, let the tracker drop down the grille at the foot of the screen.

Danny returned to his Mazda and checked the *Racing Post* database for trainers with the initials B.N. There were three: Brian Nettles based at Hampshire, Boris Naylor at North Yorkshire and Barry Naismith at Ayr. There was no B.N. of L.

Who were the gasses meant for?

He clicked his phone into the dashboard holder. Driving back to Cardiff, he regularly checked the flashing dot of Barton on the screen.

Turning off Gabalfa roundabout, he saw the dot edge from the centre. Raymond Barton was on the move.

Was he aware Danny was after him?

Danny watched intently, hoping the circle wouldn't leave Cardiff heading north towards Caerphilly Mountain and Silver Belle Stables beyond.

It appeared Barton was sticking to Cardiff city centre.

As he joined the early morning flow of commuters round the city's one-way system, he could see he wasn't closing on the dot. It seemed Danny wasn't next on Barton's list. He took no pleasure in this as it meant another one of the nine was in danger.

155

CHAPTER 15

Danny got some funny looks back for staring into cars as he passed. The GPS suggested he was now right on top of Raymond.

And then, a chance glance in the rear view mirror, he saw the fat head of Barton in the driving seat of a hulking, green Range Rover right behind him. Looking through the passenger window, Danny had been too low to get a clear view of the driver as he'd overtaken.

Why hadn't he chosen a less conspicuous mode of transport? Danny wondered, as he slowly sunk lower in the seat. He turned the mirror slightly, so Ray couldn't see enough of the reflection to recognise his face.

Danny slowed and slipped into a gap in the left lane of the one-way system rounding the castle walls, and the white of the museum and art galleries on Park Place. When he saw Ray accelerate past in the right lane, Danny didn't react. He wanted to catch Ray in the act.

They entered the Pontcanna area of Cardiff just north of the Millennium Stadium in the centre of the city and soon turned off into quiet tree-lined street of semi-detached houses with generous walled gardens. Danny pulled over when he saw the Range Rover's rear lights flash red.

From afar Danny could see Ray had mounted the pavement outside one of the houses. He got out and straightened his seemingly favourite blue suit jacket. He looked to be smiling. *Sick bastard.*

Perhaps it was his way of improving the chances of gaining entry by looking smart and turning on the charm.

Barton disappeared behind a wall of hedges. He'd walked between red brick pillars presumably at the mouth of a driveway. Danny sprinted to the nearest pillar and looked on as Barton rapped his knuckles on the door before putting his large face to the glass of the bay windows.

156

If the occupier was one of the nine, Danny hoped they were out.

Again Ray banged the door and then shouted something through the letterbox. He then clenched the fist and thumped the door one more time, seemingly more out of frustration. Any harder and he'd have knocked the door off its hinges.

He then wrote a note using his thigh to press on and shoved the folded paper through the letterbox. Mercifully he was looking down at the driveway as he turned. Otherwise he'd have seen Danny duck behind the pillar.

Danny hopped over the knee-high wall and buried himself in the thick hedge overlooking the pavement and road. Covered by foliage, Danny heard Raymond drive away in the Range Rover.

Perhaps he'd have better luck getting an answer. He pulled himself from the bushes and brushed himself down. It felt like he'd been dragged through Becher's Brook backwards. Like Barton, he wanted to look at least presentable or he'd no doubt get a door in the face.

Danny looked at the number on the pillar. He now hoped the owner of one-eight-nine was in and hadn't answered Barton's aggressive call, fearing he was some loud high-pressure salesman.

He walked down the paved driveway and knocked the door. There were laced curtains blocking the window but he could tell the lights were off. He knocked again and then called through the letterbox, 'Hello? Is anyone home?'

He looked around him. The hedges either side of the garden and driveway were as tall as those fronting the property. It was a semi but he wasn't overlooked where he stood on the doorstep.

Danny removed the hooked wire and picked the lock of the front door. He kept furtively glancing back at the gap between the pillars showing the road and path.

Suddenly the door clicked open invitingly. Fearing a passer-by on foot or on wheels, he quickly stepped for cover inside. He didn't know whether to play it quiet or making his

157

presence known. Either way, it was going to be an unwelcome shock if anyone was home. He looked around a wide tiled hallway with a wooden staircase ahead. He heard a rustle and looked down. He was stood on Barton's note. He picked it up and shook his head when he read it.

The only sound he could hear was the tick of a clock from a room at the end of the hall. Danny checked a half-open door to his right and stepped into a large lounge. There was a computer on a desk to the wall facing the door and a large flat-screen TV in the corner with a tan three-piece leather suite angled towards it.

Danny slowed his breath. He could hear his heart was ready to burst. He kept telling himself he was here to help but right then it didn't feel like it.

'Hello?' he called out.

Danny heard a distant bang of a door upstairs and thud of feet stampeding down the stairs. Their bold approach suggested the person wasn't aware a stranger was in the lounge, unless they were brandishing a weapon. As the lounge door swung open, he didn't know how to lessen the inevitable impact.

A thirty-ish woman appeared as if in a hurry. 'Where'd I put my bloody brush?' she muttered and then shut the lounge door to the cooler air in the hallway. The strong smell of her perfume soon filled the room.

He quickly raised his hands as a futile symbol of surrender. 'I'm here to help.'

When she saw Danny stood there sweating in combats and a black t-shirt, her whole body froze, apart from her blue eyes widening in horror. Her blonde hair was dark and straggly and her wet skin shimmered above and below a towel covering a shapely body. But right then, he felt as exposed as her. 'Don't panic, I know how it looks.'

She screamed and then said shakily, 'There's some money in the pot by the TV, not much but it's yours. Please, take it.'

'No, it's yours,' Danny said. 'I don't want it.'

'What do you want?' she asked, clutching the top of her towel tighter.

158

'I'm not after your body either.'

She screamed again.

Aware there was an adjoining wall feet away, Danny panicked and rushed to cover her mouth.

'Stay back!'

It was Danny's turn to freeze.

'Yeah… of course. But the front door was open,' he lied.

'That doesn't mean you had to walk through it!'

'But I needed to speak with you desperately. Just hear me out and I'm gone.'

Danny could see she was shivering, almost convulsing, and her eyes were now as wet as her skin.

'I've never seen you before in my life,' she screeched. 'Why? Why me?'

'I know you're in real danger.'

'I think I bloody know it too,' she said. 'Now get out of my house!'

Danny opened up Barton's note and glanced down.

'Give me one reason why I shouldn't call the police now.'

He edged forward to hand her the note. She fearfully backed away slightly. 'I'll leave it here.' He dropped it on the coffee table halfway between them.

Wordlessly she came forward and picked up the note, eyes never leaving his. For several seconds, she looked down at the note. 'I have to get my glasses.'

She went to fish in her bag on the settee and suddenly turned on her bare heels brandishing a can of pepper spray. 'Who sent this?'

Danny's hands came up again. 'Not me.'

'Prove it.'

'I'm not a serial killer.'

'You've given me a note that says, "If you ignore me, you will end up dead. I won't give up",' she said. 'Why the hell should I believe you?'

'If I was you'd be dead by now.'

159

She had stopped shaking but Danny was well aware she was closer to the hallway door and could easily make a break for the neighbours. He knew chasing after a near-naked woman down the street would take some explaining. He kept his distance to stay out of range of the spray. He needed her on side quickly.

'Are you into racing?'

'What?'

'Horse racing.'

'I go to Ely with work sometimes but I'm not a regular and … what has that got to do with this?' she asked, waving the note.

Danny glanced over at the PC on the desk. 'You went there on Welsh Champion Hurdle trial day.'

'Are you a stalker?!'

'No!' Danny said, shaking his head. 'That night, you went on the computer over there and watched a twenty-seven second clip showing the fallout after the race.'

'I was curious,' she said defensively. 'I'm not normally like that. I'm not one of those rubberneckers when there's a bad crash on the motorway.'

'I'm not blaming you, I watched it too,' Danny confessed. 'The trouble is the nine that witnessed the footage also witnessed the murderer's face fleeing the scene.'

'I wasn't looking at faces.'

'Neither was I but the gunman doesn't know that,' Danny said. 'Are any of these usernames yours?'

Skipping SBOnline and Concorde21, Danny read out the third on his list: LP189.

'That's mine,' she said. 'Lucy Parker.'

Danny knew this was number one-eight-nine. He was pleased she now trusted him enough to willingly share this without coercion. He now felt more confident she wasn't going to run. 'What exactly did you see in the clip before it was taken down?'

'Probably as little as you, seeing as you need to ask,' she replied.

160

Danny went over to peer again between the curtains. 'Please, we haven't much time. He wouldn't have risked returning to the UK without finishing the job.'

'What job?'

'He wants us both dead,' Danny said. 'There are nine of us.' He glanced at his watch. 'Now tell me, what did you see?'

'I told you, nothing,' she replied, still wielding the spray. 'I was more annoyed that a complete amateur had wasted my time by uploading some shaky footage.'

'Did you see any suspicious faces clear enough to ID them?'

'I don't remember any faces being clear enough,' she replied.

'There must be one,' he said, 'otherwise he wouldn't be killing all those who witnessed the twenty-seven seconds.'

Danny went over to boot up the laptop and then resumed his lookout post at the window. Seeing the dark shadow of a masked man peering through the glass and lace, he backed away and nearly fell over the coffee table. Moments later there was a thudding on the front door, followed by a creak.

'You didn't lock it then,' Danny whispered.

'Excuse me for being distracted,' she hissed and then gave a look.

She hitched up her towel and quickly swiped a tear from her cheek.

'Leave, back door,' Danny mouthed and then nodded towards a door at the other end of the lounge, presumably leading to the kitchen.

'What about you?'

'Just go, I need to meet him, end this one way or another.'

'Don't! Come with me,' she cried. 'Let the police arrest him.'

He stared at the hallway door. When he looked back, she was gone.

He heard a click. He hoped it was her escaping from the kitchen and not the masked man closing the front door.

161

Danny rushed for the wall alongside the shut hallway door. He had nothing to combat the intruder except the element of surprise.

While he couldn't make out any features of the dark figure through the net curtains, he saw enough to know the intruder held the size advantage.

When the door opened, Danny tensed up, like a wildcat ready to pounce. As soon as an empty hand swung into the room, Danny spun and grabbed the hand and slammed it against the wooden frame with a finger-snapping force.

It was only then he saw the other hand come in and then the butt of a gun's handle as it came down on his face with a bruising blow.

Danny's legs went from beneath him as the beige carpet came rushing up to him. He groaned as his hands came out to protect his body.

He lay there shaking his banging head, worse than a hangover after a night of mixing drinks.

He squinted up at the intruder in full black biker leathers with badges sewn down the sleeves. His face was masked by the tinted visor of a silver motorcycle helmet. Barton had clearly ditched the cumbersome Range Rover not suited to the tight city roads and removed the bike from the back of his four-by-four.

Before he could roll to one side, the biker dropped his considerable weight onto Danny, legs straddling his chest.

Danny could barely breathe, as if winded. He filled his lungs with enough air to say, 'Go on, cross another off the list.'

'This pains me as much as it will you,' the intruder replied, muffled like talking through a partition wall.

'Before you do, see that laptop over there.' The silver helmet turned. 'Maybe you can't see from down here with a visor, but there's a button camera above the screen. It can definitely see you.'

'The screen is black.'

'It's just turned to screensaver mode,' Danny said, 'but the processors are still working, along with the camera capturing all this in a live stream to my website. And there'll be more than nine witnesses to this.'

There was a breathy growl behind the helmet, and the handle of the gun was cranked up again. Pinned there on his back, Danny had no choice but wait for his skull to be caved in.

But there was a moment of stillness, as if the intruder was pausing to consider his actions.

'Ray, don't do this,' he pleaded one last time.

The helmeted man shoulders dropped slightly, as if realising the game was up.

'I know who you are,' Danny added.

'Who else have you told?'

'The police,' Danny bluffed. 'You're a wanted man, haven't you seen the posters? Take that helmet off and we can make a deal.'

'Like you did with George. No, we end this here. With you gone, another risk will also be gone.'

He turned the gun on Danny and put the mouth of the barrel between his eyes.

Danny suspected he'd be back in B7 sooner than he'd hoped. He shut his eyes and said, 'Say cheese for the camera.'

'My face is hidden.'

'But those leathers barely disguise your size,' Danny said, 'and I'm presuming those badges affiliate you to some club or gang. The viewers have already heard your name.'

Suddenly the intruder froze again, as if pinned there too, probably realising he couldn't go to switch off the computer without releasing Danny from the hold.

'If you slowly remove yourself before I suffocate, we can both leave quietly, forget this ever happened. Lucy won't be any the wiser,' Danny reasoned.

From the other side of the wall to his right, Danny heard footsteps pace along the hall. Had the masked man come with back up? Perhaps to clear up any mess left behind.

Danny purposefully didn't react and thankfully neither had the biker, whose hearing had clearly been hindered by the protective plastic and foam padding of the helmet.

'I can't hear the computer working,' the intruder said. 'You're lying.'

'If you take that thing off, you might,' Danny suggested.

The intruder pushed the gun deep in his jacket pocket. Danny's relief was cut short when he saw a shimmering blade emerge from one of the many zipped pockets in his jacket, much longer than the one George had used to puncture Danny's skin.

'The police will be chasing my scent like a pack of dogs. By changing my MO, I'm merely putting a stream in their way,' the man said. 'The police won't make the link to the Galbraith murders.'

'They will,' Danny said, 'when I've already told someone about the clip. The TV channel cut to an ad break, but you didn't bank on the crowds with their smart phones.'

'Who?'

'And soon the police will know why you came here.'

'You shared it with Lucy,' the man said. He sniffed the air. The perfume still lingered. 'She was here.'

From behind the helmet, Danny caught a glimpse of Lucy growing larger. His eyes quickly returned to the visor, not wanting to reveal her presence.

'It's over,' Danny said, trying to hold the intruder's focus. 'Admit it.'

'For one of us,' came from the helmet.

There was a creak of leather as he leant over Danny, who then felt the cold of a serrated steel blade press his stubbly neck. It hurt to swallow as his Adam's apple bobbed against sharp metal.

Suddenly Danny contemplated all he'd leave behind. He'd never get to see baby Cerys and little Jack grow up, and Meg was too young and inexperienced to cope with the yard and two kids. Her exuberance and enthusiasm alone wouldn't see her through. He couldn't let that happen. For the first time he felt he properly belonged in a family unit and he knew this wasn't how it should end.

'No, don't,' escaped Danny's dry lips. 'I'm a new father.'

'And that's supposed to affect me how exactly?'

'Man to man,' Danny pleaded, 'you must feel something, even if it's for the kids.'

'We live, we die,' came the cold reply. 'This will soon be forgotten, you will soon be forgotten.'

Lucy had now crept to stand silently directly behind the biker. He hoped her lengthening shadow hadn't given her away. She'd obviously come from the kitchen, tiptoed down the hallway and, instead of escaping out the front door, had crept into the lounge via the door near the bay window.

Her arm came out. Two handed, she held something weighty and pleasingly solid. It was only when she swung her arm Danny saw it was a rolling pin.

Thud.

The intruder slumped to the ground near the coffee table and then groaned as he tried to reach for the pain between his shoulder blades where he'd been struck.

She let the rolling pin slip from her hand. 'What have I done?' she cried, hand covering her mouth as if about to retch.

'You've saved my life.'

'But ended his!'

'He's just stunned.'

'I would've sprayed him if he hadn't worn the helmet. I've never hit anyone in my life I swear!'

'It didn't show,' Danny said, looking down at the writhing man. 'You chose a good time to start.'

'The police!' she blurted.

'Don't get them involved, not yet.' Danny then heard distant sirens from the road out the front. 'You already have.'

'I called silently from the kitchen. You looked in trouble on the floor. I put the phone to the crack in the kitchen door. The operator had clearly heard enough to send a car out.'

165

'I'll leave the back way,' Danny said, hearing the sirens clearer now. He could no longer hear the intruder's groaning from behind. He turned. All that was left was a red stain in the cream carpet. Danny felt the back of his head and his fingertips were covered in blood. Clearly the intruder could hear well enough to know the police were on their way.

'What do I do?'

'Shift the coffee table over that stain, tell them it was a false alarm, keep that note as evidence and double-lock doors for the next few days.'

'What about you?'

Danny was distracted by the flicker of blue lights colouring the lace curtains. 'Is there a way out the back?'

She shoved him through the back door and whispered, 'Over the fence, turn right at the end of the lane.'

'Ta,' he mouthed and forced a smile.

'Please, get him, for me.'

Danny nodded and then sprinted down the garden before clambering over the rear fence, aggravating his already bruised ankle.

***

Danny drove a safe distance from the crime scene of Lucy's house. He'd parked up in a side street while he recaptured his composure. He was about to face the snaking roads back to Rhymney when he saw Barton's marker on his smartphone's GPS map. He was still in the area. Danny zoomed in. Barton was at a small shopping area nearby in Roath. Had he stopped off for a coffee or bite to eat on his way back to the airport?

Danny left the Mazda on double yellow lines. Getting a ticket was furthest from his mind as he studied Barton's flashing beacon on the small screen. He'd slipped on some old shades he'd found in the glove compartment though it was cloudy and grey. He hoped to locate Raymond without being spotted himself. Pacing along a row of small independent shops, Ray's flashing circle was now fully eclipsed by his own but there was still no sign of him in any of the cafes or the pub.

He had to be here somewhere, Danny thought, no one can simply vanish. He was tempted to hang around for a pint but he needed a sharp mind and couldn't risk missing out on this chance to confront the killer. He may not get a better one.

He stopped at the end of the parade and turned to see a white sign showing three gold balls besides the lettering: 'S.R. Williams Pawn Brokers'.

Perhaps Ray was in there trying to offload the biker leathers or the helmet before returning to sunnier climes, Danny thought. He pressed the shades to his face.

A two-note chime rang out as he entered. When he saw the shop floor was empty, Danny checked the GPS map. The circle was still flashing.

The shop was as small on the inside as it looked from the outside. Even though the shelves were straining under all manner of random stuff from metal detectors to tennis racquets to clocks, there was no place for Ray to hide in here. At the end there was a cabinet full of gold and silver jewellery.

Nearby, sitting behind a counter and glass window, was a spindly old man with a sad comb-over and an expression that suggested business was down. He rested his magnifier. He'd been studying something small and shiny in his bony hands.

Silently Danny approached the counter. The old man glanced above Danny's eyes.

Danny ran a hand through his hair. It was then he saw his own reflection in the glass and hastily wiped blood from a cut where he'd been struck by the biker entering Lucy's lounge. He could now understand the trepidation in the old man's eyes. He looked more like an axe murderer than a prospective customer.

'Has a big man in leather and a helmet come here trying to sell something in the past hour?' Danny asked.

The pawn broker shook his head.

'Brown hair, fifty-ish.'

'Who's asking?' the broker replied. 'You don't look like police.'

'Have you seen him or not?'

'Debtor? I'll need some genuine ID, client confidentiality you see.'

Danny fished in his pocket and put down one-hundred pounds in five twenties. 'How's that for ID?'

Mr Williams' hand reached out to grab the notes from a metal well in the counter under the glass window. 'He came in about twenty minutes ago, pawned some cufflinks.'

'Can I have a look?' Danny asked and nodded at the broker's hands.

'If you really want, they're nothing special, enamel and gold plate.'

Danny picked them up from the metal well.

'I'd have told you for fifty,' the broker beamed. Having one over Danny seemed to make his day.

They definitely looked the same size and colours he'd seen on Barton's shirt locking up at the Greyfriars Road branch. 'How much?'

'Racing stuff sells well mind,' the broker replied. He changed his tune quick, Danny thought. 'Let's see, forty.'

Danny put the cufflinks in his pocket.

'What the... don't even try it boy!'

'I've already paid, you can keep the tenner change,' Danny said as he walked from the counter.

He didn't want the spectacle of being harassed by an old man in public, so decided to take refuge in the hardware shop next door.

Inside Danny sought out a display of hammers. He picked out the sledgehammer and pounded his palm to test it was up to the job.

He turned and was faced by Mr Williams. The pawn broker looked as startled as Danny felt. He'd probably come to warn the other shops there was a thief on the loose.

'Any problems?' Danny asked, still gripping the sledgehammer.

The broker raised his gnarly hands. 'No problems.'

He then hobbled from the shop.

Danny turned to see a plump shopkeeper in brown overalls. His rosy face was frowning from behind the till in the corner. He shakily said, 'It's on the house.'

'Very generous round here,' Danny replied. He wiped his forehead again and saw more blood on his bare forearm. 'But I'm not the thug you think I am.' He walked over to the counter. The shop keeper sought refuge in the corner. Danny placed his last twenty down. 'And I'm no thief.'

Danny left to find the nearest side alley to get away from the other shoppers. He dropped the cufflinks on the rough tarmac and then let his anger out as he smashed the hammer down with all his might. The gold clips soon warped and buckled, and the enamel cracked and then split open.

Danny picked up the cufflink and picked out the small black tablet of a tracking device. It was similar to the false foot on the chessboard. He checked the GPS map. The circle was still red and flashing.

Danny dropped the tracker and then brought the hammer down on it with a single crushing blow. The device was flattened. Danny checked the app and saw the flashing dot had died.

Danny had lost his only way of keeping up the chase. Although still very much alive, Barton had become a ghost.

With no fixed address in Britain, Danny knew the only realistic way of tracing Raymond was to find his new home.

CHAPTER 16

From the top of the ridge Danny stood looking down the six furlongs of gallop strip.

Off in the distance, he could see Salamanca's bold head over the fence of the lower field. Even after tendons in his near fore had flared up, he was still full of life. His legs were fine with a light canter and the take-off part of the jump, but they wouldn't be up to absorbing the impact on landing. His jumping days were over. That didn't stop him try to match strides with his younger stablemates as they thundered by on the other side of the fence every morning. Earlier in the summer Danny added an extra rung to dissuade Salamanca from clearing the fence to join in the gallop sessions. He knew how the horse felt. In his own mind he still felt twenty.

He held a digital timer hung from his neck. His eyes were tracking the climb of Powder Keg, though it wasn't the yard's best hurdler he was most concerned about. This was Meg's first proper gallop since giving birth. He punched the stop button as they breezed past at the end of a lung-burning uphill piece of work.

Meg pulled up Powder Keg. As they walked back, her whoop between breaths broke the still morning air. She punched the air weakly. 'God, it's good to be back in the saddle,' she panted and wiped her watery eyes with the back of her riding glove. 'That will blow the cobwebs away.'

'I bet,' Danny said and showed her the stopwatch. 'That's the fastest she's completed the full six furlongs upslope.'

'A bloody PB,' she beamed and hugged Powder Keg's black neck. 'Did you hear that Kegsy? I knew it felt good.'

'Keep up the exercise routine and special diet while I'm away and you'll both be in prime condition.'

He'd told Meg he was going to the Deauville sales to potentially snap up a few promising hurdlers to strengthen the squad. He was in fact booked on a flight from Birmingham to Gibraltar.

'You try and stop me,' she said. 'Saturday will be the most important day of my career.'

Danny jogged alongside Meg, who returned Powder Keg in a hack canter back to her stable for a well-deserved hose down and feed.

'Perhaps we don't need any new blood from France,' she said as she dismounted by the stables.

'Don't be surprised then if I come back empty-handed.'

He didn't enjoy lying to Meg but he reckoned telling the truth would only make things worse. She was worried enough without knowing he was going after the Galbraith murderer. She hadn't said anything more about the break in, but one look at her face when she thought no one was looking told him enough.

He hated hurriedly leaving his staff in the lurch too. He'd filled out and pinned up a colour chart showing work riders, led by Jordi, which of the horses needed morning gallops and those on the easy list. He also left comments to instruct the level of workout required for each horse. It wasn't ideal as he was happiest when present to see it done properly.

On the coach up to Birmingham, he called Stony to let him know about the cover story, in the unlikely event of Meg calling. Stony seemed more interested in sharing that Gibraltar's airstrip was one of the most dangerous in the world. He knew Danny wasn't the best of flyers. It was probably his way of getting back for laughing about his ban from art class.

Lost in thoughts and plans, the smooth flight seemed to pass quicker than the scheduled three hours. Danny needed evidence linking Raymond Barton to the nine witnesses of the online clip. His planning, however, was put on hold when he saw something two rows ahead that made him pull down the peak of his cap and slide down the back of his seat slightly. Just after take-off, he'd noticed a fat head and slick brown hair but it wasn't until it turned to take a drink from the flight attendant just then that Danny saw the face. Raymond Barton.

171

Having failed to kill Lucy, he'd clearly aborted and was returning to base. With only a handful of flights each week from Birmingham, which is the nearest airport to Cardiff serving Gibraltar, Danny knew there was a risk of crossing paths but he'd assumed Barton would be extending his stay in Britain to make up for the failed attack on Lucy. Danny had wanted to follow him but not this closely and not without an escape route nearby.

Thankfully it seemed Raymond hadn't seen, or at least recognised, Danny, who was just yards from his back. Danny wanted it to stay that way. He put his headphones on and pulled his cap down to cover most of his face.

Hearing the captain announce the imminent landing, Danny looked out of the window at the famous Rock rising up by the Strait of Gibraltar off the southern Iberian peninsula.

On the approach to Gibraltar airport, Stony's fun fact of the day came back to haunt him. Time seemed to slow right down as the plane skimmed over a road crossing the runway. He gripped the armrests and shut his eyes tight as they touched down with a screech of burning rubber on the thin strip jutting into the sparkling sea.

As the plane stood on the tarmac, Danny hadn't the time to breathe out when he saw Raymond unclick his belt and stand to leave for the exit behind them both.

Remaining seated, Danny would surely be seen. He quickly stood but then took longer than necessary to remove his hand luggage from the overhead compartment. Suddenly a wave of sickly aftershave tickled his nostrils. Barton had been wearing something similar in his shop door. When he sensed Ray squeeze by in the aisle, Danny breathed in and pressed his slim stomach against the headrest of a seat.

Ray's bag brushed Danny's back.

'Sorry, pal,' Raymond said.

Danny couldn't acknowledge the apology. He just kept wiggling his holdall as if it was wedged in the compartment.

'Manners cost nothing you know,' Raymond added as he moved on.

172

Danny turned his head slightly to remain facing away.

He then let an old woman by with sun-dried skin like a prune. He wanted at least one person between him and Raymond walking out of the airport.

'Do you need a hand with that?' a perplexed attendant asked.

Danny stopped wiggling the bag and removed it. 'I'm good, ta.'

Outside the airport, Danny looked on as Raymond shook hands with a driver in a grey suit and a matching peaked hat. As they got into a black Chrysler, Danny saw Raymond share a joke and then laugh. He was probably relieved to find the tracker in those cufflinks.

Danny hailed a taxi.

'Follow that black Chrysler,' Danny ordered. 'But keep your distance.'

The taxi driver shook his head until Danny handed over a hundred euro note.

They sped past glamorous marinas with cafes and restaurants. Danny could see it wasn't just the tax regime that made this place so attractive.

Soon, apartments were being replaced by square, plainer buildings. Danny could see they were entering Gibraltar's business district.

They followed the Chrysler until it turned down a ramp beneath a grey stone square building with four floors of windows. He heard the grind of a retractable metal door.

'Stop,' he ordered the driver.

Barton was clearly checking in at the headquarters of RBOnline before returning to his hillside villa.

Danny recalled the address inked on the back of George's card. 'Take me to the Upper Rock area.'

He then asked to be dropped a good mile from Barton's place. He didn't want the driver to speak up if the imminent break-in made the *Gibraltar Chronicle*.

It didn't take him long to find the lengthy whitewashed perimeter wall surrounding Barton's villa, broken only by a tall wrought-iron gated entrance. Danny wiped his sweaty palms as he looked up and down the winding road. He pressed the brass plate with an intercom on one pillar to make sure there wasn't a cleaner readying the villa for his lordship's return.

He looked up to see security cameras looking down. He pulled down his cap and then hoisted his light frame up the wrought-iron gate high enough to hook a leg over the top of the wall. Danny pushed himself up to straddle the wall and was then able to swing his other foot over. He grabbed the gatepost as a steadier and pushed himself off to fall on to the cushioning shrubs.

He reckoned he'd have a safe hour here. He circled Barton's huge white villa. Round the front, he was met by the crystal clear waters of an infinity pool dominating a sun terrace that looked down over the Old Town, the towering marina apartments and the jetties beyond. He looked across to the sparkling Strait of Gibraltar. On such a stunningly clear day he could see the coastline of Africa dividing the vivid blues of the sea and sky. He would've enjoyed the stunning vista had he been invited here.

Even through the soles of his trainers, he felt warmth from the patio tiles. Part of him wanted to rest on one of the blue sun loungers facing the pool and catch Ray off guard on his return from the office.

But he knew he'd be in a cell for trespassing before he had chance to get answers. He had business to do inside.

He was ready to pick the locks of the panoramic patio doors but they slid open invitingly. That wasn't all good news. He didn't want company. Tentatively he stepped in hoping it had been left unlocked by an absent-minded cleaner or pool man.

The interior more than matched the exterior. This was a playboy's villa. He scanned a sprawling open-plan living area, big as the footprint of many detached houses, with parquet floor scattered with plush rugs. There was a fifty-inch TV stuck to the wall and tall standalone speakers either side, facing a white leather suite and walnut drinks cabinet. Off to his right, the sleek kitchen was all chrome and granite tops. The panoramic patio window turned the room into a goldfish bowl. The villa had clearly got it all, apart from perhaps a female's touch. He was surprised the bookie didn't seem to be sharing the good life with someone. Perhaps it was a personality flaw.

Powder Keg would have to be another Istabraq to afford a place like this, he thought. This wasn't a man with money worries.

Why then would he risk it all by having Campbell Galbraith killed? Why did he argue with Campbell Galbraith at the awards? And why, once sobered up and calmed down, did he make good on his promise to see Campbell pay for his support of the bill?

Perhaps all this was bought on tick. Or maybe he was just a miser who resented giving a percentage of his profits back to racing.

One by one Danny inspected the cupboards and drawers in the kitchen. Next to the tall fridge, he found one stuffed with half-opened letters, junk mail, gambling magazines. He had a similar drawer in his own office.

His hands explored in there and fished out a clutch of fiftieth birthday cards. When he opened one to see the message, a photo fell out. He picked it up. It showed Maria in nothing but skimpy black knickers and high heels. She was lying on an unmade bed, legs opened invitingly. Beneath was penned, 'I'm wet just thinking about you, won't be long now sexy, your M xxx'.

Happy birthday indeed, Danny thought, most I ever got was a badge reminding me of my age.

Danny already knew they were friends from the smiley awards photo in Maria's lounge but he hadn't reckoned on this friendly.

Looks like this was the actual third person in the Galbraith marriage Maria had spoken about. No wonder she 'wasn't sorry' about the affair. Perhaps she should've been.

With his phone, he took a photo of Maria in her birthday suit. He returned the cards as he'd found them.

He then delved deep into the other kitchen drawers. Most were empty, even the cutlery drawer. Ray had clearly yet to fully move in or did most of his eating out.

He opened the final drawer next to the sink and pulled out two folded sheets of paper. The inner sheet had nine names and addresses written by hand. Among them were Danny, Micky and Lucy. Micky's name was crossed off. There was a question mark against Lucy. Danny was next on the list. The paper began to quiver in his hand.

Removing a reminder note stuck to the fridge, he could see the list of names had been written in Barton's hand. There were grainy imperfections on the shiny paper. It looked like a photocopy. Barton had clearly taken the original to Britain. But why leave a copy in his villa?

Finding the contact details of those witnessing the Ely Park murder would be like an admission of guilt. He opened up the outer sheet and flattened it out on the black granite surface by the sink. It was another list of names. Danny counted twenty. Were these more witnesses?

He then recognised one of the names, George Wheater. Danny reckoned he'd found where the money was being sourced for the betting coups on the doped horses.

On the counter he'd seen the same photo from the awards do as he had on Maria's mantelpiece.

Danny checked another drawer and saw the solicitor's deeds for the villa. The sale price was £1.2 million. There was a mortgage agreement from the bank for one million. Applying for a mortgage before the bill was passed, Barton could easily convince a bank to shell out on the promise of levy-free profits. But perhaps the loan had since been withdrawn, following the

176

introduction of the levy extension bill and the inevitable reduction in projected future profit.

By the kitchen there was a dark corridor. Danny presumed it led to the bedrooms. He glanced at the digital clock in the fridge.

He slipped the folded sheets full of names securely inside the buttoned knee pocket of his combats. He planned to return with the evidence later. He wanted to see Raymond squirm his way out of this lot.

CHAPTER 17

Danny retraced the taxi's route as he jogged most of the way down back to the business district of Gibraltar. He stopped only to duck into bushes or to pretend tie his lace-less shoes when oncoming traffic climbed the Upper Rock. He didn't want his face seen in the area of a suspected burglary.

He strolled along the marina basking in the brilliant blue sky. He listened to the lapping water and the clink of ropes on the masts of the yachts moored quayside. There weren't many better ways to mark time, he thought.

He stopped and stood there, eyes shut. He felt the warmth of the sun stroke his cheeks and saw the inside of his eyelids turn a fruity pink. Stress seemed to seep from his body. Knots between his shoulder blades began to loosen. He'd forgotten what that felt like. For months, he'd been too busy wrapped up with the never-ending cycle of jobs just to keep the yard ticking over. When the sun strayed up to the valleys for directions, he didn't even see it, let alone appreciate it.

He kept walking to the business district. From inside the taxi, he'd spotted a coffee house and eatery facing Barton's new offices, an ideal spot to spy the exit to the undercroft car park. Without a tracker, he needed some way of telling when Raymond was returning home.

A chalkboard outside cafe read: Coffee and bacon roll £2.99. Full English and free orange juice £4.99. He was no longer in any doubt this was the heartland for the exodus of British bookies.

He ordered an orange juice at the counter but refused the offer to buy a full English to get the drink 'free'. He didn't want to be bloated by a fry-up if Barton suddenly left his offices.

He found a window seat with the clearest view of the grey unassuming office block and dropped his rucksack on a spare seat in case anyone even thought about joining him.

As he slowly turned the chilled glass on the table, his reverie was broken by a young cockney voice off to his right. 'Casing the joint are we?'

It was only then Danny knew he wasn't alone with his thoughts. He looked across to see a rakish man, mid-late twenties, gelled brown hair and clean shaven. He could've been Barton's love-child. He had the smartness of a man out to impress. He held a bacon sandwich in one hand and had already returned to staring at his laptop on the table as if hypnotised by the silvery screen.

Danny looked down at a leather computer bag on the terracotta red floor tiles. There was R.B. embossed on its side.

'Would I be telling an employee if I was?'

'Good answer,' the man replied, grinning. He still didn't look back, as if already bored with Danny, who suspected the man would make a good character witness. 'What're the odds?'

'Eh?'

'Meeting an employee of Raymond Barton Online,' Danny said, 'How do you rate your boss?'

'Sorry, who's asking?' the man replied, grin gone. He then looked up from the screen.

'Sean,' Danny said, offering a hand. The man showed his palm covered in streaks of red sauce. Danny could see enough of the laptop screen to make out a grid of betting odds. He wanted to bond with the man before he returned to work from his brunch break. 'I'm an odds compiler looking for work. Let me guess, senior trader?'

'Near enough,' the man said and then smiled. 'Mr Barton is a good man.'

'Very wise,' Danny said. 'Never speak ill of the dead or your boss.'

'He gave me a job, that's enough to make him a good man in my book.'

'Speaking of books, which betting markets do you specialise in?'

179

'Tennis, snooker and golf mainly. Working on match betting for the second round of the Valencia Open right now. Why? Are you offering a second opinion?'

'I'm more a racing man myself,' Danny said.

'Shame, I need all the help I can get, need to make a big impression.'

'You're new then,' Danny said.

He nodded. 'But I can at least say I was there from the start.'

'So it's a new company,' Danny said, playing dumb.

'I'd do your research about the firm before applying,' the man advised. 'It's a cut-throat business, only the best will survive. What makes you think you can make it?'

'I love my betting and want to finally make it pay, so thought I'd join the other side.'

The trader smiled. 'Welcome to the dark side.'

'I've heard Raymond's a ladies man.'

The man looked over both shoulders and then leant across. 'One of the original traders in Cardiff to come over reckoned he'd found the one. He overheard Mr Barton boasting Wales' number one bachelor was officially off the market.'

'Her name is Maria.' Danny showed her photo on his phone. 'Is that her?'

The trader had a longer-than-required look. 'Blimey!'

'I'm guessing that's a "yes" then,' Danny said.

'Where the hell did you get that?'

'As you suggested, I did some online research.'

'I'm surprised they haven't requested the search engines to remove it.'

'You know Ray, he'd regard it as showing off his latest trophy to the world.'

'She's alright, for her age. Don't know what she sees in the multi-millionaire.'

Danny smiled.

'Who are you really? Some jealous ex-husband of hers?' the trader said, shutting down his laptop. 'I think I've already said too much.'

'Nah, happily married me,' Danny said. 'One more thing to help me in the interview, why did he move out here?'

The trader nodded to the window. 'Look around the marina down the road and the Upper Rock district. And have you seen his pad? Flash Harry's got nothing on him. The sun, the sea,' he said and handed back the phone showing Maria's photo, 'the sex.'

'You're telling me a canny businessman and bookie that'd spent his life building up a chain of shops in South Wales would up sticks for anything but money?'

'I guess some things are more important at his age.'

At his age? 'He's fifty!'

The trader glanced over at the counter where the waiter was pouring himself a coffee and then, as if preparing to share a lifelong secret, leant even closer to Danny. 'That same lad also told me the dryer, warmer air and laid-back lifestyle here eased the boss's health problems but remember, I never said that. Don't want to lose this job before I'd got a tan, let alone a promotion.'

Danny didn't pry. He knew a prospective jobseeker wouldn't be interested in the private life of the company owner. He didn't want to waste a question as he'd still to ask about the list of twenty new names. With his hand, he ironed out the photocopy found in the villa's kitchen on the trader's table, next to the laptop.

The trader took a look and then shakily shoved the paper back in Danny's hand. He then slipped his laptop into the company's bag.

'Are these employees at Raymond Barton Online?' Danny asked.

'I'm not supposed to talk to government officials.'

'What?'

'They're all currently serving British MPs.'

Danny looked harder at the list. He knew George Wheater was among the names. 'If I was a government official do you really think I'd be asking who they were?'

'I'd get out of Gibraltar while you can,' the trader said. 'Your type aren't welcome here.'

'Who are you to tell me where to go?'

'I didn't say my name,' the trader replied and raised an eyebrow. 'I'd rather come across as rude, than find out you were some hack, or inspector.'

'I'm no grass, spent years inside.'

'And that's supposed to reassure me how, exactly?' the trader said. 'I think it should be me asking your real name.'

'What's the point?' Danny replied. 'I think we both know it'll be made up.'

'If the boss was still in the office, I'd be reporting this,' the trader said and stood to leave.

Danny looked out of the window. It seemed the boss had already left the building. Their paths had crossed again. The Chrysler must have been one of the oncoming cars he'd ducked on the descent from the Upper Rock.

The trader left with a rattle of the glass door.

Danny was left there staring at the twenty names. He suspected this was the 'something' Ray had on George that could topple the government.

At the top of the photocopy Danny penned 'members of betting scam led by ringleader' and then drew an arrow to George Wheater's circled name.

Twenty MPs weren't enough to topple a government, Danny thought. They'd most likely plead ignorance to the horse doping and argue it was merely an investment opportunity advised by their accountant. A sincere apology and a slap on the wrist would be enough for many, like after the expenses scandal, Danny reasoned. He didn't even know whether these twenty were members of the ruling party.

It was then he recalled Wheater's parting words in the Audi at the delivery depot. 'It's not just me you'll have let down; there are twenty *others* banking on you to deliver winners.'

Others, Danny thought.

He counted the names again. There were still twenty names, including George Wheater. There was a name missing. If Barton was part of this, he wouldn't have needed to put his own name on the list. Barton could be the twenty-first member of this very private club. The members would've needed a means of placing large bets without any alarm bells ringing at the bookies. Wheater wasn't prepared to take any risks. Bookies were always laying-off hefty bets with other bookies and betting exchanges to reduce liabilities on any given event. There wouldn't have been an eyelid batted had Raymond tried to get money on with others. If the betting scam was ever uncovered, he would've looked like the victim trying to force down the on-course price with the rails bookies to limit the damage from having seemingly taken big bets in the first place on the targeted horses in this scam.

Danny was about to confront the man behind the killings. He put the folded sheet deep in the lining pocket of his jacket. If he was going to be next of the nine to die, he wanted the first officer on the scene to have a lead as to why Danny's body was discovered at Ray's villa, though he suspected if this turned into an investigation back at the Met, George could somehow ensure files went missing so none of this got out, just like the blood samples at the racetrack.

Danny winced as he finished off the bitty orange juice. He planned waiting for the cover of nightfall before returning to Upper Rock. He wasted the afternoon nervously sipping mineral waters in the bars on the Wharf until it was time.

CHAPTER 18

Danny didn't buzz the intercom this time. He suspected Barton would regard Danny as an unwelcome disruption to his evening, whether or not he recognised the face.

Instead, Danny walked far enough along the curved perimeter wall to go beyond the view of the CCTV above the pillared gates.

He nestled his rucksack between two roots jutting up at the foot of an orange tree on the grassy verge by the wall.

Should be safe enough there in the dark, he thought, as he turned to tackle the wall. He pulled the torch from his jacket and tested it on his open palm before slipping it in his back pocket.

He then took a run up and jumped, high enough to hook both hands over the top of the wall. He hoisted himself up and over, landing with a bump on what felt like firm ground the other side. He tugged on his riding gloves.

Keeping small and silent, he made it to the villa. There were no lights on. Perhaps Barton had retired for an early one after the flight.

Danny was about to flick on the torch when the dazzle of a security light saved him the effort. He'd tripped a sensor beam. He quickly fled for cover to the white of the side wall near the front door. He felt confident that's all he'd triggered as an alarm would be constantly set off by all manner of foraging wildlife, including the apes of the Rock.

Danny saw there was an alarm box, however, above the blue front double doors. He circled the villa to try the glass patio doors round the other side. When he pulled at the handle, the doors were not only unlocked but also slightly ajar. As a housebreaker in his youth, he made doubly sure to leave a property as he'd found it. Must've lost my touch, Danny thought, as he pulled the doors further apart.

He stepped into the dark of the open-plan lounge. As he shut the glass doors behind him, there was a clap of another shutting. He swore it had come from the black hole leading off the lounge.

Maybe Ray had seen the white of the security light illuminate his bedroom blinds. He dived for cover behind the kitchen island. He waited there on his haunches, listening for footsteps. He tried to control his pulse with slow breaths but his heart had other ideas.

In the sparse light of the flashing fridge-freezer clock, Danny craned his neck above the island. He didn't see anything appear from the hallway. But he did spot something closer by on the granite surface of the island. He stood and looked down on a wallet, a Chrysler car fob and an open bottle of Rioja.

He picked up the wallet. It was brown leather with lighter frayed edges. Like the trader's laptop bag, there was an R.B. motif embossed in one corner.

Surely a man of Barton's means would've replaced it years ago. He probably got them as a job lot, posting them out to his high-roller clients, at least the losers among them.

Inside, Danny pulled out several twenty euro notes and the stub of a gold VIP suite ticket for Ely Park's Welsh Champion Hurdle Trial day, now remembered only for the murder.

When Danny's gloved finger wormed into the corner of each little pocket, out fell a silver foil containing several pills. Danny began to think the George Wheater scam was more about money laundering for a narcotics ring. He squinted to see the tiny black writing running diagonally across the silver. *Humira.*

Danny made a mental note and then carefully returned the contents and then the wallet.

It was only then he caught a flash of light from the granite top. There was a gleaming handgun, just casually lying there as if it was perfectly normal. At first he hadn't seen it against the black of the granite.

Danny looked over at the mouth of the hallway beside the kitchen. He picked up the gun and gripped it in both hands against his chest. As he slowly crept along a wide passageway with back to the wall, he could make out the dark wood of the doors, all four of them.

He didn't flick on a light as it would seep under the crack in the doors. There were two on either wall. Three of them were open at varying degrees.

Danny kicked the first door. He flashed light in there before stepping inside. It was as dead as it was dark. The size of the room, with its king-size bed and doors to a dressing room and en suite, suggested this was the master bedroom where Ray and Maria had slept. Danny had a quick look around but didn't touch or move anything. An eagerness to complete the job done without delay had stayed with him since his days as a housebreaker.

He moved on down the hallway and kicked the second and third doors leading to spare bedrooms, both as still and silent as the master.

He pictured the wallet and car keys on the kitchen island. They were the first two things he made sure to pick up when leaving Silver Belle Stables. Barton must be here somewhere. With only one room left to check, Danny felt added nerves.

He stood by the fourth door. He recalled the clap of a door when he stepped inside the villa. This was the only one shut tight. There simply was no place else to hide. Barton had to be in there.

The turn of a handle would forewarn Barton inside. Danny edged closer to the wood and broke the silence with, 'Ray? I've got your gun and I'm coming in, so don't dare try anything.'

Danny stretched an arm out and turned the silver handle until it clicked and then kicked the door to swing wide open. He stayed silent as he released the safety catch on the gun to make sure Barton had heard.

He didn't need the torch as there was enough white light from a laptop whirring on the desk inside. Danny stepped cagily into a smaller room, currently being used as a study.

Gun pointing at arm's length, Danny spun on his heels to cover all angles, fearing an ambush.

It was as empty as the others. Danny glanced down at the laptop screen. It showed a screen capture of a man shouldering a

186

rucksack and staring up at the CCTV cameras above the gated pillar. Looking closer, he saw it was his face looking back.

Was Raymond down the police station giving a name to the face?

Danny sighed at the prospect of an international arrest warrant being granted. He could see enough of the black keyboard to press Escape and then Control-Alt-Delete but the screen was stuck there, as if the computer had a virus.

Danny began to slap the keyboard out of anger. Perhaps he'd fluke some key combination to close the system down, or at least minimise the image. Perhaps it was locked by a passkey. Danny was more comfortable picking a real lock than a digital one.

He unplugged the computer at the wall and, while the screen merely dimmed slightly, he hoped the internal battery would run out before he'd boarded the plane.

Danny left the study. He was glad he'd taken his riding gloves as he carefully rested the gun by the wallet and keys.

When he opened the patio door, he heard another clap of a door. His heart went berserk until it became clear the culprit was fresh air gusting through the villa. But that didn't explain where Ray had vanished.

As he slid the door behind him and turned to sprint back to the perimeter wall, he afforded one last glance across at the view of the glittering Old Town and marina, and the sea lit by white moonlight.

His eyes stopped at a large black shape floating at the end of the infinity pool, though the irony of this was lost on Danny right then.

He hoped it was a bloated black bin liner of destroyed evidence that had split and leaked.

At the far side of the pool displaced water was allowed to cascade over the edge. From the patio, there was no way of getting close enough to fish out the black object floating there. And he couldn't flash light on the shape as it would shine like a lighthouse against the black surroundings up here.

187

Danny wrestled off his jacket and shoes. He bit the torch between his teeth again and lowered himself into the freezing water. He held his arms up to at least keep part of him dry. He hoped the stink of chlorine would make the forensic team's work harder.

As he slowly waded over, ripples grew and spread. And the shape began to bob in the water.

Up close, Danny flashed a light down on the water's surface. He fell back with a splash from the sight. He was confronted by the large body of a man, floating face down with jacket puffed up by trapped air and surrounded by a blood-red moat. He knew there was no point in resuscitating. The wrinkly hands were white as a ghost.

Had Barton crossed another off the list?

He realised he was standing in a murder scene. He looked down to see if the edges of the blood had lapped against his t-shirt.

In and out quick, Danny reminded himself. He took several rapid breaths to oxygenate his blood but it only made him lightheaded. Last thing he wanted was to pass out and be found floating next to the body, giving Barton a viable suspect to point the finger at.

He ducked under and spooned water to move along the pool's floor. He pulled the torch from his teeth and, eyes stinging, stared up at the black shape directly above him. When he flicked on the torch, a stream of bubbles escaped his mouth and he paddled more frantically.

He'd lit up the white and grey of Raymond Barton's bloated face. There was a bullet hole in the middle of the forehead. His large eyes and mouth were open wide, as if capturing his last moment of terror. Danny's expression was something similar as he flicked off the torch and tried to resurface away from the slick of blood on the surface.

As he waded from the pool a good deal quicker, he felt as sick as when removing the sheet in the morgue. He pulled on his

188

socks and shoes but kept his jacket away from his sopping wet t-shirt, knowing he hadn't a spare.

He didn't mind leaving wet footprints over the patio tiles as they'd dry by the morning but he hoped there'd be no residue of blood left as he knew how difficult it was to shift having needed to wash his spattered silks several times after a heavy fall.

He made an ugly shape clambering over the wall and then, swiping up his rucksack, set about pacing down from the Upper Rock.

When he started to shake, he found a lay-by sheltered by bushes, shrubs and overhanging trees. From his rucksack, he pulled out a dry change of t-shirt and combats. Gooseflesh had spread down his strong arms and lean, muscular torso. With fistfuls of dried grass and leaves, he towelled his naked body down in the chilled night air and then changed into his spares.

Once he'd stuffed the potentially incriminating clothes into his bag, Danny removed his own mobile from his jacket he'd hung from a branch.

There were several missed calls from Meg. He knew his voice would be shaky and his mind was racing. Whatever her concerns, he was in no fit state to calm them. He felt a sinking feeling but he was safe in the knowledge the killer was out here, a long way from his family at the yard.

Instead, he called Stony, who would be less perceptive something was seriously wrong, particularly at this hour.

'Stony? It's Danny.'

There was a silence. Danny could almost hear the cogs begin to whirr into action.

'What time is it?' Stony croaked.

'I need you to check something.'

'I'm asleep.'

'You don't sound it.'

'I sleep talk as well as sleepwalk.'

'Can you search for something online? The reception is murder here.' Danny cringed. It was the one word he wanted to avoid.

189

'Why? Where are you?'

'Gibraltar.'

'Wha—' Stony said. 'Funny time for a holiday when the jump season's just kicking into gear.'

'I'm not on holiday.'

'And I'm not going to ask,' Stony said.

'Please, do this for me and I'll sub you say... a dozen pints.'

Danny heard the springs of a mattress and the snap of a few bones.

'Go on, let's have it,' Stony said, voice stronger.

'Humira,' Danny said.

There was a rustle of foil and then silence.

'Stony? Are you going to your computer?'

'Don't need to,' Stony replied and then yawned. 'The answer's right here, in my hand.'

'What is it?'

'I've taken that drug since the hip op. It's for my arthritis. Good stuff it is mind. I swears by it.'

So that was the health problem the trader had mentioned, Danny thought. Raymond had brittle bones. No wonder he'd picked a villa with a large pool. It would help his joints as well as his stress levels and bragging rights.

'Are you sure?' Danny asked. There was another silence. 'Are you nodding?'

'Oh, sorry,' Stony said and yawned again. 'I was, brain hasn't got going yet.'

'You're doing great,' Danny reassured. 'Just one more thing, have you still kept that cardboard cut-out from Raymond Barton's shop?'

Silence again.

Danny added, 'Don't worry, I'm not going to judge you.'

'I've kept it in the study, for target practice you understand.'

'Can you go there and take a closer look at it?'

There was a sound of footsteps and grunting down the line. Away from the Old Town at this time of night, everything sounded so clear up here. The steps even made Danny glance over both shoulders into the blackness. He edged deeper into the shelter of the layby.

'I'm in there,' Stony explained.

'Tell me, how is he standing in the cut-out?'

'On his feet.'

'But is he slouched or leaning against something.'

'No, he's stood proud and smiling.'

Doubt it's a dodgy hip, Danny reckoned. 'What about his hands?'

'They're out in front of him, the right one is cradled by his left, like he's hurt it.'

'What about the fingers?'

Danny heard a louder grunt.

'Doubt I'll get up from down here. Now, let's see. His fingers are all curled up. Do you reckon he's got arthritis too?'

'I know he's got arthritis.' Danny recalled the strength in the hands of the masked man pinning him to the floor of Lucy's lounge. Barton clearly wasn't capable. He recalled the bookie handing over the cut-out awkwardly with his left hand from the shop door. At the time, Danny had assumed there was something in his other hand. Little did he realise it was arthritis.

He wouldn't be able to hold a gun for long, let alone take deadly aim between Campbell's eyes.

'I can hear grasshoppers.'

'I'm outside on a hill.'

'Go on, tell me why. Won't get back to sleep otherwise,' Stony said.

'I'm here to find the killer of the Galbraiths.'

'You've had a wasted journey.'

'Not completely, I can now rule out Barton.'

'I could've done that,' Stony said and then chuckled.

'Why?'

'Haven't you heard? Don't suppose it made the news out there,' Stony said. 'Keith Gosworth was arrested two days ago. He was questioned down Cardiff police station and then released on bail.'

'Perhaps he'd proved his innocence in that interview.'

'Funny way of showing it, he went missing straight after walking out of the cop shop. The alarm was raised when he failed to report for duty at the racetrack and he then skipped bail. God knows where he's got to.'

'I think I just missed him,' Danny heard himself say.

'What?'

'Nothing,' Danny retracted, 'What do you make of it?'

'I reckon the police had enough on him and the interview didn't go so well for Gosworth. Guilty as sin that one.'

'It's good to speak, Stony. I've got to keep on the move or I'll seize up.'

'I know the feeling,' Stony replied. 'And I'll be waiting for those dozen pints.'

Danny descended back to the Old Town and laid low waiting for the return flight.

Danny sat on a bench in the marina and unfolded the photocopied list of MPs and the nine witnesses to the race-day footage. It seemed he was trying to track down the maker of these lists. Like Danny, he was tracking the killer. He could see why Barton had become a wanted man.

He pictured Ray banging on Lucy's door and the note. 'If you ignore me, you will end up dead. I won't give up.'

It wasn't a threat but a warning. He had her name and address and was there to pre-empt the masked killer on his way to her house.

He then pictured Barton's bloated white face staring down at him. It seemed the killer had caught up with him. Perhaps Barton was close to revealing all to the police.

He couldn't believe Keith Gosworth was capable of a killing spree. From the censored diary entries in the clerk's office diary, it was clear Gosworth and Galbraith were sworn enemies. Perhaps that was the something the police had on him.

Campbell Galbraith is a complete *blank*. Danny now found it even easier to fill in that blank.

But why had George accused Raymond Barton of the murders. The new Minister for Gambling had more questions to answer.

CHAPTER 19

Danny was breathing hard and sweating as he rushed into the parade ring behind the stands at Ely Park.

He was greeted by Meg. 'What part of "this is the most important day of my career" did you forget?'

'I'm so sorry, sweet.' He'd been so consumed by pinning the murders on Raymond Barton that he'd pushed Powder Keg's big race to the back of his mind.

She pulled her curly blonde hair back into a bunch and then fumbled with the chin strap of her riding skull cap covered in her red-and-white quartered silks, matching the colours of her favourite ballroom gown.

Danny was buttoning one of the manky tweed jackets he'd seen hanging in the store room beside Gosworth's office. Despite being two sizes too big, he'd been forced to hire it at the entrance. He then pinned an owner's and trainer's pass on the frayed lapel.

'Where are your clothes?' she asked.

Danny looked down at his t-shirt and combats. 'Racecourse security was being a pain in the arse at the gates. Guess they're paranoid there'll be a repeat of what happened two meetings ago. They took my rucksack and jacket away to examine in their hut.'

'Why?'

'Probably the stink of chlorine.'

'Chlorine?'

'They had a pool at the Deauville hotel I stayed.'

'You wore them in the—' she said and then added, 'You know what, I won't ask.'

'I came straight from the airport.'

'I can see,' Meg said looking Danny up and down dismissively.

Danny tugged for some slack in the tie knotted round his neck. Ties made him feel strangled and he didn't want to be reminded of being pinned to Lucy Parker's floor.

'Looks like you're ready to go, with or without me,' Danny said, looking at her pristine silks, correct saddle and tack. It shows you're a proper assistant trainer now.'

'But all of that is pointless if Powder Keg wasn't declared for the race.'

Danny put a hand to his furrowed brow and mouthed, 'Sorry.'

'Danny, this isn't you,' she said. 'Sod getting new recruits to fill the empty boxes from France if we can't even get the best from the ones we have.'

He couldn't believe he'd overlooked declaring Meg's star hurdler into Wales' number one hurdle race at the final forty-eight hour entry stage for this Grade One.

'I left loads of messages on your mobile to check you'd named her among the decs but when you didn't reply I used your ID and password to make the declaration on the Weatherbys website.'

A bell rang out. Jockeys began to leave their connections on the grass island to go find their rides.

'I'll make it up to you, I promise,' Danny said and gave her a leg up into Powder Keg's saddle.

As Danny led them slowly round the parade ring, she made herself comfy in the saddle and adjusted the length of rein.

She looked down at Danny and voice small, said, 'Danny, I'm scared.'

Danny didn't want to hear those words. Any hint of nerves or hesitancy would transmit down those reins to Powder Keg, who needed to know who was in charge, or she'd soon do the bossing.

'I've never forgotten this is the biggest race for both of you and could springboard you to a career of outside rides. Part of me is scared of losing you to other yards, but every fibre still wants you to win and I know you will,' Danny explained. 'But above all else, I need to know you believe the same. Like in the rest of life, confidence is everything. You can make it happen up here.' Danny tapped his temple. 'So what do you say?'

She smiled down at him. 'I believe I can.'

'Then let's do this,' Danny said and mirrored the smile.

As they continued to circle the asphalt ring awaiting orders to go down to the start, Danny looked across at a small satellite group of bookies pitches by the Tote offices. He could see Powder Keg had weakened from two-to-one favourite out to three-to-one in the early betting shows. Danny wasn't overly concerned; he'd witnessed the recent PB clocked on the gallops by the bouncing horse and beaming jockey to his side.

He was, however, concerned about the more likely reason for the market drift. There was growing confidence behind number one on the racecard Angel's Trumpet, a winner of six of his eleven starts over timber and coming here on a four-timer in Graded company. There were flipping favourites as Angel's Trumpet had been backed right into nine-to-four from seven-to-two. Danny turned to eye that rival's jockey Scott Kemp, who was sat tall in navy and white checked silks and looked a lot calmer than Meg as he listened intently to pre-race instructions from his Lambourn trainer Robert Naylor. The gelding between his whites was also walking on springs.

Instinctively, Danny ran a reassuring hand down Powder Keg's glossy black neck, though he felt he needed it more. Nerves had set in but he was determined not to show it. It must've been the loss of control. When sat on the horse, his destiny was in his own hands. Looking through high-powered binoculars from the owners' area in the stands, he could do nothing but cheer and occasionally look away from a mistimed jump or being shuffled back due to interference.

He scanned the other runners, including the third favourite Stonebelt, who came here on the back of a promising fourth in an Irish Grade One at Fairyhouse.

It was then he clocked George Wheater by the sponsor's podium in the centre of the ring. Danny began to doubt whether he'd got rid of the tracker device down the grille of the Audi.

196

Danny groaned internally. He didn't want Meg to hear any negative noises at this tense time. Right then it seemed they were surrounded by dangers, not just the opposition.

Man up, Danny thought. He wasn't exactly living up to that team talk.

'Did you really mean those words?' she said, as if picking up on his anxiety.

'Every one of them,' Danny reassured.

She straightened the neck pin fastening the collar of her silks and tugged on her black riding gloves.

Over the racecourse speaker system, there came, 'Would the trainer Daniel Rawlings please come to the jockeys' changing rooms immediately, thank you.'

'I weighed out correctly on the scales, spot on ten-stone seven pounds with Powder Keg's sex and age weight allowances. I can't claim my conditional jockeys' claim in these Graded races. That is right, isn't it?'

'Yeah, it's not that,' Danny said. 'They'd ask for you as well if it was. This'll be some clerical error, or something.'

'You go sort it out,' she said.

'You sure you're okay now?'

'I'm ready to go.'

'I can't leave without seeing you both off.'

Along with the seven other runners, Danny led Powder Keg down the offshoot in the shadow of the stands.

She looked down and said, 'Weighing room, now!'

He let go of the reins and slapped Powder Keg's narrow rump as she quickened into her flicky galloping action to the two-mile starting pole at the far end of the home-straight. There was just over a lap and eight flights of timber between Meg and potential glory. Even daring to dream made the nerves return.

Danny turned and headed for the jockeys' and stewards' building facing the parade rings to answer the call of the speakers.

When he pushed the door of the weighing room, the young jockey Carl Downing was being led from there by the grisly old valet-turned-usher Doug Rees.

Danny let them by and then stepped in to see the changing room was eerily empty. There was a steaming mug of coffee on the slatted-bench bordering the room, while reeking kit bags were left unzipped and lead weights were scattered over the valet's table in the centre. *Racing Posts* were lying about open. Why was he the only one being allowed in?

'What is this? A fire drill?' Danny turned to ask, though the only alarm bells were ringing in his head. But the valet had gone and the door had clicked shut. There was a jangle of keys the other side and a clunk of the lock turning.

Danny spun back into the room. None of this felt right. The only part he couldn't see was the showers and sauna beyond a gap in the far wall.

He couldn't hear any rush of water or see any plumes of steam.

Must've misheard the announcer, Danny thought and was about to leave when he heard the slap of leather on tiles.

Danny backed a step nearer the only way out. Was this a trap? Was he being set up?

The large suited frame of George Wheater filled the gap in the shower wall. A laminated VIP pass was pinned to his lapel.

'Racing again,' Danny said. 'Haven't you got a home to go to?'

'Several actually,' George replied smugly and stepped into the changing area.

'Why do it?' Danny asked.

'Do what? *I'm* not the one who's done anything.'

'Send me on some wild goose chase after Barton.'

'I didn't order you,' George said, 'I merely shared some truths about the bookie. Now Danny, why did *you* do it?'

'What?'

'Raymond Barton was found lying face down in his pool by cleaners letting themselves in first thing.'

'I wasn't there,' Danny said. 'I wasn't even in Gibraltar.'

'Racecourse officials found return plane tickets from Gibraltar to Birmingham in your rucksack. I had them search your stuff on a government tipoff from secret service.'

Danny swallowed. 'Yes, I went there, but that's no crime.'

'Remember what I said about trust, Danny. No more lies.'

Danny looked over at Doug Rees' green valet jacket. He must have a spare set of keys in there.

'Are you planning your escape?'

'Just wondering how much you paid the valet as a tip to clear this place.'

'Tell me, do you make a habit of swimming in the hotel pool fully clothed. Surely a man of your physique wouldn't shy away from showing it off.'

Danny recalled the smell of chlorine from the damp clothes. 'Were you in the security hut with them?'

'It's easy to ask favours when you're in a position of power, just ask the valet.'

'Are you wired?' Danny asked.

George removed his shiny grey suit and hung it from one of the saddle-tree pegs. He then loosened his collar and spread his arms. 'No secret service listening in. Just us. Search me if you have any doubt.'

'I'd rather not,' Danny replied, 'and I never killed Ray. I found him there, along with a list of twenty names.'

'Where is that list?' George asked.

'Safely in my jacket with secu—'

Danny looked on as George removed the folded paper from his trouser pocket. 'Did it look like this?'

'What was Ray doing with it?'

'Several monitored cash bets taken in Barton's shops on targeted horses were permitted by the trading department but later flagged up as highly suspicious by their security department. When Ray looked at the shop CCTV showing the placers of these bets he saw they all had one thing in common, other than they were backing the same horse each time.'

'They were all serving politicians,' Danny said.

199

'If you knew Ray like I did,' George explained, 'you'd know he was a bloody-minded businessman who wouldn't stop until he'd unearthed and then made public all the politicians that had picked up six-figure sums at his "win" counters.' He looked down at the list in his hand. 'Very thorough.'

'Except there's one name missing,' Danny said. 'Did Barton get sucked into the scam, enticed by the returns? He could easily use this inside information, take a limited hit on laying wagers placed by these faces and then place larger bets on the same horses using all his other accounts with the other big bookies and make a tidy sum himself.'

'He played no role in this,' George said.

Danny recalled Barton disappearing into the BHA entrance on High Holborn just before he'd been whisked away in the silver Audi. 'Did he even report it?'

'According to contacts high up in the BHA, Raymond delved deeper into the workings of our betting ring and discovered Campbell was letting samples go untested. He was convinced the Ely Park murder was in some way linked to the MPs placing these remarkably accurate bets. He viewed a clip on a video-sharing website and soon discovered he'd unwittingly witnessed the killer's face in the clip. He made a list of the other witnesses,' George said and then pulled out another sheet. 'One that looked something like this.'

'Barton was one of the nine,' Danny said, picturing him floating in the pool. 'Give the list here.'

'I don't think so,' George said, shaking his head. 'Unfortunately for Raymond, in revealing the whole story to the BHA, he had to break the unpalatable news that their recently departed chief Campbell Galbraith was involved in a doping scam. Obviously they dismissed it as an attempt to besmirch the good name of their former glorious leader.'

'Where is Keith Gosworth?' Danny asked.

'On the run I presume, isn't that what fugitives do?'

'He launched a failed leadership coup on Campbell, who posted him out to be the new clerk of the course at Ely Park as a punishment.'

'A punishment?' Danny asked incredulously. 'Bunch of privately educated snobs. Ely's got a dress code you know.'

George looked down at Danny's frayed old tweed jacket over a green t-shirt with a slack tie. 'Really?'

Danny made for the door but it was locked from the outside. He turned to check Rees' pockets when he felt a strong hand grab his jaw in a vice-tight grip. He was dragged helplessly to the side where he was pinned to the wall, back of his skull smacking the wooden backboard supporting the saddle trees.

'You can't escape.'

'Why lock me in here?' Danny asked.

'To make sure I know where you are.'

'Why? It doesn't make sense.'

George's strong hands held him firm. Danny couldn't move if he tried.

'Let me breathe,' Danny hissed.

Suddenly George looked over at the TV on a shelf in the other corner of the room. He eased his grip as the speakers blared, 'And they're off and away for the first Ely Park running of the Welsh Champion Hurdle and it's Stonebelt that takes an early lead, tracked by Angel's Trumpet and Lonely Eyes. Powder Keg is sitting a handy fourth and a few lengths to the rest content to bide their time at the rear in these very early stages.'

Danny saw his chance and threw a fist that connected with the mole on George's cheek. The politician lost his balance and slipped on soles wet from the shower. He fell to the ground and lay there shaking his head.

Danny knew George had the size and reach advantage. He scanned the room for a weapon but he found nothing more than a whip. The air cushioned persuader would barely leave a mark on Wheater's hulking frame. Even the mug of coffee had gone cold.

Danny leapt on the floored man and tried to keep him there with a headlock. But George soon wrestled free and then fired back with a right hook that connected cleanly with Danny's chin. He saw a galaxy of red dots as his head snapped back. And then came the searing pain. He quickly rolled out of arm's reach as another hammer blow came down.

'They clear the second flight and as they pass the grandstand for the first time, Powder Keg under the inexperienced conditional jockey Meg Rawlings makes a stylish forward move up on the outside to dispute the lead with Stonebelt.'

Danny's blue eyes were now transfixed by the screen showing Meg's arms and legs moving as one with the mare. Occasionally her right hand offered up a gentle tap with the whip down the mare's shoulder, just to keep her mind on the job.

George said, 'You've taught her well.'

'It's natural,' Danny said.

It was then Meg let slip the whip.

'And did I mention clumsy too?' George said and laughed.

Instinct made her reach back which threw the flow of her riding action out of synch. 'Leave it Meg, Kegsy will respond to the reins!'

Powder Keg had lost her momentum for a few strides but was soon back on an even keel again.

Danny was lost in the happenings out on the track long enough for Wheater's hand to grab his neck again and push him to the floor. George's considerable weight anchored Danny there on his back.

It's like Lucy's lounge all over again, Danny thought, except she wasn't in the weighing room to save him this time.

From the speakers came, 'They stream over the first in the back straight and a mistake from Powder Keg sends her back to third behind gamble Angel's Trumpet.'

George smiled as he sat on Danny's torso, twisting to see the screen.

'Sad bastard,' Danny croaked. 'Not only are you content ruining my life, you wish the worst for my wife.'

Danny felt his left side of his chin begin to swell. He also felt pain in his right hand but could still clench it enough to fire a body blow into Wheater's soft belly. A roar filled the room as the large politician bent double wincing.

With his remaining strength, Danny pushed George, who fell back limply. Danny got to his feet again and with the one part of his body that didn't ache, kneed George in the face. There was another groan and blood dripped from George's mouth.

'Enough?!' Danny asked.

When George nodded, some more blood splashed to the tiles.

'Then tell the valet to let me out,' Danny said. 'I want to greet Meg with an arm around the shoulder, whether to comfort or congratulate.'

Danny was well aware he was nearer the showers than the exit door and in the way was George, who was now feeling his mouth, perhaps for missing teeth.

'They near the third flight down the far side and all clear it cleanly enough,' Danny heard and looked up at the screen. 'Though just the first signs of distress from Lonely Eyes' jockey in fourth, no immediate response to urgings from the saddle for that one as he struggles to keep pace with the market leaders.'

'Come on, Meg, keep it together,' Danny said and then gave a cursory glance to see George, who'd gone quiet but was still bent double.

'Swinging into the home straight and there are still three horses in contention for the prize. Angel's Trumpet rails the best and enters with a length lead over long-time leader Stonebelt, who's starting to back-pedal after the early exertions, and there's Powder Keg out wider in search of better ground in a close third, moving as well as the leader.'

'Over two out and the duel is on as Stonebelt fades out of the picture. On the right as we look, Angel's Trumpet wings the flight and extends the advantage over the only possible danger, Powder Keg.' Danny looked again at George, who was now staring up at the screen with similar intent. 'Rawlings is working hard to claw back the deficit and the tiny mare is responding, now on the heels of the leader… half-a-length in it, now a neck.'

203

'Come on M—' Danny was shunted violently to hit his back on the separation wall to the showers. He looked down at George, who was using his broad shoulder as a battering ram.

With the shower wall as a support, Danny pushed George, who stumbled back on the shiny tiles.

'They close in on the final hurdle and it's Angel's Trumpet with the quicker jump.'

'Come on,' George called out.

Danny wanted to go over there and make sure he never got up. 'What's Meg done to you, spiteful shit.'

'But Powder Keg won't go down without a fight and rallies to the cause, back to a neck down.'

'Do this Meg, believe!' Danny yelled, holding his jaw.

'As they flash past the post, it's Angel's Trumpet just, from Powder Keg inches away, Stonebelt a distant third.'

Still grounded, George found the energy to punch the air in delight.

'As if I couldn't hate you anymore,' Danny muttered, though it sounded like he was straight out of the dentist. There was a tinny ringing in both ears.

George was still staring at the screen, now showing a replay, with the one-two-three of the result superimposed.

Bruised and winded, they both watched in silence as the completed runners filed off the track. The TV picture switched to the racecourse announcer waiting in the winner's circle, 'Congratulations to Angel's Trumpet on completing a hat-trick of wins, also providing her trainer with a third winner on the card, a certain Robert Naylor of Lambourn.'

Bobby Naylor, Danny thought. *B.N. of L.*

He looked at George, who was smiling with a gap in his teeth.

'You weren't cheering Powder Keg to lose, you were cheering Angel's Trumpet to win. He was the next targeted horse with another yard.'

George looked over at Danny. 'I always win.'

Danny staggered round the battered politician. 'Not this time.'

On his way he swiped the folded piece of blood-spattered paper from the floor near the valet's table. They must have ended there at some stage in the scuffle.

He then fished in the pocket of the valet's green jacket. He found several twenties in used notes. He now knew how much convincing the valet took to clear the room. Also in there, he found the weighing room keys. Danny unlocked the door.

'Where are you going?'

'To lodge a formal objection to the winner,' Danny said. 'You didn't want me about the track when the chief rival was a targeted horse. Fearing I'd make the link and take some kind of revenge, you had me holed up in here until the result could stand.'

'You're too late, the result is already official,' George said and pointed up at the screen.

'It's not official until the jockeys weigh in.'

'We'll still get paid, bookies pay double result now, win or get disqualified, we'll be winners, have you been out of the betting loop for that long?'

'But this is about us winning the race, it will stand in the formbooks that Meg won the Welsh Champion Hurdle. But that's not all I'll be telling them.'

George stopped smiling and scrambled to his feet. He staggered towards the open door. Hurriedly Danny slammed it shut and turned the lock from the outside.

He saw the handle rattle but it refused to turn. He didn't want George to silence him any longer and dragged a nearby bench up against the door.

'Danny!' George shouted. 'You'll regret this day.'

Danny joined Meg as she walked Powder Keg into the berth reserved for the runner-up in the winner's enclosure.

'Danny, what happened?' she asked.

Danny felt his face and saw blood on his fingertips. He wiped some more away on the sleeve of his jacket.

She wiped her nose on the back of her glove. It was then he saw her watery eyes as she removed her riding goggles. 'You would've won on that,' she cried.

She dismounted. Danny hugged her.

'Trust me, I don't think Tony McCoy could've got past Angel's Trumpet today.'

'Why?'

'Come with me.'

'I've got to see the clerk of the scales to weigh in.'

'Then join me in the stewards' room.'

'But Angel's Trumpet didn't bump me, there wasn't any contact made.'

'It's not that I'm objecting to.'

'What's happened?'

'You'll see, just let me do the talking in there.'

'But making an official objection costs money,' she said.

'Only if you lose it.'

'I lost fair and square, it hurts but you can't defend me just because you didn't like seeing me upset.'

'There was nothing fair about that result.'

'Who did this to you?' she asked, studying Danny's damaged face.

'The person who made Angel's Trumpet unbeatable.'

She gave him a look. 'I'm scared again, Danny.'

CHAPTER 20

Danny felt the weight of eyes on him as he entered the stewards' room.

Behind a desk to his left, there were two men and a woman sat beside a bank of four flat-screen TVs showing race footage from different angles on a loop. To his right there were two cameras on tripods in front of a small gathering.

The male steward in the middle held some forms and a Parker pen. He wore gold-rimmed specs and tufts of grey hair sat perched either side of a bald head. His studious eyes were probably trying to figure out why a man dressed like a vagrant, with face cut and swelling, had entered as if it was a boxing ring. Danny was indeed up for a fight to get some justice for Meg. With renewed hope and expectation, he felt the pre-race buzz was back.

'Yes?' the middle steward said sternly.

'I'm representing Megan Rawlings. I'm her husband, Daniel, and the trainer of Powder Keg. I lodged the objection to the winner but I didn't know we'd have to perform to a gallery.'

'You'll be performing to the nation,' the stewards' secretary said. 'The objection will be televised live on a terrestrial channel, so please mind your language and manners. The reputation of racing's good name will be at stake.'

You got that one right, Danny thought.

A man with an earpiece and a clipboard stood behind one of the cameras pointed a finger as a cue to the stewards.

'Could you let the jockeys and trainer Robert Naylor in please,' the end steward ordered.

Racecourse security let Meg, Scott Kemp and Robert Naylor into the room. They settled on padded wooden chairs facing the desk. Meg glanced briefly up at Danny, who stood near the end of the desk.

'Mr Rawlings, could you please reiterate your reasons for lodging an objection to the result of the three-thirty at Ely Park.'

Scott stood before Danny could speak. 'No interference took place, just look at the footage on those screens, both our horses kept a straight line. Agree Meg?'

Meg looked up to Danny, who shook his head.

'Mr Kemp would you please calm down and respect this enquiry. Answer only when asked a question. I was addressing Mr Rawlings, please proceed.'

'It's not the interference I'm objecting about.'

'But Mr Kemp and Mrs Rawlings have both weighed in correctly, so please explain yourself.'

Danny turned to Robert Naylor, who was staring ahead in silence, perhaps hoping he'd go unnoticed.

Danny asked, 'After this, Bobby, do you fancy a game of chess?'

He studied the look of shock and then guilt on the rival trainer's face. Danny knew then he had his man. Naylor was in on the scam.

'What is this about Mr Rawlings?'

'Seems one of us here has spent too long in the owners' and trainers' bar,' Naylor said.

'Mr Rawlings, I will remind you, this is being broadcast. Please do not bring this process or our sport into disrepute.'

'It's not me you should be worried about,' Danny said and removed the crumpled and blood-flecked sheet swiped from the weighing room floor.

Danny flattened it out on the desk in front of the three racecourse officials.

'Who are they?'

'I'm surprised you don't recognise the names,' Danny told the middle steward. 'You were probably old chums from Eton, that's where all you lot went to right. All you toffs come from those posh private schools, even the prime ministers are weaned there.'

'This hearing is being terminated for contempt—' the steward barked.

The missing name was 'too famous to forget, too important to be named', Danny recalled George saying.

'That's it,' Danny interjected as a thought struck him. 'The PM.'

'I'm beginning to agree with Mr Naylor here, you are acting as if under the heavy influence of alcohol.'

'Hugo Forster is the twenty-first on the list.'

Doubt condoning cheating, risking animal welfare and defrauding punters would go down as well with the working-class voters as a pint and a gig, Danny thought.

'Please explain yourself, making such wild, fanciful and I might add, slanderous accusations,' the stewards said, slapping his Parker pen on the desk. 'And start making sense, or I'll be forced to halt this hearing with immediate effect.'

Meg was sat between Kemp and Naylor. She was shifting her pert behind in the chair. She was probably wondering why her husband appeared to be making a fool of himself and the yard on live TV.

Danny leant over the desk and using the Parker he added Hugo Forster to the foot of the list of MPs. He slid the pen to the steward and then stepped back. 'The twenty-one names on this list are not only serving members of parliament, they are also members of an illegal betting syndicate.'

'There's nothing illegal about having a bet, Mr Rawlings,' the stewards remarked. 'Whether it's pooling stakes together on a tip or a racecourse whisper. Offices and pubs up and down our land run syndicates on horses, pools and lottery. It's part of the joy of our sport and what helps fund it in part.'

'But none of them bet willingly on horses drugged up on steroid-carb cocktails or by inhaling similarly performance-enhancing gasses.'

'Are you seriously suggesting the politicians on this list were investors in an illegal doping operation?'

'I'm not suggesting, I'm telling you.'

209

'I think we should stop filming please,' the steward said and ran a finger across his neck as if to signal cut to the murmuring gallery at the back.

'I doubt they will,' Danny said, 'this is TV gold. And Mr Robert Naylor here was one of the trainers involved. Isn't that right Bobby, or should I address you as B.N. of L.'

'Rubbish,' Naylor said.

'I'm sure you won't like to be seen dismissing these accusations,' Danny said to the steward. 'Seeing as the sport needs to be seen to be run fairly for all.' He then turned and said, 'I'm sure Naylor here won't mind eliminating himself from your enquiries by letting the security and race-day police search your horse box. And you won't mind them finding a chess box holding gas canisters containing argon and xenon.'

The secretary whispered something in the steward's ear. 'Well? Mr Naylor?' Naylor crossed his arms and looked away. 'Do you refute these allegations?'

'Angel's Trumpet had breathed in these gasses before the race. I've just come from watching George Wheater, who is the Minister for Gambling and is circled on that list as the ringleader, cheer home Naylor's horse.'

'Where is he now?'

'Recovering in the weighing room.'

'I was duped into it,' Naylor cried. 'George threatened to end my career if I didn't comply.'

'By forging his signature on a form terminating his trainer's licence,' Danny said. 'He's done it before.'

Naylor continued, 'He also warned me if I ever dared walk away from this he had contacts in the integrity unit who could falsify positive drug results for any winners I might have in the future. What could I do?'

The steward batted that away with, 'I'm afraid that doesn't happen in our organisation. We have installed watertight procedures.'

'They won't mean a thing if there's a lab technician willing to follow orders from up high.'

'Employees are overseen to ensure there is no foul play at any level.'

'By who?' Danny asked. 'It's no use being overseen if those doing the overseeing are just as corrupt. As much as this hurts to hear, your former leader Campbell Galbraith played a vital role in this mess. He ensured those targeted trainers were exempt from post-race sample testing.'

'Campbell was a man of honour, he wouldn't betray the sport for any amount of money,' the steward snapped.

'I don't doubt, but Campbell wanted more than money. He wanted a bill to pass that would dramatically boost the racing levy by charging foreign bookies for bets placed by Brits on racing in this country. It would help secure racing's financial future and make Campbell a hero in the sport he loved.'

The man with the clipboard called from the back, 'Can we stop for a commercial break?'

'No!' Danny replied. 'This isn't a bloody soap opera.'

'Language!' the steward barked.

The secretary stopped making notes to ask, 'How do you know all this?'

'I was targeted as a potentially vulnerable trainer willing to break rules but unlike Naylor here, I never administered any drugs to my horses.'

'All licensed trainers are told repeatedly to come forward to us with any information the moment you are approached with offers from suspicious persons or groups. Why did you let it get this far?'

'I needed to get inside their operation to uncover the truth,' Danny said. 'And even if I did flag it up, there was no way you'd have launched an internal enquiry when one of the lynchpins of the scam was also one of your own. Raymond Barton came to you with that list and was turned away.'

'We have never seen that list.'

'No offence but you're a part-timer working on behalf of the BHA. Barton went straight to High Holborn with this.'

211

Danny's phoned bleeped. He looked at the screen showing the GPS map. The blue circle locating the tracker Danny had slipped down the windscreen grille of the Audi had now left the track and appeared to be heading east on the M4. George Wheater had clearly been released from the weighing room and was escaping before the stewards came after him.

Danny turned to look down the lens of the camera with the flashing red light. 'To conclude, I am demanding you look into the current lab technicians working at the integrity unit and you might also want to look into Mr Naylor's horse box if he's willing to hand over the keys.'

'Well, Mr Naylor?'

Bobby shrugged. He knew it was over.

'I have full faith in the judicial process and expect Powder Keg to be promoted as the winner at a future hearing,' Danny said confidently.

'In light of the confession I cannot see how Angel's Trumpet can keep the race,' the steward conceded. 'I will personally ensure a full enquiry will be carried out at headquarters.' The steward began to tidy his sheets like a newsreader. 'We must work to keep British racing the cleanest in the world.'

Danny saw the red light on the cameras go out. The clipboard man had already removed his earpiece and picked up his coffee.

As Danny made for the door, Meg rushed after him. She wrapped her silky arms round his stiff shoulders and whispered in his ear, 'You've more than made it up to me.'

They kissed.

'Don't wait up,' he said and was gone.

CHAPTER 21

Danny pulled up outside the gates of the Galbraith manor house.

He looked again at the blue dot flashing at his current location. He'd followed the Audi across country and had ended back here.

He killed the engine and then sought cover behind one of the pillars. Peering between the bars of the gate, he could see a man in biker's leathers reversing the Audi into a triple garage, alongside an equally flash motorbike.

Danny then saw an inviting yellow glow from the mouth of the manor's front door. Maria must've been expecting visitors. Was she having an affair with the MP too?

Danny saw his chance. He leapt over the chest-high wall and in the dusky gloom, bit back the pain as he sprinted across the manicured front lawn.

From the open front door, he could hear the clack of heels on tiles come from the lounge at the end of the grand hallway lit by chandeliers. He recalled the lounge was mostly carpet and wood. She must be in the tiled kitchen. It was then the smell of grilling steak reached him. Perhaps George had phoned ahead.

Danny stepped in from the cool night air and was about to head straight for the lounge before the biker had chance to park up. He was halfway down the hall when he also heard footsteps from behind. When he looked back, he saw a shadow eating into the chandelier's light out on the driveway.

He was suddenly cornered both sides. He spun on his heels and to his left saw a small door blending tastefully with the wood panelling. He hoped for enough space to hide, but the blackness inside made it hard to tell. He stepped in and closed the door. A couple of rapid breaths later, he heard the creek of the oak front door slamming shut.

The biker would surely want to hang his jacket, gloves and coat. Danny hoped this wasn't the cloakroom.

When he took a step back to give him some room, the ground disappeared beneath him. Falling back he desperately reached out to stop himself. His fingers scratched cold brickwork before catching hold of a wooden handrail. His body swung round and his arse landed painfully on the sharp edge of a stone step. He stretched his leg out and felt another step lower down. He wished he'd thought of taking the torch from his car, but he guessed every stairwell had a light.

When his finger flicked a switch on the wall, a single naked bulb flickered into life far below.

Danny glanced back at the door. George would've removed the gun from the Audi, he reckoned. Perhaps he could find a makeshift weapon of his own from the basement.

Silently he climbed down the stairwell. In the half-light of the bulb, he scanned a cellar full with piles of dusty and cobwebbed furniture, boxes, old paintings and crates full of clutter.

In the far corner, he heard a muffled squealing. Danny assumed it was rats. But when he stepped into the room the squeals grew louder. Rats would've fled for cover.

As he stepped in to investigate, he could see some familiar white hair poking above the crates.

Danny rushed the rest of the way, clearing a path to face the clerk.

Keith Gosworth was sitting on a metal chair in a small gap between the wall and the crates. A scarf had been tied over his eyes. When Danny dragged a box out to clear the way, Keith's head lifted.

As he closed in, Danny saw his hands were tied to the padded arms of the chair by gaffer tape and he was gagged. Keith's dimpled chin glistened with dribble.

Danny quickly pulled the gag from his mouth.

'I told them I saw nothing on track,' Keith whimpered. 'Please don't hurt me.'

Danny untied the scarf.

'Oh, thank God, I never thought I'd be so glad to see your face,' Keith whispered and then smiled past tired eyes. 'Pull me out, give us both some room to move.'

It was only then Danny realised the clerk was strapped into a wheelchair. The smell of rubber of the tyres put Danny right back in the boot of the Audi.

'How long have you been here?' Danny asked as he pulled on the arms of the chair to inch Keith out of the gap.

'Long enough.'

Once in a clearing, Danny's fingers began to work on wrists and ankles cocooned in tape. 'Why did they take you?'

'I was picked up by a biker after leaving the police interview and bundled into the back of an Audi. He clearly thought I was in there confessing.'

'But that would help put Campbell's killer in the clear, so why kidnap and hide you down here?'

'I meant confessing to pushing the killer in this thing round the side of the track seconds after the shooting. With the gunman still at large, I thought I was helping a vulnerable racegoer flee the danger, I didn't know I was moving the danger itself.'

'What did he look like?'

'I couldn't see behind the beard, shades and cap.'

Danny pictured the staged BHA vet raid. 'Try pulling your hand now.'

Gosworth funnelled his fingers to make his hand small and then strained. Suddenly his wrist whipped up as the tape snapped.

He began to shake his hand, trying to push some fresh blood there.

Danny rushed round the back of the chair. He noticed there was a large rip in the canvas back-support.

'I was already in shock when he stood up from the wheelchair, turned and said I'd be next to die if I didn't tell the police Campbell had been pushed to his death and that I hadn't helped him escape. The police called me back in when they knew I was lying and saw my hate for Campbell in the diary.'

Hearing the pound of footsteps, they both looked up at the low ceiling.

'They're in then,' Gosworth said.

'The Audi's parked up and I heard a woman in the kitchen,' Danny whispered. 'Do you think they can hear?'

'I don't intend to hang around to find out,' Gosworth said as he freed his other hand and headed for the foot of the stairwell. There, he needed the wall as a steadier as he shook his head. 'They're going to kill us both.'

'You go, I've got some unfinished business here.' He searched a crate on the floor and pulled out a rusty metal file and stuck it down the back of his combats.

'That won't do you any good, they've got a bloody gun.'

'Just get help,' Danny said, 'please.'

Gosworth offered a hand. 'Goodbye and thanks.'

'I *will* be seeing you again,' Danny said.

'Of course you will.'

Keith's attempts at comforting were having the opposite effect. The clerk climbed the steps, put an ear to the door and seconds later was gone from there.

Danny hoped he'd made it to the front door and down the driveway without getting a bullet in the back.

Danny climbed the steps and then waited there. He couldn't hear anything from the hall. Perhaps George was upstairs putting antiseptic on his wounds.

Danny slowly opened the door and crept down the empty hallway. The sidelights in the lounge were on and there was music playing softly nearby. He guessed Maria was still in the kitchen.

Danny sucked in a lungful and then stormed the room. He saw Maria, who put down a bottle of red wine and picked up a handgun near the sink. It looked like the one in Wheater's glove compartment.

'Where is he?' Danny asked and then heard the creek of floorboards above their head.

'He'll be here soon, don't you worry about that.'

Backing away Danny bumped his way past the coffee table and ended by the mantelpiece. As he felt his legs wobble, his hand sought the mantelpiece and knocked something over. He looked across to see it was the awards photo. 'You managed to find it in my lounge then.'

'My husband's murderer was in the photo,' she said. 'He didn't want to be associated with his victim.'

'Raymond and Campbell are dead,' Danny said, glancing again at the photo. 'That just leaves you and George.'

'Look harder.'

Last time he was here, he'd recalled her say there were five at the awards that night. He'd put it down to the drink. But in the mirrored wall behind, he could make out the shape of another figure. He looked up from the photo. 'The killer was taking the photo.'

Where I go, he goes, Danny recalled George had said of his driver, Roy.

George was at the murder scenes of Ely Park and Worcester. Roy was also there.

'Roy was taking the photo.'

He saw movement in the glass of the framed photo. When he turned, Roy was also pointing a gun at Danny. His cropped hair was wet.

'Except that's not my real name,' Roy said.

'He told me it was a nickname that stuck from his days in the TA,' she said, smiling. 'After Roy Rogers, as he was always happiest with a trigger in his hands.'

'But when you held me down on Lucy's lounge, you reacted when I called you Ray.'

'I couldn't hear for the helmet,' he said.

'So it was you.'

'George gave me a day off, said he had a meeting at an M4 services, allowing me time to hunt down Lucy Parker.'

Danny noticed that *1er* tattoo on his neck. Hoping to stall for time while Gosworth found help, he asked, 'Army tattoo is it?'

'Biker tattoo,' Roy said. 'It's an old saying, one per cent of bikers cause ninety-nine per cent of the trouble.'

'You didn't find driving George around fulfilling enough for you, so you've branched out as a hit-man,' Danny said.

'When I got chatting that night, I agreed to my riskiest job yet.'

'Maria said you were talking to her most of that evening,' Danny said. He turned to Maria. 'You ordered your husband's public execution.'

Two loaded guns versus a rusty metal file; he didn't like the current odds.

He wished he'd taken Keith's advice and escaped while he could.

'I couldn't find George at Ely Park after the Welsh Champion Hurdle, but I knew something was wrong when I saw you covered in blood heading for the stewards. Your wife rode a good race, shame she'll lose a race and a husband in the same day. I took the Audi and fled to the safe house here,' Roy said.

'I can't believe you ordered your husband's death,' Danny said.

She nodded. 'I was desperate to be with Raymond.'

'But I saw you in the clip,' Danny said. 'You were the only one on the balcony trying to save him.'

'I was also the only one there who knew for certain there would be no more gunfire, the contract had already been fulfilled,' she said. 'And I needed to make it look to the audience below that I wanted him alive. I could have held on for longer.'

'Why make it so public?'

'He deserted me and humiliated me after our second child was still born.'

Danny recalled the fresh scars when she flashed him. They weren't on the birthday photo of her in Raymond's villa.

'He just buried himself deeper into his work,' she said, 'too busy with impressing his colleagues at the BHA to even notice me. He shunned me at social gatherings like that. I needed support. I needed love.'

218

'So you called on Raymond Barton to fill that void,' Danny said. He removed his mobile and brought up the revealing photo of her. He then placed the phone on the table between them.

'I wanted to join him in Gibraltar,' she said. 'He meant everything to me. Campbell was the only problem.'

'And when you got talking to Roy, he was the answer to your problem,' Danny said. 'But I bet Barton didn't feel the same when he found out you were behind Campbell's murder.'

'He called it off,' she said. 'Even changed his mobile number and locks at his villa.'

'I was in the villa, waiting in the shower unit while you checked the bedrooms,' Roy said.

Danny was glad he hadn't looked in the en suite.

'Why didn't you kill me, get rid of another one of the nine while you were in the villa and kill two birds with one stone in a few hours.'

'I was too busy framing Barton's murder by capturing a still image of you in the CCTV system.'

Danny recalled seeing himself in the study.

She said, 'He was good enough to get rid of that problem for me, too.'

'He killed Barton for his own reasons,' Danny said.

'Raymond was pleasantly surprised to see a familiar face greet him at Gibraltar airport,' Roy said, grinning. 'At the awards do, he wouldn't shut up about his improved lifestyle. I told him he'd won me over and I'd got a driver's job out there. Inviting me into his villa was his final mistake.'

'Raymond was one of nine to witness an online clip showing Roy's face being pushed by Gosworth down the ramp from the viewing area,' Danny explained to Maria. 'He fired the gun through a rip in the back of the wheelchair.'

Roy smiled. 'I used the base of the rip as a steadier to take aim. All eyes were on the race and in any case, no one wants to be caught casting a suspicious eye on a disabled person, one worse off than themselves. I pulled the gun from the hole and

219

immediately it was hidden again. I turned and wheeled from the viewing platform.'

Danny recalled it lay in the triangle he'd shaded on the racecourse plans.

'I then escaped round the side of the track.'

'With a little help from the clerk of the course,' Danny said.

'Why didn't you tell me this?' she asked.

'It wasn't your problem,' Roy replied, glancing over but still directing his gun at Danny. 'It was my mistake that needed fixing.'

If she didn't know there was a wanted list of nine names, she also didn't know Micky was on it. He didn't need a weapon when he could turn Maria on Roy.

Danny removed the list of nine names and addresses also found at the villa. 'These are the nine witnesses on death row.'

As they both held their guns firmly on Danny, his legs trembled some more. He knew the bloodied paper was his last hope.

Roy said, 'The witnesses were a mere unintended waste. What we'd call collateral damage in the force.'

Maria was nodding.

'Maria, Micky was on that list. He witnessed the twenty-seven seconds of online footage. The hired hit-man stood next to you blew your son's head off at Worcester racetrack.'

He saw her shoulders drop slightly and the gun was now pointing at the coffee table.

'Think about it, Maria,' Danny said and nodded at the gun. 'I was only trying to find your son's killer, and there he is!'

'Is this true?' she whimpered.

Roy shook his head. 'Can't you see, he's trying to play us off on each other, drive a wedge between us, it's mind tricks, don't get sucked in, they're all lies.'

Danny looked down at the list of nine and then up to Maria, 'See for yourself, Maria. The ink is dry and the writing is your ex-lover Raymond's. Micky's name is already crossed off, I was next.'

Roy lunged for the coffee table, beating Maria to it.

As Roy tried to stand up, he was stopped by a gun pressed against his cropped scalp.

She wiped tears from her eyes. 'Collateral damage you said, nothing to worry about you said. It was my only son! My only living darling boy! All I had left.'

Danny added, 'And this cold-blooded monster blew his brains out.'

'Say it isn't so.'

'He's lying, can't you see what he's doing?' Roy growled.

Danny looked at Roy's eyes shifting left and right. He was searching for a way out. His survival instinct from the army training was kicking in.

When he reacted and swivelled on his knees, he knocked Maria off her feet. She fell back on to the leather suite, but kept a grip on the gun.

Before Roy had chance to take aim, Maria pulled her trigger. A deafening bang filled the room, rattling the mirrors and coffee table. Roy held his bloody chest, pasty face grimacing. He managed to lift the gun high enough to take revenge but she fired again and he fell to the ground like a rag doll.

'You killed my son!' she raged again and again.

In slow movements Danny went to comfort her. She was sobbing into her hands.

'I'm sorry,' he said. 'For Campbell and Micky.'

'And Micky's little brother,' she cried. 'Poor little Jake. There were complications, because of my age. He was induced and... was stillborn.'

Danny kept silent, fearing she'd turn the gun on him again. But she didn't. She just rested it on the glass surface of the table, alongside the birthday photo and the list of names.

Danny looked down at Roy's body, motionless in a heap, blood leaking from his chest and corners of his mouth.

Outside he heard the screech of sirens grow louder. Keith Gosworth had clearly kept his promise. It was in his interest to tell all and clear both their names. Perhaps he was going to be a good clerk to deal with after all.

'I just wanted Campbell to pay for deserting me.' She started sobbing into her hands again. 'And now I have nothing.'

Danny slowly reached out for the gun.

'No!' she screeched and snatched it from his grasp.

Danny stepped back. Did she plan to finish him too? She was going to get a life sentence whether she did or not. 'I don't want your fingerprints on the handle. I need to pay for what I have done.'

She looked up, eyes pink and glazed. 'Danny, if I can give you some advice, never let grief eat you up, as it will. Don't ever look back.'

Danny nodded. He began to head for the sirens and the flashing blue patterns of light shining through the glass pane above the front door at the end of the hallway.

As he opened the door and stepped into the cold evening air, he put his hands on his head and heard another loud bang ring out from behind in the lounge.

Danny waited for the searing pain in between his shoulders but nothing came. The sobbing had stopped.

Danny didn't look back.

Printed in Great Britain
by Amazon